STARS

CYNT

Life in the England an exciting and dange eldest Washington ch cover when they become involved in a secret plot to help young Princess Elizabeth flee the country.

Known to the children by her code name "The Lady", Elizabeth is kept a virtual prisoner in nearby Woodstock by her elder sister Mary Tudor. The plan is to smuggle her by sea to Italy. Discovery would mean death on the scaffold to the Washington boys.

But such is the fascination of the beautiful princess that Robert and Laurie Washington cannot keep away from Woodstock. Their younger sister Anne becomes an active plotter too, helping them to conceal everything from their parents. And behind the scenes the mysterious astrologer Doctor Dee plays his own special part. . . .

Carnegie Medal winner Cynthia Harnett has written a gripping adventure story about Tudor England. The *Stars of Fortune* are those on the coat of arms of the Washington family, which developed into the stars and stripes of the American flag. Had the adventures in which the children took part gone just a little wrong, England might never have had her Good Queen Bess or America her George Washington.

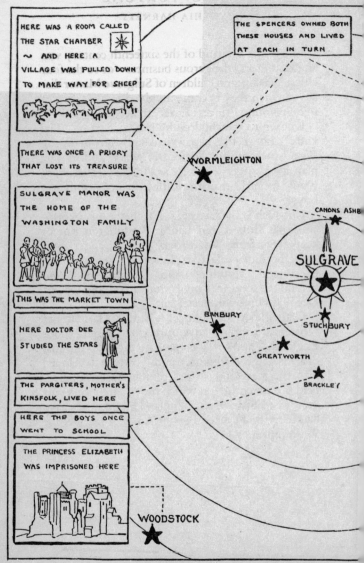

HERE WAS A ROOM CALLED THE STAR CHAMBER ~ AND HERE A VILLAGE WAS PULLED DOWN TO MAKE WAY FOR SHEEP

THE SPENCERS OWNED BOTH THESE HOUSES AND LIVED AT EACH IN TURN

THERE WAS ONCE A PRIORY THAT LOST ITS TREASURE

SULGRAVE MANOR WAS THE HOME OF THE WASHINGTON FAMILY

THIS WAS THE MARKET TOWN

HERE DOCTOR DEE STUDIED THE STARS

THE PARGITERS, MOTHER'S KINSFOLK, LIVED HERE

HERE THE BOYS ONCE WENT TO SCHOOL

THE PRINCESS ELIZABETH WAS IMPRISONED HERE

WORMLEIGHTON

CANONS ASHB

SULGRAVE

BANBURY

STUCHBURY

GREATWORTH

BRACKLEY

WOODSTOCK

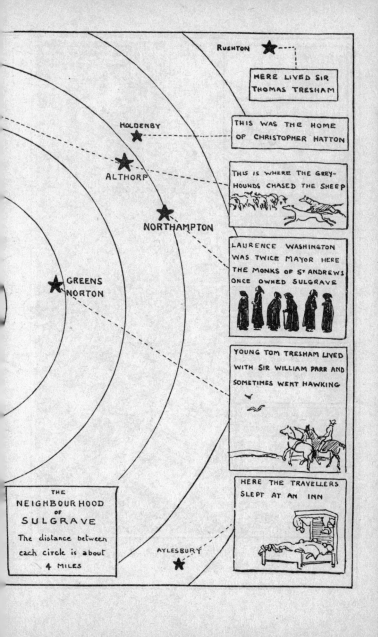

RUSHTON

HERE LIVED SIR THOMAS TRESHAM

HOLDENBY

THIS WAS THE HOME OF CHRISTOPHER HATTON

ALTHORP

THIS IS WHERE THE GREYHOUNDS CHASED THE SHEEP

NORTHAMPTON

LAURENCE WASHINGTON WAS TWICE MAYOR HERE THE MONKS OF ST ANDREWS ONCE OWNED SULGRAVE

GREENS NORTON

YOUNG TOM TRESHAM LIVED WITH SIR WILLIAM PARR AND SOMETIMES WENT HAWKING

HERE THE TRAVELLERS SLEPT AT AN INN

THE NEIGHBOURHOOD OF SULGRAVE

The distance between each circle is about 4 MILES

AYLESBURY

Father's coffer bumped down several steps

Stars of Fortune

WRITTEN AND ILLUSTRATED
BY

CYNTHIA HARNETT

mammoth

First published in 1956
by Methuen & Co Ltd
Reprinted 1962, 1967, 1971 and 1977
Magnet paperback edition published 1981
Published 1990 by Mammoth
an imprint of Egmont Children's Books Ltd
239 Kensington High Street, London W8 6SA

Reprinted 1999

Text and illustrations copyright © 1956 Cynthia Harnett

ISBN 0 7497 0514 0

A CIP catalogue record for this title
is available from the British Library

Printed in Great Britain
by Cox & Wyman Ltd, Reading, Berkshire

CONTENTS

Sulgrave Manor

CHAPTER I

Stars and Stripes

With the back of his wrist Francis Washington pushed back the hair from his hot forehead. Though there was always shade under the elms at Sulgrave, it was a blazing August day, and he wondered how his sister Anne could endure it, gathering lavender out there in the sun. His legs were stiff from sitting on the ground and the midges were devouring him, though until now he had been too engrossed to notice them. Regardless of dirty finger marks he indulged in a good scratch. He was busy making his "mud pies", as his brothers called them; modelling in the moist clay which the builders had left with the rest of their gear in the stable yard.

It was wonderfully quiet, so quiet that he could hear the swish

I

of the scythe as old Jake mowed the lawn. Even the house itself looked deserted, with no sign of life in any of the windows, and nobody running in and out. Sulgrave Manor was not often as quiet as this; but Father was away in London on some business about the sale of wool; Robert and Laurie, the two elder boys, had ridden off with their friend Christopher Hatton on an expedition of their own; and yesterday Dame Katharine Spencer, Father's "Cousin Kit", had fetched the younger ones in her big chariot waggon, and taken them back, all five of them, to share the nurseries at Wormleighton with her own brood. So today of the nine Washington children only he and Anne, his twin sister, were left at home.

Nine children? As he said it Francis corrected himself. He should have said *ten*; for last night, while he and Anne were asleep, Mother's new baby was born. New babies were not very exciting. Francis himself could remember the arrival of four, and Anne insisted that she could remember five, though he was sure that she was making it up. After all she was the younger by two hours, so how could she possibly remember more than he could?

But this baby *was* interesting. It was a boy. At long last he had a younger brother. Though he scorned to show it, he was really pleased. He'd been the youngest boy for so long. It was always his business to fetch and carry for Robert and Laurie; now there would be someone to fetch and carry for him. It would be fun, too, to teach his little brother to string a bow, or to bait a line, or to show him the proper stance and the true swing of the bat at trap-ball.

Father would be pleased about the baby. Father always said that the Washington family was like a lizard. It started off well with four good legs—Robert, Laurie, Francis and Anne, for though Anne was a girl she was the first girl, and being Francis' twin grew up with the boys. But after that the lizard became just a long tail, five more little girls, with the tail growing smaller all the time. Yes, decidedly another boy was a good addition to the family.

He stretched himself and once more gave his attention to his clay. This time he was not trying to model a knight in armour, like those he'd seen on tombs in the churches. He was doing something which was easier and yet more important. He was modelling a shield with the Washington coat of arms on it. It was to be a surprise for Father on his feast day—St. Laurence's Day. He had measured it out very carefully and mounted the slab of wet clay on to one of the stone tiles that the builders had left over when they put the roof on the house. The house itself was finished now, but they were still at work on the entrance porch.

The Washington family was like a lizard

He'd heard Father say that he really must have the family arms over the porch door, as other people did.

It was difficult to keep the clay from hardening in that heat. He splashed it liberally from a bowl of muddy water beside him, and then wiped the sharpened stick, which was his best tool, with a handful of grass.

He was lost in his work again when Anne came and flung herself down beside him, her face the colour of a peony and her arms full of lavender.

"It's hot," she gasped. "Old Jake says that it will end up with a thunder storm. What are you doing, Francis? I wish you'd help me strip the lavender. Marta wants some to mix with the rushes for Mother's room."

He grunted and held out his muddy hands. "How can I? It would all stick."

"What are you doing?" she repeated, and kneeled up to look over his shoulder. "Oh, I see; the stars and stripes."

"*Stars and stripes.* Isn't that like a girl," he scoffed. "Whoever's heard of stars and stripes in heraldry? Can't you say *Mullets and Bars?* Surely you must know the Washington arms by now: *argent, two bars gules, in chief three mullets gules.*"

"You can call them what you like; they *are* just stars and stripes. What are you doing it for?"

Francis said as shortly as possible that it was to go over the door of the new porch.

"It ought to be carved in stone," she pointed out. "The arms over Grandfather Pargiter's door are stone; and he's got the date too."

"I can put the date easily enough," said Francis, ignoring the question of stone. "Here you are."

He picked up his stick again and carefully traced the figures on the clay, two on each side of the shield. They were a little crooked, but Anne could read them quite plainly.

She nodded approvingly. "That's nice. I suppose the porch will be finished soon. Robert's to have the little room over it all to himself, because he's the eldest. Isn't he lucky? There's another little place over that, right up in the roof, but it's got no windows and no stairs."

"It's going to have a ladder," he said quickly. It wasn't often that he could tell Anne any news. "It's to be a sort of secret place. I heard Father talking to the master mason about it."

He waited for this to sink in, but Anne wasn't listening. She had begun to strip the lavender.

"I wonder what they'll call the baby. If it had been another girl Mother was going to call it Katharine Mary—Katharine after Cousin Kit and Mary after the Queen. I think it's a little bit like Cousin Kit."

"It's not like anything. Babies never are," said Francis sweepingly.

Anne took no notice. "Father *will* be pleased that it's a boy. I want to be the first to tell him, Francis."

"You can't. *I'm* going to tell him. I'm older."

"You can tell Robert and Laurie. They'll be home to-night. Father won't be back for ages. It takes him three days to ride from London."

Francis heaved a sigh. He might as well give in; it was never any good arguing with Anne. "I wonder what time they'll get in from Woodstock. I wish I could have gone with them. It's only just over twenty miles and I've often ridden further than that."

"Don't talk so loud," said Anne quickly. "You know it's a secret about their going to Woodstock and old Jake might hear. If you'd been going Mother would have wanted to know more about it because you are younger. Robert and Laurie always ride with Chris Hatton; so when he arrived and asked if he could take them to spend the night with his friend Francis Verney she said 'Yes' at once. Woodstock wasn't even mentioned."

"I don't see why it had to be so secret. We've never been *told* we mustn't go there."

"Francis, you are dreadful about secrets. You know perfectly well that they go because the Princess Elizabeth is prisoner in the Palace of Woodstock and Father always says he'll have no meddling in State matters. She's been in the Tower of London for plotting against the Queen. Lots of people think she's a traitor and ought to have been beheaded with Lady Jane Grey and the rest of them."

"She's *not* a traitor," cried Francis hotly. "Chris says she's a loyal sister to the Queen and it's a shame to hold her prisoner."

"There you go, you see," retorted Anne. "You're getting as bad as Chris. Father says that all the boys are losing their senses. Because she's a young princess and locked up, they all fancy themselves as knight errants. If he knew that Robert and Laurie were in it they'd get the beating of their lives, so for goodness sake be quiet. Why can't you help me with this lavender? Your hands are dry enough now."

Grumbling to himself Francis pushed away his coat of arms. He rolled over on to his front, seized a handful of lavender and began to strip it into a cloth which Anne hastily spread before him.

Lying like that he could see out from the shady tent of the elm trees across the sunny lawn to the manor house, with the unfinished porch which was to carry his coat of arms. It was a long low house with walls of new creamy stone. The sun had moved round and the garden front was in shadow which made the cream look a shadowy blue. But the stone roof and the high chimneys still caught the golden light, and the diamond panes of the windows shone grass green or bright blue, as they reflected the garden or the sky. It was a lovely house, thought Francis to himself. Wormleighton, Cousin Kit Spencer's home, was much bigger and much grander; but to his mind it was not a patch on Sulgrave.

"Cousin Kit said yesterday that they were counting the sheep again," remarked Anne suddenly. Francis had just been thinking about Cousin Kit, but that sort of thing was always happening between him and Anne so he did not even bother to notice it. He let her run on. "They think they really have reached twenty thousand this time, and you know when they get to twenty thousand Cousin John has promised to have the biggest shearing supper there's ever been."

"You can't have a shearing supper unless it's shearing time," objected Francis. He was still feeling a little sore about Woodstock.

"Well, a supper anyway, in the biggest barn. Cousin Kit said that they might even hire mummers to give a show, and we'd all be invited. . . . But it takes such a time to count all those sheep. They have to do every flock separately and somebody always gets one wrong. The flocks at Althorp were wrong last time. Now it's the Wormleighton ones."

"Cousin John's always talking about twenty thousand sheep but he never gets them." He was determined not to be cheered. "Old Jake says that Sir William Spencer, Cousin John's father, was just as set on twenty thousand, but they always fell short. Either there was murrain, or the lambs got sick, or someone stole them." He sat up suddenly and listened. "Hark! Can you hear horses? Here they come."

He scrambled to his feet but Anne shook her head. "It can't be the boys. It's only one horse."

"It might be Father."

"Father wouldn't be alone either; he took Will and Henry with him to handle the wool samples."

"Anyway it's coming here," cried Francis. He raced across the lawn to peep through the planched beech hedge which divided the garden from the stable yard. In a moment he returned shaking his head.

"It's only Will. He's alone. I suppose Father sent him home with letters from London."

"Yes, that must be it. There'll be a letter for Mother and she'll send one back about the baby and then we'll none of us be able to tell him. What a shame!"

Francis picked up his coat of arms and looked at it.

"Anyhow this is finished," he remarked. "If Father doesn't like clay he can give it to the mason to copy in stone. It's not so hot now. I think I shall go to the stream and see if I can get a fish or two. Are you coming?"

"Oh yes!" she cried. "But you might help me finish the lavender first. It won't take long if the two of us do it."

This time Francis decided to be obliging and they both set to work in earnest. They had stripped all but the last few stalks when Anne glanced up.

"Here comes old Marta with a pitcher," she remarked. "I suppose it's milk for us. Oh goody! She's brought some raspberries too."

Old Marta, her plain stuff gown covered with a large white apron and a tight white coif over her smooth grey hair, was wrinkled and tanned and rosy, like a ripe russet apple. From her girdle hung a string of large rosary beads which clattered as she walked. Marta had worn her beads even in the years when the old religion was forbidden, and no one had dared bid her put them away. She was officially the cook-maid at Sulgrave Manor but in reality she ruled the family. In her youth she had been a nun, just as old Jake had once been a monk. Long ago, in King Henry's day, when all the monasteries and convents were destroyed, Laurence Washington took them both into his house. It was his habit to employ monks and nuns whenever possible. He said they made the best servants.

Francis rubbed his hands together to get rid of the mingled lavender and clay, then swiftly wiped them on the seat of his hose. Quick as he was old Marta saw him.

"Hey, my young lord, what are you at?" she cried. "A pretty picture you've made of yourself. You look as though you'd been smacked as you deserve to be. You'd best go and change your hose before your father sees you."

"Father? Has he come?" cried Anne.

"Nay, but he'll be here before long. . . . He sent Will riding ahead to warn us that he's coming to-day. He's bringing a guest with him. Won't he be pleased about the baby!"

Anne clapped her hands. "Then I'll be able to tell him. Francis, do you hear? *I*'m going to tell him about the baby. I think I'll go and meet him."

"You'll do nothing of the sort," scolded Marta; "not until you've changed your gown and combed your hair anew. You look like a pair of vagabonds, When you've drunk your milk you'd best come in and tidy yourselves."

She handed them the pitcher and the platter of raspberries and gathered up the lavender into her apron, grumbling that they'd scattered nearly as much as they'd saved.

They had stripped all but the last few stalks

Francis drank and then passed the pitcher to Anne. She leaned back against the tree and as she sipped she gazed at the house, as Francis had done. She loved it every bit as much as he did. There could be no other house in the world like it, so peaceful and safe and secure. It was *home*. She looked up at the window of the Great Chamber, where Mother lay with the new baby, and wished that she could see inside. Anyway soon Father would be back from London, and the boys from Woodstock, and presently the Tail would return from Wormleighton, and they would be all together again. It had felt so odd to have nobody about except Francis and herself and the servants.

Suddenly an idea crossed her mind. She set down the pitcher.

"The boys are not back yet," she said uneasily. "If Father sees them come in, he's sure to ask where they've been and they'll get the most awful beating; at least Robert and Laurie will; I

Old Jake spotted them

suppose Father can't beat Chris. Oh, Francis, what *can* we do?"

"I might go and meet them," Francis suggested. "Father's certain to take the short cut through the farm, and they'll come the other way by the village."

"That'll do. You can warn them to tie up their horses in the barn and slip in by the back door if he's got here first. Oh, Francis, hurry. I'll come with you as far as the lane."

Stealthily, keeping under the shadow of the trees, they skirted the lawn so that they should not be seen from the house. Old Jake, swinging his scythe, spotted them and called out "What be you two up to?" but they took no notice of him. At the bottom of the garden there was a gate. Francis reached it first and left it open for Anne.

Together they looked up and down the dusty lane. On the

left it disappeared between the thatched barns of the home farm where it became just a track across the water meadows, linking up a mile away with the main road towards Helmdon and London. That was the short cut which Father always used. In the other direction it led straight to the village street, and it was through the village that the boys would come.

There was not a soul in sight. They stood for a moment listening intently, but except for a sheep bleating in the field they could hear nothing.

"D'you think I'd better take the pony?" said Francis. "It wouldn't take half a minute to saddle Meadowsweet."

But Anne gripped his arm. "Listen!" she hissed, pointing to the way through the farm. "I'm sure I heard voices. I believe it's Father."

They strained their ears again and heard the drum of horses' hoofs.

"No, it's the other way," cried Francis. "Look! Here they come." He started to run towards the village waving his arms and shouting. "Hi! Robert! Laurie! Make haste; Father is coming."

Three figures on horseback had actually turned the corner into the lane. Christopher Hatton was in front on Juno, his own tall grey, with Robert and Laurie strung out behind him on stout country cobs. They were too far away to hear what Francis said but they spurred their horses and came clattering along the lane, raising a cloud of dust behind them. Anne watched, hopping about with excitement. When Chris Hatton was only a few lengths away he pulled up so suddenly that the others almost piled on top of him, and all three horses plunged about perilously.

Anne turned round quickly to see why they had stopped like that. At the same moment a voice rang out behind her.

"Steady, you young fools. What in heaven's name are you at? Must you perform like a horse fair in a narrow lane?"

Anne clapped her hands over her mouth, and dropped a curtsey at the same time. Father, on Rosemary his chestnut mare, had just emerged from the farm. At his side rode a stranger, a tall thin man in a black riding cloak so large that it enveloped his horse from flank to tail. A little party of servants with baggage horses were gathered behind them.

The three boys gradually managed to get control of their mounts and came to a standstill in front of him. They looked tired and dishevelled. Their faces were red, their hair rough and their horses sweating and covered with dust. There was an unmistakeable air of guilt about them. Obviously they had come a long way.

Laurence Washington looked from one to the other.

"Those horses are over-hot," he declared. "Haven't I told you before that I won't have you riding them to death? Where have you been?"

The boys looked at each other but nobody answered. Anne saw that Father was frowning. He was beginning to suspect something.

"Come," he said sharply. "Have you all lost your tongues? Where have you been?"

Robert, the eldest, edged forward, but before he could speak Anne had an idea. She darted to her father's side and laid a hand upon his foot.

"Sir!" she cried, "have you heard the news? There's a new baby. It's a boy."

Laurence Washington turned from his sons to his daughter.

"What did you say? A boy? Praise be to God! When did it happen? How do they fare?"

Without even waiting to hear the answer, he turned his horse and started off briskly towards the house. Only when he reached the corner did he remember his guest.

"Your pardon, Doctor Dee," he called, swivelling round in the saddle. "Follow me at your leisure. Robert will show you the way."

The party in the lane all waited without speaking. Anne stole a glance at her father's companion and discovered to her embarrassment that he was looking at her. Though he was not at all old he had a fair beard trimmed to a long point. His eyes were brown and very bright. They watched her so keenly that, had it not been for a twinkle in them, she might have been frightened.

"That was prettily done, mistress," he said. "You are, I think a resourceful little maid."

She dropped a curtsey

Anne blushed. She did not understand what he meant by resourceful, but she realised that he had seen through her device. She dropped a curtsey and was thankful when Robert arrived to lead the guest to the house.

The screens passage

CHAPTER II

"Hush, you little fool"

By the time that Francis and Anne got back to the house everybody had vanished. They went in by the new porch; tiptoed along the screens passage, which led straight across from the porch door to the courtyard door, peeped into the great hall through the opening in the screen, and even popped their heads into the pantry and the buttery opposite. But everywhere was deserted.

The courtyard door stood open. Outside in the yard they found old Marta, instructing the maids where to take the cloak-bags and saddle-bags. The master had led the visitor upstairs to the guest chamber, she told the twins, and the boys had gone to see to their horses. Francis did not wait to hear any more. Turning a deaf ear to her order that they should go and tidy themselves, he made for the stables, followed closely by Anne.

The three boys were all hard at work rubbing down their hot and weary horses. They all looked up as the door flew open, and then, as they saw who it was, returned to their task again.

"Did you see the Lady?" demanded Francis breathlessly.

Robert, a dark boy with a square determined chin, looked round quickly.

"Hush! you little fool," he exclaimed. "Somebody will hear you. You've already caused trouble enough, acting like a mountebank in the lane."

"I did but try to warn you that Father was coming home," protested Francis with an injured air. "If I hadn't stopped you, you would have ridden straight into him without knowing anything about it."

"What are you going to say if he asks at supper where you had been?" interposed Anne quickly, to keep the peace.

Robert hesitated, but Chris Hatton with a friendly smile peeped at her over his horse's back.

"That's easy," he answered. "I shall say that they came with me to see Francis Verney. It's quite true. There's no need to say *where* we saw him. His home's in Hertfordshire. I expect your father knows that, so he's not likely to guess that we've been to Woodstock."

"You did go, then?" she ventured.

"To Woodstock? Of course we did. We spent the night in Verney's room, all four of us head to tail in one bed. We were nearly stifled but it sufficed. He's got a room at the 'Bull'. That's the inn where all the Lady Elizabeth's people stay. There's Master Parry, her treasurer, and that Florentine fellow, Castiglione, her Italian tutor, and some of her kinsmen on her mother's side. Old Bedingfield, her jailer, won't have them dwelling in the Palace; he thinks they're hatching mischief, and who can blame him?" He chuckled to himself. "But that doesn't prevent her from seeing them now and again. She knows how to get her way. She's not old King Hal's daughter for nothing, I can tell you."

"Chris, you prattle too much. You're almost as bad as Francis," objected Robert. "If you're going to answer my father, for your life's sake say as little as possible or he'll suspect something."

"Who is this man he's brought home with him?" inquired Laurie, speaking for the first time. He was a slim pale-faced boy who looked as though his thoughts were always far away. "Father called him Doctor Dee. He looks as solemn as a judge. He seemed to have a lot of baggage. I wonder if he is staying long."

"I don't think he's solemn," said Anne. "He notices things very

"We spent the night in Verney's room, all four of us"

quickly. He saw that I'd told Father about the baby just to stop him asking questions. He was laughing. I like him."

Just at that moment the stable door opened and Jenkin, the scullion boy, came in.

"If it please you, my masters, you're to hasten and make ready for supper," he said. "Marta sent me to fetch you." He paused and his freckled face broke into a grin. "There's duck for supper, and they're good, I can tell you. I've got them basting on the spit." He sucked his greasy fingers noisily, as if he liked the taste. Then he turned and vanished across the yard.

"We'd better go," cried Anne. "Come along, Francis; I'll race you. The one who gets to the garde-robe first washes first."

"Don't make a noise," Laurie called after them. "Mother might be asleep."

Ashamed of herself for forgetting, Anne caught Francis by the arm and slowed him down. It was like Laurie to remember Mother.

They were all of them down in the hall, clean and tidy, before either Father or his guest appeared. The boys had taken particular pains to make themselves spick and span. Robert and Laurie both wore short full jerkins, cut in the London style, over their best doublets and hose. Chris was still wearing riding clothes, but he had rolled his soft Spanish leather boots right down to show their rich linings of scarlet silk, and as his hose were of scarlet too, the effect was so gay that no one noticed his doublet of plain tanned hide.

Old Marta was in the hall, presiding over the laying of the table, and she soon set everyone to work. Laurie and Chris must fetch the flagons of white Rhine wine which were cooling in the cellar; Robert who was strong could set Father's great chair at the head of the table and put the cushioned one for the guest at its right hand, while Francis and Anne arranged stools for everybody else. She wished that the master would hurry up, she complained. The ducks were done to a turn and the sun was going down. Unless they were quick there'd have to be candles before supper was done.

Almost before she had finished her grumble, Laurence Washington came into the hall. He appeared to be in great good humour.

"Well, my young game-cocks," he exclaimed rubbing his hands gleefully, "this is right good news to come home to. Your mother is well and the babe is a sturdy brat. I had begun to think that this family was destined to fill a nunnery. Marta, your pardon; I had forgotten you. If we turn Sulgrave into a nunnery you shall be its prioress and Anne shall be mistress of novices under you. What say you, my poppet? If our gracious lady, Queen Mary, fills the country with monks and nuns again, will you lead all your sisters into the convent, like a row of ducklings into a pond?"

Anne laughed nervously as he pulled her to his side and gave her a little squeeze. She was never sure whether Father wanted an answer to his funny questions or not. This time, apparently, he did not, for he turned without waiting to Chris Hatton.

"Chris, my boy, I am in truth glad to see you. 'Tis an odd chance that you should be here when this new boy of mine arrives, for I was at dinner with your father, God rest him, the day *you* were born. That was fourteen years ago—or was it fifteen? Times goes so quickly. A thought-has struck me; we'll call the new baby after you. Robert, bring the wine. I'll give you a toast. Christopher Washington, and may good fortune follow him."

He poured some wine into his silver cup, took the first sip himself, then passed it round, watching with a smile as each of them raised it in turn, answering "Christopher Washington". When it came to Anne he held it for her, then himself drained it to the bottom.

"That was well done," he said with satisfaction; "though maybe it was unmannerly to drink without our guest. Francis, go up-stairs and knock at the door of the guest chamber. Tell Doctor Dee with my deep respect that we are waiting for him. Go quietly, so that you do not disturb your mother."

There was silence when Francis had gone, and the boys looked at one another. Anne knew that they were afraid of silences. Laurie rather awkwardly asked a question, just to keep Father talking.

"Did you say *Doctor* Dee, sir?"

"Yes, my son; Doctor John Dee, Doctor of Laws. He is a very learned man, a mathematician and an astronomer. I'm told that he knows more about the stars than any one alive. He was made Fellow of Trinity College, Cambridge, when he was but one and twenty, and now the University of Oxford would have him as Lecturer in mathematics. He has not yet made up his mind whether to accept or not. He has work to finish and he wants time to reflect, so I have offered him the use of the little house at Stuchbery. It is only a mile away and yet it is as quiet as he could desire. If he wants to study the stars he can climb Barrow Hill, and he is nearer to Oxford here than he would be in London."

The boys all nodded their heads with an appearance of keen interest. Their father looked at them with a smile.

"In exchange for my hospitality, Doctor Dee has suggested that he will guide your studies while he is here—yours, Robert, and Laurie's, and possibly Francis's too."

This was quite a different matter. Robert's interest suddenly became very real.

"But, sir," he protested, "I have left school. Of course it's as you wish, sir; but you said that I was old enough to be done with lessons and be apprenticed to the wool trade."

"The wool trade can get along without you for a little while longer. A chance like this must not be wasted. You learned your Latin and your sums at Brackley Grammar School, but since you left I have not noticed much anxiety to learn anything. You spend your time roaming about the country. By the way, I have not yet heard what you were doing when I met you in the lane just now, carrying saddlebags and all covered with dust. Where had you been?"

Anne held her breath. So it had come! But Chris was as good as his word.

"I hope you do not mind, sir," he began, without so much as a quiver in his voice; "but I took Robert and Laurie to visit my friend Francis Verney. He's the son of Sir Ralph Verney of Pendley in Hertfordshire—or I should say he *was* the son—his father is dead, God rest him. You were away so we could not ask leave. You knew Sir Ralph, sir, I believe?'

Anne just managed not to gasp. Chris was so marvellously natural.

"Yes, I knew Sir Ralph well. But his sons are a pair of young hotheads. I heard that they had a hand in Wyatt's rebellion. Have a care, Chris, that they do not lead you into mischief."

Laurie was rather white; Robert's face was red, but Chris was as cool as a cucumber. Anne wondered at him. He was clever; there was no doubt of that. It was all quite true, and yet it was so untrue that she did not really like it.

But anyway it was over; and there was no time for Father to ask more questions. From the buttery a string of men and maids in snowy aprons appeared bearing the supper dishes. At the same time the door at the bottom of the stairs was thrown open by Francis, and Doctor Dee came in.

The family supped alone in the hall. When the servants had set down the dishes they withdrew and the boys waited at table. Anne, who usually waited on Mother, had nothing to do. Father pulled up a stool for her at his left side, facing Doctor Dee. The

The great hall at Sulgrave

two men were deep in conversation, so until her supper arrived she just sat still and looked about her.

The great hall at Sulgrave, like the rest of the house, was newly built, and smoke had not yet darkened the oak beams of the ceiling. The stone floor, where it showed between the rushes, was a dull blue. Father was proud of it. He'd taken a great deal of trouble to procure stone of just the right colour. Anne thought it very pretty. The great window had coats of arms painted on some of the glass. There were the "Stars and Stripes" again. And there were three fishes, standing on their tails, which was the arms of Margaret Kytson, Father's mother. They were Cousin Kit's arms too, because she was a Kytson before she married Sir John Spencer. The same three fishes were painted on a wall at Wormleighton, where Cousin Kit lived, and there'd once been a terrible row because one of the boys had drawn in three fish hooks and three lines. Anne giggled inside herself as she remembered it; there was always fun at Wormleighton; Cousin Kit's children, the little Spencers, were much the same ages as the Washington children.

But the huge fireplace was the part of the hall that Anne liked best. The only pity about summer was that there were no fires.

Father's special corner

That chimney place was so lovely when the logs were blazing. There was a little seat right inside, let into the wall. It was Father's special corner, with a hollow scooped out to fit his elbow, and a ledge to hold his mug of ale. On winter afternoons when Father was out and the boys not yet home from school, Mother would often gather the six little girls, from Anne down to baby Margaret, the last baby before this one, and tell them stories in the firelight.

She was recalled from her dream by a great platter of roast duck with green peas and a slab of pasty which Laurie set in front of her. She looked at it a little worried. This was such a grown-up supper party that she did not want to disgrace herself. The duck was easy; she had a knife and her fingers, and she had been taught how to eat without getting herself too greasy. But how about the peas? If she collected them with her fingers she got covered with gravy. She glanced at her Father. He was eating them with his knife, but she was strictly forbidden to put her knife in her mouth in case she should cut herself. Then she noticed that Doctor Dee was using a spoon. There was another one on the table just opposite to her, so she stretched out her hand and got it, and then everything was easy. She set to work happily with one eye on her father's guest.

However learned he might be, Doctor Dee was certainly not a frightening person. There was a boyish look about him. He was thin and lanky, and his gown was long and black and very old, with hanging sleeves. Beneath it he wore a doublet of sky blue, which made his eyes look bright and twinkling. As he talked his fair pointed beard waggled in front of him, just as Father often wagged a finger to drive home what he said. It made Anne want to laugh.

But best of all he was full of stories. Right through the meal, until the platters were wiped clean, he hardly stopped. Everybody, from Father down to Anne, sat enthralled. He started by telling them that when he was a boy at Cambridge he used to work eighteen hours a day, taking only two hours off for meals and four for sleep. Robert and the others stared at him blankly, as if they just didn't believe him, but he stuck out his beard at them and asked them what they would have done in his place. The days just weren't long enough for both books and stars, so he read his books during the day and studied the stars at night.

"Have you ever studied the stars?" he asked them suddenly. "I suppose you stick your heads under the bedclothes and snore the nights away without it ever occurring to you that all the secrets of the universe are laid bare in the heavens, waiting for you to discover them?'

The boys looked sheepish. They didn't know how to answer that, so he left them alone and went on to describe how he'd been to some learned professors of mathematics in Holland, stout solemn old men, who had been rather shocked at him because he was young and always laughing. While he was there he heard that he'd been made a Fellow of Trinity College, so back he went to Cambridge, determined to settle down and take life seriously.

"But it was no good; I couldn't keep it up," he said mournfully. "Within a year I was in trouble for bewitching all the dons."

"What did you do?" demanded Anne breathlessly.

"I staged a play," he answered, smiling at her. "It was a learned play—the *Pax* of Aristophanes. You'd have thought that would have been sober enough for them, wouldn't you? I took an immense amount of trouble but they didn't like it. You see, there's a scene in the play where the Scarab—that's a sacred beetle—flies off to heaven with a man and a basket of victuals on its back. Well, I made it go."

"Made *what* go?"

"Made the Scarab go. I contrived it with lights and a mechanism of my own inventing. It was a great big scarab; it had a man on its back, and it flew away—at least it appeared to. They saw it go. But they didn't like it. They said that it was witchcraft. They all turned on me like a pack of hounds. I barely got away with my life. If I had remained I believe they would have burned me at the stake."

"How did you do it—the beetle thing I mean?" asked Francis. He always wanted to know how things were made.

"That's a long story, my boy; too long for now."

"Where did you go when you ran away?" inquired Anne, afraid that he was going to stop.

"I went abroad again, to the University at Louvain. They were good to me there. They made me a Doctor of Laws, and I met the map-makers—Phrysius and Ortelius and the great Mercator." He turned to Master Washington who nodded his head and looked wise, though Anne suspected that he did not know the names any more than she did.

"What are map-makers?" questioned Francis.

"People who make maps," said Doctor Dee with a grin. "Almost every year sea captains are discovering fresh lands that no one has known before, and then somebody has to make maps so that other sea captains can find the way and discover a bit more."

"How do they make maps?" Francis was leaning forward. Robert and Laurie groaned aloud. When Francis started asking questions there was no end to it. But Father came to the rescue.

"That's enough for to-night," he decreed. "Doctor Dee will be weary of you. How about some more wine? Robert, bring the other flagon. This is some Spanish sack, sir; a brown wine. It rounds off a meal nicely, I think. Have you a fancy for some music?"

With L.W. carved on the door

This was a sign that supper was over. The boys began to carry the dishes away. Anne, who knew what was expected of her, went to the little cupboard beside the fireplace, Father's own special little cupboard with L.W. carved on the door. There, on a shelf, lay his flageolet. She placed it carefully on the table beside him. When he was in a good mood he enjoyed playing tunes so that they could all sing.

That done she slipped away. She had a bright idea. The boys had all been horrid to Francis, shutting him up when he asked a lot of questions, and she was determined to put it right. The house door stood open and nobody saw her go. It was still hot in the garden; there seemed to be no evening freshness, though it had clouded over and the sun had vanished. As she ran across the lawn to the elm trees she heard a distant rumble of thunder. There was going to be a storm.

Marta had taken away the lavender, but Francis's coat of arms still lay on the ground. She picked it up carefully and carried it indoors.

While she was out Laurence had fetched his viol de gamba; Robert was rubbing up the mouthpiece of a recorder and Doctor Dee was trying the strings of Mother's lute. Determined to have her say before the music began, Anne went straight to her father, the clay model in her hands.

"Sir," she said quickly, "look what Francis has made; the Stars and Stripes."

He smiled at her. "Stars and Stripes? What are Stars and Stripes? Oh, I see; the Washington arms." He took the slab from her. "This is very good. Did Francis make it himself?"

She nodded. "It is to go over the porch. You said that you wanted one like Grandfather's."

"Yes, I remember. Francis, my boy, it is excellently made. When did you do it? It must have taken you a long time."

Francis, his cheeks red and his eyes bright with excitement, came to his father's side.

"Not very long, sir," he said in a clear voice, "I made it while they were at Woodstock."

The great chamber

CHAPTER III

The Storm

In the deathly silence that followed Anne could hear Francis catch his breath and even hear the sudden creak of Chris's leather doublet.

"So!" said Laurence Washington at last. "It was from *Woodstock* that you had come."

He looked from one to the other of the boys, but nobody answered. He continued with a deadly calm. "I seem to remember that you said you had been to see Francis Verney."

"That was true, sir," Chris broke in quickly. "We *had* been to see Francis Verney. He is staying at Woodstock. We spent the night with him."

"It was a truth intended to deceive, eh? I will say naught of that to you, Christopher. I am not your father. I hope it is an excuse for *you* that you have none; but I fear my own sons gave consent."

Once more there was silence. Then quite suddenly he turned and roared at them.

"You young hypocrites," he cried. "You knew perfectly well that you were doing wrong, otherwise you would not have concealed it. You knew that I should not allow you to go. Therefore you went when you thought that I was out of the way. You richly deserve the greatest beating of your lives."

Chris Hatton took a step forward. "If you beat them, sir, beat me too. 'Twas I who planned it. They did but come with me."

Laurence Washington grunted. "They came readily enough, I'll wager. If I could beat some sense into them I'd beat with a will. But one might as well expect sense from scarecrows. You knew well that I should forbid you to go to Woodstock. What did you think would be my reason? Come now, speak up. Don't leave it all to Christopher."

"Because the Lady Elizabeth is there," ventured Robert.

"And isn't that reason enough? The Lady Elizabeth is held prisoner because only six months ago Wyatt and his rebels stormed London and tried to put her on the throne. More than four hundred poor wretches suffered death for that bit of folly, doubtless many of them hot-headed boys like you."

"But the Lady Elizabeth had no part in it, sir. She has sworn that she knew nothing of it."

Master Washington tossed his head impatiently. "You talk like children. Whether she had part in it or not matters nothing to those who are dead. Possibly half of them did not even know the object of their rebellion, to make a marriage between her and young Edward Courtenay and crown them King and Queen. Why, you lack-wits, this is no stuff for boys to meddle with. 'Tis an evil deep-rooted in the past before you were born. It started when old King Henry wanted to set aside his Queen, Katharine of Aragon, and take another wife. To do that he had to cast off the Pope and the old religion, and of course cast off his daughter, the Lady Mary. The new Queen, Anne Bullen, did not last long; she ended on the scaffold. But she left him another daughter, the Lady Elizabeth. The bitterness between these two sisters lies at the root of all the troubles to-day. Not only were their mothers deadly enemies, but they are, as it were, of different worlds. The Lady Mary, our present Queen, stands for the old religion and the old way of life; the Lady Elizabeth stands for the new. They may well split the country in twain and the only course for a wise man is to go his own way and stick to his own business."

He pushed back his chair. Anne held her breath. Were the boys about to get their beating? But her father turned to Doctor Dee.

"Your pardon, sir," he said. "It must be irksome for you to have to listen while I try and knock some sense into these dolts."

Doctor Dee shook his head. "Nay, you put it very well. 'Tis not everyone who can see the case so clearly."

"If it is clear enough to get through their thick skulls I shall be the more happy. It is not only their own lives that they risk; they put all of us in danger, their parents and their family and even their home. Why, Sulgrave itself might be lost to us by this tom-foolery." He sighed wearily, and turned to the boys again. "Now, listen all of you, and remember what I say. The Lady Mary is our lawful Queen; of that there is no question. We have the old religion back and there is no reason why we shouldn't live peacefully. But unfortunately there are plenty of people who have other fish to fry. England is full of knaves who care not a jot for Mary or Elizabeth, Catholic or Protestant, if they can fill their own coffers or add to their lands, or at least hold on to what they have already grabbed. So long as their own ends are served they take no heed who they bring to the scaffold, be it the Lady Elizabeth or a parcel of beardless boys."

It was growing dark in the hall. In the distance the thunder growled. As her father paused for breath Anne looked round. Her heart was thumping uncomfortably. She had feared that the boys would get a beating, but she had not dreamed that it was as serious as this. Sulgrave might be lost, the whole family be in danger. Obviously they couldn't have known what they were doing. She glanced quickly at them, one after the other. Robert and Laurie stood with Chris, glum and silent. Francis was still by his father's chair, the fatal coat of arms lying on the table in

28

front of him. He looked deathly pale and his hands were clenched till the knuckles stood out white. Anne knew that he was in despair because he had given his brothers away. She forgot all about Woodstock and thought only of Francis. At ordinary times they squabbled between themselves, but if anyone else attacked him she was ready to fly to his defence.

A flash of lightning suddenly lit up the room. Laurence Washington absent-mindedly crossed himself as he turned from his sons and began to talk to his guest again.

"It is odd that in an out-of-the-way place like this we should be troubled by politics," he remarked. "A few years ago the Court and its affairs seemed as remote as the coasts of Barbary. But to-day not only have we the Lady Elizabeth at Woodstock but Courtenay, the poor fool they would marry her to, locked up at Fotheringhay, at the opposite side of the county. And as if that weren't enough, my lord the Marquis of Northampton has settled at Greens Norton, a bare eight miles away. Our air must be specially suitable for prisoners newly from the Tower."

"The Marquis of Northampton? Isn't he Sir William Parr?"

Master Washington nodded. "Quite right. The brother of Queen Katharine Parr, old King Hal's last wife. His title was forfeited when he was condemned to death for helping to put Lady Jane Grey on the throne, but our Queen pardoned him and allowed him this manor of Greens Norton from among all his property so that he might live quietly. I've known the Parrs all my life. Their family place is at Kendal, in the north country, quite close to Warton where I was born. They are people of good substance, but we never dreamed in those days that they would produce a queen." He looked round the room. "I'faith, it is dark. Have we sat into the night or is it the storm? Anne, child, run to the kitchen and bid them bring lights."

Anne started off, thankful that he seemed to have forgotten about Woodstock. Perhaps the boys would escape punishment after all.

She had barely reached the buttery door when the hall was lit by a blinding flash. At the very same instant the thunder cracked with a deafening roar. Before she could recover her wits there was another rending crash, so violent that the whole house shook with it.

"Saints in heaven, have we been struck?" cried her father. It was almost too dark to see but she heard him stumbling across the hall.

" 'Tis a tree, sir," called Robert from the direction of the window. "One of the elms is down."

The place was in turmoil. Servants came running through the buttery door, terror-stricken, to know what had happened.

"Marta, go to your mistress and calm her. Robert, quickly, give me a cloak. I must see what the damage is."

They all crowded into the porch while Father, refusing to be held back, plunged out into the storm. The thunder rolled again; it was further away now, but the rain was cataracting down. In a few seconds he was back.

"Yes, it is one of the elms," he gasped, shaking the water from his face. "It lies right across the lawn. Phew! One could almost drown in the rain. This cloak is sodden just in that minute."

Somebody took the cloak and hung it to drip while somebody else brought a towel. When he was dry the family returned to the hall and the servants to the kitchen. There was now just enough light to see the confusion, chairs pushed back and stools overthrown. They had barely begun to put it right when old Jake appeared in the opening of the screens, a sack across his shoulders.

"Your pardon, sir, but there's a gentleman with a young boy and a groom sheltering in the barn. They popped in when that big crack came. I thought as you'd wish to be told. They're terrible wet."

"A gentleman? What gentleman? Did you ask his name?"

The old man shook his head. "Nay, sir; he gave no name. I think he comes from Greens Norton, sir."

"*Greens Norton!*" Father wheeled round to face Doctor Dee. " 'Talk of the devil——' " he said under his breath. "If the old saying runs true it is Sir William Parr." He raised his voice again. "I'll come myself, Jake. You boys, fetch wine and wine cups, and bring lights."

Seizing his wet cloak again he charged past old Jake who

"I am plain Sir William Parr"

followed him. Indoors everyone began to bustle about. Robert and Laurie hurried to the pantry; Christopher helped Doctor Dee to arrange chairs and stools, while Francis and Anne ran for the candles. They had only just got everything to rights when the courtyard door opened and Father ushered in the travellers, a man and a boy, both of them dripping with water. They paused in the screens passage while servants carried away the wet cloaks and Robert and Laurie assisted in the peeling off of long riding boots.

"Now, my lord marquess, come you in," cried Father, leading the way. "A cup of wine will warm you, or perhaps some mulled ale. Your cloak must be a good one; your doublet looks quite dry. But I fancy the boy is wet. He looks about the same size as my youngest son. Francis, go quickly and fetch a warm jerkin."

His "youngest son"! Francis exchanged delighted glances with Anne as he ran off to get the jerkin. Father had forgotten the baby.

"Nay, do not 'my lord' me," declared the guest as he advanced into the hall. "The Queen was graciously pleased to give me back my life but she took away mine honours. I am plain Sir William Parr. Good Master Washington, we are in truth beholden for this welcome. We were riding back from Banbury and we missed our way in the storm. Tom here was frightened out of his wits." He pulled the boy forward. "Tom Tresham is a young kinsman of mine who serves me as a page. Make your bow, Tom."

Standing unnoticed behind her father Anne had a good view of Sir William Parr. She looked at him with some awe, because he was the brother of King Henry's last queen. Except that he had very small ears instead of long ones, his face reminded her of a rabbit. He had prominent teeth, small eyes of very pale blue, and his round head and bony jaw were covered with soft stubbly hair the colour of a rabbit's fur. He was tall and elegantly dressed, with little bits of jewellery that glittered in the candle light. He took the cup of wine that Father offered him and looked round smiling at everyone in turn, as though he expected them to bow to him.

Father hastened to do the honours.

"May I present to you Doctor John Dee, Doctor of Laws, a most learned scholar of Cambridge."

Sir William Parr paused, with his cup in the air as though startled. Then he waved a gracious hand on which a diamond shone.

"Doctor Dee needs no introduction. We have met before in happier times. You are the astrologer that Master Secretary Cecil brought to court; the man who works magic with the stars. My nephew, the late King Edward, thought highly of you."

Her help was needed to make it go on

John Dee bowed low. "I am honoured, sir; but do not say *magic*, I beg you. I study the *science* of the stars."

Anne could see that he was annoyed about the word "magic", and Father saw it too, for to cover up the awkward moment he hurriedly presented "Master Christopher Hatton of Holdenby" although, as they were neighbours in the county, Sir William Parr knew him very well already. Then Francis returned with the jerkin and called her. Tom Tresham was broader than he was and her help was needed to make it go on. Afterwards the two boys began to talk, and she stayed listening while they compared notes about ages and lessons, and about how far each could shoot a crossbow bolt, and how often they had succeeded in hitting a rabbit. Tom had plenty to say for himself. He was a Northamptonshire boy too, the grandson of Sir Thomas Tresham of Rushton, a very great man, sheriff of the county and representative of the Queen. But Tom's father was dead and as he had no brothers or sisters he was sent to his 'Cousin Parr', as he called him, to be his page and learn good manners. Anne did not think that he had learned very much, for he boasted all the time about his hawks and his hounds and the sword that his grandfather had given him on his last feast day; and when Francis produced his own little short dirk, he pushed it aside with a lordly air and said, "You should see mine." She decided that she did not like Tom Tresham, so she left the boys to their own devices and returned to the grown ups.

Sir William Parr was now sitting in Father's great chair, a mug of mulled ale on the table beside him and Mother's lute across his knee. Though he did not actually pluck the strings, he was passing his long fingers gracefully over them as he talked. Anne remembered that he had been a prisoner in the Tower. He might have some exciting stories to tell, so she crept to a stool in the shadows and sat with her eyes fixed on his face.

He was holding forth rather pompously about the great people at Court.

"Everything is changed nowadays," he lamented, shaking his head, " 'twas vastly different when old King Henry was alive. My sister, Queen Katharine, was a tender step-mother to the royal children; the Lady Elizabeth and the little prince Edward doted on her. He was a sweet boy, of a wisdom beyond his years. When he became king he made me his Lord Great Chamberlain, you know. He used to call me his 'honest uncle', just as his father dubbed me 'my old integrity'. But alas! he had a poor frail body. It was a bitter blow that he should have died so young."

"Indeed, sir," said Father sympathetically, "it was a blow to many in this realm."

"Ah, well; what is the will of heaven must be borne." He sighed deeply. "I have left the Court. All my desires are for a quiet life. I stood trial in Westminster Hall and heard myself condemned to death; I languished in the Tower thinking every day would be my last. That cures a man's tastes for courts, I promise you."

Father leaned forward to pour out more ale. "But now you have settled at Greens Norton, I hear?"

"Yes, Greens Norton at least is left to me; and I have books and music and the joys of the chase, so there is yet some sweetness to be found in life. You must bring your hawks over one of these days, Master Washington. I can offer you good sport, though not so good as it used to be, thanks to these plaguey sheep everywhere. Half the woods are being cut down for pasture and the shepherds' dogs are always disturbing the game. The place is nothing but a great sheepfold."

Anne looked quickly at her father. What would he say to that? At Sulgrave the sheep were considered more important than anything else.

But Laurence Washington only laughed good-humouredly.

"You must not be too hard on the poor sheep," he said. "Remember that the wealth of England is on their backs."

With one sudden chord upon the lute, Sir William Parr sat up straight.

"A thousand pardons, sir," he cried. "I spoke without thinking. You are a sheep owner yourself I believe."

"I am a wool merchant by calling," said Father simply. "I keep a few sheep, but most of the flocks you see on my pasture belong to my kinsman, Sir John Spencer."

"Of course, I remember. I heard that he aims at twenty thousand. I ask your pardon, sir, for my untimely words. In token of your forgiveness I beg you come and stoop your hawk at my pheasants, or course a hare or two with my hounds. Bring your sons, if you will. Tom would enjoy their company."

"Thank you. I should be honoured. But the boys ought to stick to their books. Doctor Dee has offered to take charge of their studies while he is here. It is a chance not to be missed."

"In truth it is. I wish that Tom could join them. Would you extend your favour to him too, good Doctor, if Master Washington is willing?"

Anne looked at Doctor Dee. He had been sitting in silence all this time, abstractedly swinging his signet ring backwards and forwards on a strand of thread. He put the ring back on to his finger and pocketed the thread before he replied.

"I will gladly have him. One boy more or less will make small odds. I have your leave to beat him if I have cause?"

"Beat him and welcome. It will doubtless do him good. When we were young the best education for a boy was for him to serve as page in a noble house." He spread his hands as though bewildered. "Now it seems that learning is everything. Tom, come here and be presented to Doctor Dee. Mind that you are obedient and appreciate your good fortune."

Tom did not look too well pleased, but he bowed as he was told and then stood in silence while it was being arranged which days he should come and which way he should ride. Sir William thought that he ought to have a groom with him, for the woods were full of vagabonds who could not find a roof to shelter them. Master Washington suggested that when the weather was bad he might sometimes sleep at Sulgrave, but the suggestion was dismissed with an elegant wave of the hand.

"You are very good, sir, but he is hardy enough and he has a good cloak. Which reminds me—the sky seems to be clear now. There is still a glimmer of daylight. It is time we were on our way."

Indeed when Anne went out with the boys to call for the horses there was a golden glow of sunset behind the barns. They all went to the gate to see the visitors ride away. Sir William Parr, full of effusive thanks, swept off his cap with a grand air, and Tom, at last showing signs of friendliness, stood up in the stirrups to wave good-bye.

Walking back to the house Anne found herself beside Doctor Dee. To her astonishment he picked up the edges of his old black gown and tripped a few mincing steps. " '*Now it seems that learning is everything*'," he piped softly in a high-pitched voice.

Anne stared at him completely taken aback. Then she giggled. It was so exactly like Sir William Parr. But Doctor Dee frowned at her, his lips pursed and his finger raised. Obviously it was to be a secret between them. Anne gave a little skip. She *did* like Doctor Dee.

As they re-entered the house Father looked round and his eye lighted upon Anne.

"Child!" he exclaimed, "it is high time you were abed. Without your mother to send you packing you would sit the clock round. Be off with you; yes, and Francis too."

Anne knew better than to protest. She glanced at Francis and he came to her side. Together they bowed and curtsied, first to their father and then to their father's guest, as they had been taught. Then as Anne stepped forward to receive her father's kiss, he pulled her within the circle of his arm.

"My eldest daughter is growing a tall maid," he said. "Take care that you do not outstrip your brother or the rafters will ring with it."

Anne suppressed a sigh of satisfaction. It was plain that he had forgotten all about Woodstock. She ventured to whisper in his ear: might she go and say good night to Mother? Just for a tiny minute?

"*You* may go but not the boys," he whispered back. "If she is asleep be sure that you don't wake her."

Anne promised, her face wreathed in smiles. For once she was glad that she was a girl. Francis made off towards the kitchen to find old Marta. As usual the points that tied up his hose were in a knot. Anne softly called "Good night" to him and crept upstairs.

The latch on the door of the great Chamber was rather high but she managed to lift it without making a sound. The room was still light, for the window curtains were not drawn and the last glow from the sunset lingered in the sky. The bed-curtains were open too and Anne could see her mother lying propped on pillows, the dark braids of hair showing beneath her night coif and one white hand resting on top of the bed cover.

Anne crept up to the bed, trying not to breathe. Even if Mother *was* asleep she still might have a peep at the baby in the cradle. But as she peered into the shadows she saw that her mother was smiling and that her fingers were moving gently along a string of prayer beads which lay upon the counterpane.

"Well, my Poppet——"

Anne began a curtsey but stopped it to kiss the hand her mother stretched out. The fingers closed on hers.

"Well, my poppet, and were you frightened of the storm?"

"Not very," said Anne; "only when the tree fell."

"Yes, I was frightened then; but Marta ran quickly to tell me that no one was hurt. You may come and lie down for a minute if you like."

Anne needed no second invitation. Carefully she climbed on to the big bed and lay down gently at her mother's side.

"How did the supper go? I hear that you had visitors."

Her mother's voice was so weak that Anne answered almost in a whisper. But she told her all about Sir William Parr's arrival and about Doctor Dee, and about Tom Tresham who was to share lessons with the boys. She was careful not to mention Woodstock, because trouble between Father and the boys always worried Mother so much.

When she had told all she could she lay quite still. It was so wonderfully quiet and peaceful after the storm, and after all the commotion downstairs. She thought again about what Father had said of the danger to Sulgrave. Surely when home was

A tiny oil lamp

such a lovely place, the boys couldn't be wicked and stupid enough to risk losing it.

The last glow had faded from the window; but a tiny oil lamp, standing on a shelf beside the bed, gave just enough light for her to see the prayer beads begin to move again beneath her mother's fingers.

"You've got a rosary like Marta's," she said softly. "You had one before, when I was little; you used to let me play with it."

"You've got a good memory, sweetheart. You were such a tiny girl when all those things were changed. How much else can you remember?"

"Oh, lots," said Anne. "I can remember the parson saying mass, as he does now, and wearing lovely embroidered things. And I can remember pictures in the church, and statues, and coloured glass in the windows. Then they took it all away and he just wore a white shift and said a lot of prayers in English.

Marta is very glad that it is Mass again. She cries about it. But I wish they'd put back the coloured glass. It made the church look pretty."

Her mother laughed softly. "I wish they would too, my poppet; but I expect it was all broken. I can remember so many changes that I've almost lost count of them. When I was your age there were still abbeys of monks and nuns. Old Marta was still in her convent."

"I wish things wouldn't change," sighed Anne. "I'd like them to stay always as they are now."

"God doesn't change," said Mother softly. "Remember that, Anne; whatever anybody does, our blessed Lord never changes. Now you must go to your bed. Look! It's quite dark. Would you like to say your prayers here, as you used to do when you were little?"

That was exactly what Anne would like. She slipped from the bed and knelt down beside it. She said *Our Father*, *Hail Mary* and *I Confess* out loud and then was quiet for a minute, trying to remember what she had done wrong that day. She couldn't think of anything much except being snappy with Francis, and that wasn't a very big sin. Anyway Mother never made them say it aloud unless they wanted to, so she finished off quickly, remembering just in time to say *Thank You* for the boys not being beaten. Then she got up and went close to her mother.

"May I say good night to the baby?" she begged.

"If you are *very* careful you can pick him up and bring him to me," said her mother. "Marta must be busy, with a guest in the house."

Proud to be trusted, Anne bent over the cradle. She knew exactly how to do it because she had held so many babies before. She gathered up the soft swaddled bundle and laid it in the curve of her mother's arm.

"God bless you, my poppet. Sleep well. Tell Marta that you have given me the baby and that presently she can come and put him to rest again."

Glowing with happiness Anne stole from the room. The stairs were dark and she felt her way, still as quiet as a mouse.

At the bottom of the stairs two people stood with their heads close together. Anne looked down on them. They were Christopher Hatton and Doctor Dee, talking in lowered voices.

"I pray that you will not mention it," the Doctor was saying, "but when you go again to Woodstock I would be glad to go with you."

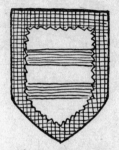

The Arms of PARR

Sulgrave Church

CHAPTER IV

The Vow

Though the thunderstorm did not come back, the night was hot and stuffy. Francis tossed and turned wearily, unable to sleep. He was lying on a straw pallet on the floor and it was very hard. His truckle bed, where he usually slept, was occupied by Laurie, for Robert was sharing the big bed with Chris.

Because Father had warned them not to make a noise, the three bigger boys were very quiet when they came up. Francis had been dreading their arrival because he was afraid they might attack him for giving them away. He lay watching the monstrous black shadows cast on the wall by the rushlight, holding his breath whenever they seemed to come near. But none of them took any notice of him. The creaking of the bed ropes announced that Chris and Robert had got into bed. Laurie took longer over his prayers; he always did. But at last he blew out the light, and soon Francis could hear from their even breathing that they were all asleep.

Francis envied them. He wished to goodness that he could go to sleep too, but never in his life had he felt more wide awake. He tried everything he knew; counting sheep going through a gate, saying the Our Father in Latin over and over again; but nothing was any good. The harder he tried the more awake he seemed to be.

He couldn't forget that feeling of deadly cold when he had come out with the word Woodstock. It was the worst moment of his whole life and he could have died of shame. Though the boys had not been beaten and they had not turned on him, he just could not get it out of his head. For he now realised that what they said was true. He *couldn't* keep a secret. It had happened often enough before, and the others had scoffed at him and called him a babbling little fool; but he'd always bluffed and refused to admit himself in the wrong. Now he faced it. He didn't know why, but words just seemed to slip out before he could stop them.

He lay turning from one side to the other for what seemed to be the entire night. The moon, shining through diamond panes, threw a criss-cross pattern over the foot of his bed. The pattern crept across the floor and slowly climbed the further wall. When it had gone the room was very dark. An owl hooted in the garden. Once he heard the new baby cry. Then the window began to show a faint light again. It must be the dawn.

As soon as he could see sufficiently he got up, wriggled into his clothes and crept downstairs without making a sound. He felt his way through the hall, and the buttery, into the empty kitchen. On the great wide hearth last night's logs still glowed among the embers. The cauldron hanging on a chain bubbled gently under its lid. The cat sat up and blinked at him sleepily. He threw on a bundle of sticks and stood by the blaze warming himself. The dawn was cold. As it grew lighter he saw that the big table was piled with new loaves of bread. Francis suddenly realised that he was hungry. He picked out a small loaf with a nice crisp crust. There were raisins in the pantry. He knew where they were kept for Marta often gave the children a few. So he took a clean clout that was hanging up to dry and wrapped up a good handful of

He stood warming himself

them. Then, with his loaf under his arm, he let himself out of
the back door.

It was already broad daylight in the courtyard. If he wanted to
get out unnoticed he must make haste.

He skirted Little Green, the meadow at the back of the house,
and emerged into the village street. As the sun rose a cold mist
rose too. Francis hunched up his shoulders and decided against
going down by the trout stream. Instead he turned off opposite
the church, avoided the mill pond and started up the hill. Before
long he had left the mist below him and felt the warmth of the
morning sun. The grass was wet from last night's storm, so he
found a tree with a convenient fork, climbed it and settled himself
comfortably, with the sun in his face and a dry tree trunk at his
back. Now for the bread and raisins.

He no longer felt sleepy, and oddly enough he was not miserable any more. As he gnawed his crust he made up his mind that
from now on he was going to be different. There was going to
be no more babbling and blurting things out. He would be care-

ful. He would think before he spoke. . . . He would watch his tongue and control it as he controlled Meadowsweet when she'd had a feed of oats and wanted to kick up her heels.

He chuckled to himself as he thought about Meadowsweet. That was a good idea. It would help him to remember. Oh, it was a glorious morning and everything was going to be all right. Sitting up there in the tree he was already quite warm. He was enjoying himself. The village lay spread out at his feet like a toy set out on the floor. Straight in front of him was the church on its little hill, with the castle mound beside it and a jumble of old thatched cottages at its foot. On the slope to his left were the corn lands, where the villagers grew their crops, cut into narrow strips of every shape and colour; some were golden with ripe wheat, some silver with barley, some green with late-sown beans and a few already cut and harvested. Beyond the cornlands there was green pasture on every side, all of it dotted with sheep. He could not see the manor house; it was hidden in trees; but evidently someone had thrown more wood on the kitchen fire for a wisp of blue smoke rose over the top of the elms.

He finished the raisins and the last bit of crust. What should he do with the inside of the loaf? It was wicked to waste it. Perhaps he might crumble it up and throw it to the carp in the mill pond. They would swallow his bait all the more readily next time.

But he was not sure that he wanted to go to the mill pond by himself, though the water glinting among the willows looked friendly enough. Beyond it, further up the hill, stood the ruins of the Grange, a farmhouse which had belonged to the monks of Northampton in the old days. Father had used most of the stones to build the manor farm. It was roofless; ivy and elder covered the remaining walls; owls and rats had the run of it, and nobody ever went near it.

One solitary old woman lived there in a cellar, with a mangy old dog for company. The village said she was a witch and gave the place a very wide berth. Francis had never ventured even to the mill pond without Anne or one of the others for company. But now from his safe perch in the tree he was able to have a good look at the ruins. He could even see the little door, down some steps, where the witch was said to live. He sat watching it. He almost wished that she would appear so that he could see what she looked like. But nothing happened. Not a leaf stirred among the walls.

Suddenly a movement in the other direction caught his eye. Down in the valley someone was crossing the field. To his astonishment he saw that it was old Jake, shrouded in a big dark cloak. Cloak or no cloak he could not mistake that tall bent old figure, crooked from many years of toil. He supposed that Jake

This must be the old witch

was coming to fetch him, though he wondered how he knew where to look.

Then he saw that the old man was not coming his way at all. He had turned up the hill and was heading straight for the ruins. Puzzled, Francis watched him as he vanished for a minute behind the tumbledown building and then reappeared at the top of the stone steps. He seemed to be carrying something under his cloak. What in the world was he doing there?

The wind set the other way, so Francis could hear no sound; but he guessed that Jake had called out, for a dark figure emerged from the door. This must be the old witch. She was tall, as tall as Jake, and she wore a long black gown and a pointed hood.

The old dog came out too, another black bag of bones, and wandered about the ruins sniffing at the ground.

The two stood talking, their heads very close together. Then something from beneath Jake's cloak changed hands. Hugging to her whatever it was that Jake had given her, the old witch turned and vanished into the cellar again, followed by the dog. Old Jake made off down the hill in the direction of home.

Full of excitement, Francis watched till he was out of sight. What *could* Jake have to do with the old witch? There was something odd going on. He wondered if he ought to tell Father. He couldn't make up his mind. Anyway it would be a grand story for the others.

He swung himself down from the tree, then stopped, remembering last night. Could this be a test to see if he really could keep something to himself? The idea grew stronger. It would be good practice to keep this business of Jake and the old witch as his own secret. He wouldn't tell anybody, not even Anne. He would use it to prove to himself that he could hold his tongue when he wanted to.

Just at that moment the church bell started ringing for the morning Mass. That decided him. He would go to church and he'd make a vow that never again would he give away a secret.

There were not many people in the church. Father was there and Anne too, kneeling beside old Marta. Laurie was on the altar steps serving the mass.

Francis kneeled by himself at the back. He'd got quite used to the mass now; they'd had it for nearly a year and the first strangeness had worn off. Robert and Laurie could both remember it from years ago, but to Francis it had all come quite new. His father, he noticed, was following in a book. Anne was praying very devoutly with her eyes closed, but old Marta looked very strange. She was gazing at the altar and he saw with amazement that tears were pouring down her face. He had seen her cry at mass before and he wondered why. At home she always seemed quite happy and she certainly wasn't the weeping sort.

He watched everybody in the church till Laurie rang the little

His father was following in a book

bell. Then he remembered what he had come for and buried his face in his hands.

When the Mass was over he waited for Laurie. He had a feeling that he ought to say something about what had happened last night, and it was easier to talk to Laurie than to the others.

The two boys left the church together and walked home by the little dusty lane. Francis took a deep breath and started with a spurt.

"I'm sorry I gave you away about Woodstock. I don't know what made me, it just seemed to slip out. I swear I'll never do it again. I've made a vow about it."

"Set your heart at rest," said his brother kindly. "There was no great harm done. We weren't beaten and Father forgot all about it when Sir William Parr arrived. You know, it was truly strange that he should have come just when he was spoken of. Chris says it always falls out like that. It seems as though everything revolves round Woodstock and the Lady. There's no getting away from it, even if one would."

Francis looked at him quickly. He had taken it for granted that last night's trouble would have put a stop to all thought of Woodstock. Now he was not so sure.

"Did you have to promise that you wouldn't go there again?" he inquired.

48

"No, not promise," said Laurie slowly. He hesitated, then turned his head away. "I don't think I'd better talk about it any more."

Francis gulped. So they weren't going to tell him. After what he'd done he couldn't blame them. It was no use for him to go on saying that he'd made a vow and was going to be different. He had to prove it. He would have to watch things happening and not say a word. Perhaps in the end he'd be able to do something which would save the situation and show them that he'd known about their secrets all the time.

"Father's not likely to remember it this morning," said Laurie as they opened the garden gate. "There's murrain broken out among the sheep. It'll spoil Cousin Spencer's twenty thousand again, and the Spencer shepherd is in a fine to do about it. He's stumping and swearing that somebody's bewitched them."

Francis stopped dead. "Bewitched?" he repeated.

"That's what he says. Of course Father said that it was nonsense. Why? What's the matter? What are you looking like that for?"

"Nothing," said Francis firmly. "I only thought that it was funny." It had been on the tip of his tongue to tell Laurie about Jake and the old witch. He had just saved himself in time. The first trial of his self-control had not been long in coming. And as if to test him further, as they walked up the garden path, there was old Jake quite close to them, unconcernedly chopping branches from the fallen tree.

Back in the house they found so much going on that Francis had no time to think about his troubles. First of all Chris said good-bye and set off home to Holdenby, cheerful enough, if a little subdued. His horse, Juno, was lame from the Woodstock outing, so he left her behind and rode Betsy, Robert's pony, which was really too small for him. But he would be over again soon, he said, and they would change back then.

When Chris had gone the boys were admitted one at a time to see Mother and the baby. Anne, very proud of herself, acted as doorkeeper, permitting each one of them to stay only while the sand ran twice through Marta's eggboiling glass. It was not often that she had the whip hand over her brothers and she made the most of it.

This ceremony was barely finished when everyone was summoned to the kitchen to gaze at the marvels of a special cooking pot which Father had brought from London. It was for Marta's use, and he said that it was something quite new, calculated to do its work in a quarter of the time taken by an ordinary pot. With all the family gathered round, he gave a demonstration of how the lid was clamped on and a sort of spring adjusted to control the steam. It must have very little water, he explained, and yet be hung on the pot hook right over the fire. Marta crossed herself and called aloud upon St. Martha, patron saint of housewives; to treat a pot like that was to invite it to burst in their faces. The pot did indeed behave in a very odd manner. First it began to whistle, then it hissed and spat like an angry goose. The maid servants all rushed for the back door, and only Father's presence prevented Marta from following them. Even Father was not happy about it, and in the end he and Robert carried it gingerly out to the courtyard to let it cool its rage in the open air.

"It hissed and spat like an angry goose"

The rest of the morning went in collecting the things that Doctor Dee would need during his stay at Stuchbery. Though the Doctor himself protested that his tastes were of the simplest, Father pointed out that the little house was quite empty, and he must at least have a bed and a table and a stool and things to cook with. So a waggon was brought round from the farm and on to it was piled everything that Father thought might add to his guest's comfort.

"If it is quiet that you are wanting, you will certainly find it at Stuchbery," he observed as the boys rolled a cask of home-brewed ale up a plank on to the waggon. "It is said that in ancient days it was quite a considerable town with a busy road running through it. But now there are only a couple of farms, a cottage or two and the remains of a tiny church, and nobody goes near it.

It is all buried in trees and the road is no more than an overgrown track, but if you follow it to the south you'll find that it leads to Oxford."

"To Oxford?" repeated Doctor Dee quickly. "How far is that?"

"A good day's ride. It might be useful for your studies."

"It might indeed. I am beholden to you, sir, for all your thought for me."

"Have a care how you speak," laughed Father. "The shoe will be on the other foot before I have finished with you. If you can knock a love of learning into these dunderheads of mine, it is I who shall be your debtor."

The waggon, well loaded, went trundling off in charge of one of the farm hands, and it was arranged that, after dinner, everyone should go to Stuchbery and help to get things straight.

Francis and Anne got there first. They took the short cut across the fields, while the others all went the long way by the road. Doctor Dee had some precious baggage which had to be taken carefully.

The little house where he was to live had a thatched roof, and was really no more than a cottage. There was but one big room with a hearth and chimney place, and a little buttery opening out of it. A steep winding stair led up to a tiny bedchamber under the eaves.

The furniture from Sulgrave had all been piled haphazard into the hall-room, and the place was quite deserted. There was a great table and a smaller table for writing, some joint stools, a small oak coffer, a bed and bedding, a charcoal stove for heating a small dish, pots and pans, platters and a pitcher, a candlestick and lots of other things.

Anne ran about delightedly exploring everywhere.

"Isn't it lovely," she cried. "Look, if I stand on this little coffer I can touch the ceiling. I'd like to live here, Francis; wouldn't you?"

"No, I wouldn't," said Francis shortly. "I wouldn't like to live anywhere but Sulgrave. And you'd better have a care of that coffer. It belongs to Doctor Dee."

Anne got down obediently. Francis was cross. He'd been funny all the morning, as if he didn't want to talk to her. She supposed that it was all because he was so upset about Woodstock last night. She was glad when he went outside again and called to her that the others were just coming.

She hurried out to join him. It seemed as if the baggage that they were bringing must indeed be important, for though there was only one single pack horse, with one solitary bundle on its back, Father himself had hold of the bridle, Robert and Laurie walked on either side steadying it, and Doctor Dee hovered round like an anxious sheep dog. When they came to a standstill at the door, the cords were loosened with the utmost care and Doctor Dee himself received into his arms two large round objects all swathed up in cloth.

"Whatever can it be?" whispered Anne peeping over Francis's shoulder. "They look like two great cauldrons."

"Cauldrons would be heavy," returned Francis. "He could never carry two cauldrons like that."

Anne had an idea. She turned tail and bolted round the outside of the house to the buttery door, with Francis at her heels. They arrived inside just as Doctor Dee set his load down on the table and began to undo the wrappers.

The two round objects seemed to be packed separately, each with a lot of straw and a covering of scrim, the cheapest cloth made of waste. He unpacked one only, and when it was completely uncovered he stepped back to admire it, almost colliding with Anne, who stood staring at it with puzzled eyes. It was a great painted globe, pivoted on a stand of ebony.

"Well," he said, rubbing his hands, "and what do you think of my treasure?"

"I don't suppose she knows what it is," said Father. "For that matter I've only once seen a globe myself. It's a map, my poppet; a map of the whole round world."

Doctor Dee touched the globe lightly with his fingers and set it spinning on its axis.

"Isn't it a beauty?" he exclaimed. "I brought it back with me from Louvain."

"Where's England?" inquired Anne, peering closely at it.

"Here," he said putting his finger on the spot. "You would
find Sulgrave in Northamptonshire
marked in the very middle if the map
were big enough. And look; here are
all the new lands I spoke of yesterday,
all lying right down the Atlantic ocean.
Nobody really knows the shape of them
yet; they are different on every map that
is made. Mark you, mariners set sail not
so much to discover new lands as to find
their way to the Indies and the spice
islands here"—he pointed with his finger
again—"on the other side of the world.
The new lands seem to lie like a great
barrier across their path and the great problem is how to find the
best way round the barrier."

*A globe pivoted on
a stand*

Robert and Laurie had pushed their way into the room and
stood peering round on either side of Father.

"Do you go on voyages yourself, sir?" asked Robert, his eyes
bright with interest.

"Not I!" laughed Doctor Dee. "I'm too fond of my comfort.
I've no fancy for food crawling with weevils or for having to
hold my nose before I can drink the water from the water tubs
because it stinks so much. Those are the sort of hardships that
mariners have to put up with, never to mention the chance of
being eaten by cannibals. There are two sides to this exploring
business, you see. The mariners risk their lives. The geographers
and the map makers stay comfortably at home and piece together
the information that the mariners bring to them. That is my
part."

"Do you draw the maps yourself?" questioned Francis, who
seemed to be hanging on every word.

"I do draw maps certainly; you will find plenty of them in
here." He lifted the lid of the little oak coffer on which Anne
had climbed. "But my work is principally to check the mariners'
findings by measurements from the stars, and so to work out

fresh courses for them to follow and suggest new routes by which they might reach the places they are aiming for." He lifted one of the rolled-up maps from the coffer and spread it out. "This is a

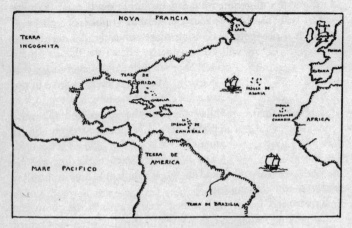

This is a map of the New World

map of the New World," he said. "Of course all the places have to be given names. Here is Nova Francia; and Florida; and Brazilia; and America."

"What funny names," said Anne, peeping at where his finger pointed.

He smiled at her. "Why funny? *Nova Francia*, New France; surely that is plain enough. It was christened by a Frenchman named Cartier, who first sailed up that river there. Then *Florida*, that means the region of flowers in Spanish. *Brazilia* is called after the valuable brazil wood that dyers use; it grows in plenty there. And *America*, that comes from the name of one of the first mariners who found the new lands, Amerigo Vespucci."

"How grand to be able to name a new land," said Robert, laying a finger on the globe and turning it gently round. "Wouldn't it be fun to see a place named Washington on the map."

Everybody laughed and Robert went very pink in the face.

"Well, my boy," said Doctor Dee with a smile, "there's plenty to be explored still. We are only at the beginning. If you have a mind that way you'd better start now. You'll have to work hard at arithmetic and geometry and you must know the stars like the back of your hand. The stars can only be studied at night, you know. It means getting up in the dark or sometimes even being up all night. How will you like that?"

"I shan't mind it," said Robert. He looked round angrily as Anne tittered aloud. Robert's lie-a-bed ways were a joke in the family.

Francis, in the meanwhile, went on examining the maps in the coffer. He could not make head or tail of most of them and he was just about to put them all back and close the lid when a familiar name caught his eye. The word Oxford was marked on the bottom corner of one of the maps. He had begun to unroll it when Doctor Dee looked round. Francis held the map out to him.

"Is this a part of England, sir?" he inquired. "I can see Oxford on it."

To his astonishment Doctor Dee snatched the roll from his hands and threw it back into the chest.

"Yes," he said lightly. "There is a new idea afoot to make maps of all the English counties. I have a friend, Humphrey Lluyd, who is busy with it. But we've had enough of that for now. There is another globe to be unpacked, a celestial globe, mapping all the stars in the heavens, but we cannot get it out until we have cleared a place to put it."

"Yes, by my troth," cried Father, rolling up his sleeves. "I would remind you all that we came here to get Doctor Dee's house into order for him, and so far we have not begun."

Everybody turned to work at once. Only Francis stood idle for another minute or two. He stared at the coffer as though he could see through the lid. There was something that he was longing to confide to Robert or to Laurie or even to Anne; but because of his vow he would have to keep it to himself.

There were a few words written at the bottom of the map that he had been looking at. He noticed them just as Doctor Dee had snatched it away. The words said plainly, in English—THE WAYS TO WOODSTOCK.

Wormleighton

CHAPTER V

Wormleighton

It was a couple of weeks before Mother was well enough for the five little girls of The Tail to be fetched home from Wormleighton. During that time Doctor Dee settled down in his little house and the boys started work with him. There was no doubt that the new tutor was an enormous success. Robert and Laurie could not keep away from Stuchbery and even Francis took to his lessons as a duck takes to water.

Tom Tresham rode over from Greens Norton nearly every day, and he and Francis became bosom friends. Anne's nose was a little out of joint. It seemed as if Francis no longer needed her. His manner was odd. She fancied that he was avoiding her, and when they did meet there was a sort of stiffness between them, as if he was being *careful*, in the way that they were both careful with grown ups. She noticed it first on the day after the Woodstock trouble, and she thought that it was only because he was upset. But when it continued, she came rather miserably to the conclusion that he did not want her now that he had Tom.

She found herself looking forward to the return of The Tail. Ninnie, the eldest, was not so very much younger than she was. They shared a bed and had most of their possessions in common. Of course Francis was her twin. Nobody, not even Ninnie, could take his place. But all the same she was very glad that Ninnie was coming home.

The expedition to Wormleighton to fetch The Tail was something to be looked forward to. It was always fun to visit the Spencer cousins. Sir John Spencer, 'Cousin Spencer', was a little frightening, but no one could possibly be frightened of Cousin Kit who was Father's first cousin. Margaret, the eldest of the Spencer children, was just a little older than herself, and Bess was just a little younger. Then came John, the same age as Ninnie, and then four smaller ones who fitted in nicely with The Tail; so there was plenty of fun for everybody at Wormleighton.

"I hope you will not be overwhelmed by the hubbub, sir," said Laurence Washington to Doctor Dee, as they rode out in the cool of the early morning. "I want to present you to my cousin, Dame Katharine Spencer, and to her husband Sir John; otherwise I should have hesitated to bring you to such a nursery party. The Spencers have seven children of their own, and to those they have added five of mine. The place is like a rabbit warren."

"Having regard to the twenty thousand sheep, it might be better to say a flock of woolly lambs," returned Doctor Dee with a side-long glance at Anne, who was riding pillion behind Father.

Anne chuckled at the joke. It was a lovely morning and she was bubbling over with happiness.

"I fear the twenty thousand will be rather a sore subject," said Father. "The murrain has spoiled the chances for the present and the news I bring from London is not very good either. The prices offered for Spencer wool are not what they used to be. It is my belief that pasturing sheep on rich land is bad for the quality of the fleeces. They grow so thick that the wool gets coarse."

"Have you always followed the wool trade?" inquired Doctor Dee.

"Ever since I was a boy in Lancashire. We are a north counrty family, you know. Our forebears lived in county Durham. From there my great-grandsire moved to Warton, where I was born. It was my mother's brother, my good uncle Sir Thomas Kytson, who brought me to London. He was a Lancashire man himself. He made his fortune trading in Kendal cloth, woven from the wool of our tough little lakeland sheep. It sold like hot cakes in Flanders and he became one of the richest merchants of his day. He had a fine house in London, and a country place at Stoke Newington, never to mention the house in Antwerp for the

The great mansion at Hengrave
in Suffolk

Flemish business and the great mansion which he built at Hengrave in Suffolk. Maybe you know it, sir? It is not so very far from Cambridge."

Doctor Dee shook his head. "I have heard of it, but I have never seen it. Sir Thomas Kytson is dead, I think?"

"Yes, God rest his soul. He treated me like a son, and so did his wife, my aunt Kytson. You will see her to-day. She is Dame Katharine's mother. She is staying at Wormleighton."

Anne looked ahead to where the boys were riding. She wondered whether they could hear this piece of news. It would not be very welcome. But none of the three looked round and she concluded that Father's voice had not carried far enough. Robert was mounted on Chris Hatton's *Juno*, to his great delight; his Betsy was not yet home from Holdenby. Laurie rode Quince, his own sturdy pony, while Francis between them jogged along on fat Meadowsweet. Will, Father's serving man, followed at the back of the party on a baggage horse which would be useful for the return journey.

"Then you received your schooling in the north of England? Forgive my curiosity, but you have the air of a man who has had a scholar's education."

Laurence Washington laughed. Clearly the compliment pleased him. "I went to Gray's Inn, sir. My uncle put me there. He held that to read law is an excellent training for a man who would make his way in the world. I'm thinking of sending Laurie there when he is old enough."

"I agree," said Doctor Dee. "A year or two at one of the Inns of Court, or at least at a Chancery Inn, is almost comparable with a university education. In fact I have always heard that as London lacks a university, the Inns practically fulfil that purpose. But tell me, if you were born in the north and educated in London, how came you to Northamptonshire?"

"Wool again. The fashion grew for grazing sheep on rich land rather than on poor. That brought trade to Northampton. My uncle was a far-sighted man. He advised me to settle there. I did so and I prospered. I was twice mayor."

"And then you built Sulgrave, and your uncle's daughter married Sir John Spencer, the biggest sheep-master of them all; I begin to see the pattern of it. Your uncle must have been pleased with the fulfilment of his plans."

"Alas, he died a long time ago. His widow has married twice since then. Though from sheer habit, I often call her my aunt *Kytson*, I should really say my aunt *Bath*. Her present husband is the Earl of Bath, and she is a very great lady, I can assure you. Even her daughter, my cousin Kit, is in some awe of her, and as for the children, they quake in their shoes. She is full of all the doings of the Court. My poor wife is heartbroken not to come and hear about the Queen's wedding to Philip of Spain at Winchester."

They were getting near Wormleighton now and with every mile there seemed to be more and more sheep. They came to the village quite suddenly, no more than a few thatched cottages dotted round a triangle of green grass, with the village stocks in the middle of it. At the back of the cottages stood a line of great stone barns, big enough to swallow the cottages up—as though sheep were more important than people, thought Anne.

The boys, riding ahead, turned sharply to the right, and there, spread out in the morning sun, lay Cousin John's great house, warm and red in contrast to the cool grey stone of the little church with its squat Norman tower, standing among the trees behind it.

Wormleighton House was built of brick, not of stone like Sulgrave, though it had stone at the corners and along the imitation battlements at the top. Anne remembered how the boys had once climbed along that crenellated parapet, pretending it was a real castle, and poured water, by way of boiling oil, on to the heads of people going to the door. The steward, Master Tungston, went up to fetch them, and they led him a fine dance over the high-pitched roof and among the tall chimneys. They were caught at last and suffered a beating that cured them for ever of a love of battlements.

"It reminds me a little of Hampton Court," said Doctor Dee, as they turned under an archway leading into a wide enclosed courtyard. "It is the colour of the brick, I suppose, and this fashion of one courtyard after another."

The boys had arrived first, and Dame Katharine Spencer and her husband, Sir John, were already waiting outside the door, with grooms at hand to take the horses.

Cousin Kit was a large plump merry woman, still with the bright hair and rosy cheeks of girlhood. Cousin Spencer was tall and grave with a neatly trimmed beard. They greeted their guests warmly and when Doctor Dee had been presented, everybody trooped into the Great Hall where pitchers of cool ale and platters of cakes were spread for them.

As they went in by the Hall passage, and under the arched doorway topped by shields of the Spencer arms, Doctor Dee looked round for Anne.

"Don't leave me," he whispered softly, his eyebrow cocked in the funny way he had. "I'm mortally afraid of all these grand people."

Anne looked at him, not sure whether he was in jest or in earnest. How could he possibly be afraid when he had been to Hampton Court and talked to the King? But she did as he asked and kept close beside him while they ate and drank.

She was still near him when Cousin Kit opened a small door in the side of the Hall and led the way up a winding stair to the room above, a great chamber as large as the Hall but even more splendid. It was panelled all over, both walls and ceilings, with panels of pale oak; and in the centre of every panel shone a beautifully painted golden star.

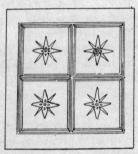

In every panel shone a star

Anne loved the Star Chamber. Two sides of it were lit by great windows and the sun poured in, making the stars glitter as though the sky had been robbed to decorate the room.

In the bay of the great window at the end of the chamber sat Cousin Kit's mother, the Countess of Bath, talking to an old man with a sun-burned face and a short white beard.

Great-aunt Bath was an imposing lady who carried herself right royally in spite of an ample figure and a great many chins. She was royally dressed too, in a gown of black velvet with a petticoat and sleeves of emerald green brocade; on her head she wore a coif of black velvet edged all round with pearls. Anne, accustomed to her mother's simple house gown with its girdle and its bunch of keys, wondered if Great-aunt Bath was wearing the dress she had worn at the Queen's wedding.

When they had all made their bows and curtsies, and Anne and the boys had been kissed on the brow, Father stepped forward to present Doctor Dee.

Great-aunt Bath received him with surprise and delight. "Why, sir, this is an unexpected pleasure. I met you once at Hampton Court, and I have heard of you at Cambridge, but what brings you to these outlandish parts?" She smiled at him

"I met you once at Hampton Court"

graciously and went on without waiting for a reply. "I wish I could persuade you to cast my horoscope. Be it right or wrong, I have an itch to learn what the future holds, and I know that none has the magic that you have in reading the stars."

Anne had no idea what a horoscope was but she could see at once that Doctor Dee was annoyed, as he had been when Sir William Parr had talked about *magic*. Though he bowed very low, the point of his beard stuck out just as she had seen it do before.

Evidently Father noticed too, for he said very quickly,

"Doctor Dee has settled at Stuchbery, Madam, because he needs quiet for his studies. He is busy on nothing less than a survey of the New World. His learning will guide the mariners who sail unknown seas, and bring new trade and new riches to us all."

"Hoity, Toity, nephew, we are very grand!" retorted Great-aunt Bath. "Your uncle always used to say that you would go far, but I doubt me if he ever thought you would reach out so far as new worlds."

"I reach out no further than I have ever done, Aunt," said Father patiently. "We do not desire these things for ourselves, but for our children. They feel the call to a wider world than ours. It is but natural. Already the boys are longing to set sail."

"Then you should check them in such vainglory," she told him sternly. She looked round at her great-nephews who were huddled close together, each trying to hide behind the other. "What is all this nonsense?" she demanded. "Don't stand there like a gaggle of geese. Come and tell me what madness is in your silly heads."

As the boys reluctantly shuffled forward, Father seized Doctor Dee by the arm and drew him away. "Come with me," Anne heard him whisper. "I want you to make your bow to Sir Thomas Tresham."

Anne pricked up her ears. So the red-faced man, who stood listening with an amused smile on his face, must be Tom Tresham's grandfather. Tom had bragged so much about his importance, but he did not look specially alarming. Though he had a big booming voice, there was a twinkle in his eyes. She decided to hear what was going on, so she edged away from Great-aunt Bath and followed Doctor Dee, keeping as much as she could in the shadow of his long hanging sleeves.

"Doctor Dee is staying at Stuchbery, Sir Thomas," Father was saying. "And by your leave your grandson Tom is coming to join my boys in their studies with him. It was suggested when Sir William Parr sheltered at Sulgrave during the storm last week. Young Tom was with him. I hope that you approve."

"Approve? Of course I approve, if Doctor Dee can have the patience. It is a stroke of great good fortune for the boy. I hope

64

you will beat him well, sir. He needs it badly. He is an only child. His father is dead and I had to send him away to stop his mother from making him into a complete nincompoop."

"Then in heaven's name, Sir Thomas, why send him to Sir William Parr?" cried Great-aunt Bath shrilly across the room. "That man would turn Sir Lancelot into a nincompoop. I have no patience with his airs and graces. What is he doing here, within a bow-shot of Woodstock? I'll warrant he's mincing round the Lady Elizabeth, playing the tender uncle, in case the wind should change."

"I would scarcely call it within a bow-shot, madam," returned Sir Thomas Tresham firmly. "It is twenty miles, and Parr is but living in his own manor at Greens Norton."

"Well, it is you who are sheriff of the county, not I." She shrugged her shoulders. "But I am a mother, and a grandmother too, and I would send no child of mine to a man with two wives. He was wedded to Anne Bourchier, my husband's niece, I'd have you know, and he cast her off like an old glove as soon as he got the ear of the little King. Yes, and he even got a special act of Parliament to allow his marriage to another woman."

"In that case, madam, he did no more than King Henry had done before him." Sir Thomas's red face had grown redder still. He turned abruptly away, muttering under his breath, while Father hurried back to Great-aunt Bath and tried to keep the peace by asking her questions about the royal wedding. Anne looked from one side to the other. She would like to hear about the wedding, but Doctor Dee *had* begged her to stay with him.

He had begun to talk to Sir Thomas in a quiet voice, as though he would pour oil on troubled waters.

"Do you find it a stumbling block that the Lady Elizabeth is in your county, sir?" he inquired politely.

Sir Thomas made an obvious effort to control his wrath. "Woodstock is not in Northamptonshire," he said. "It is in Oxfordshire, and so long as she does not cross the boundary she is none of my business, heaven be praised. I have cares enough at the other end of the shire, at the castle of Fotheringhay where young Courtenay is in custody. I had the task of fetching him from the Tower and taking him there just at the same time as my friend Bedingfield took the Lady Elizabeth from the Tower to Woodstock. He is a handsome lad, but sickly; and can you wonder? He had been in the Tower with hardly a break for twelve years, and even now he is but twenty-six."

Anne did a quick sum. Twelve from twenty-six left fourteen. What could a boy of fourteen have done to be in the Tower for twelve years?

Doctor Dee answered her question almost as if she had asked it aloud. "I suppose the poor lad's only crime was that he happened to be a descendant of the Plantagenet kings and so was looked upon as a threat to the crown?"

Tresham nodded. "That is why Henry the Eighth kept him prisoner of course, but Queen Mary set him free the day she came to the throne. He was sent back to the Tower after Wyatt's rebellion because the rebels set out to marry him to the Lady Elizabeth and crown them both. A Plantagenet king with a Tudor wife might sweep all before them. Indeed there are many who regret that the Queen did not wed Courtenay herself."

"It would have been more popular than the Spanish marriage has been," said Doctor Dee thoughtfully. "As it is both Courtenay and the Lady Elizabeth are innocent victims of other people's conspiracies. I do not believe that either of them had any knowledge of Wyatt's plot, do you?"

"I would not care to wager," said Tresham bluntly. "But be that as it may, it is my business to keep Courtenay at Fotheringhay and I suffer almost as much trouble there as Bedingfield does at Woodstock. The neighbourhood is over-run with young dare-devils who try to get in touch with the prisoner. There is one lad who leads me a pretty dance—another of these fatherless boys whose mothers cannot control them, young Christopher Hatton of Holdenby. You will not know him of course. You are a stranger here. I have been patient with him because his father was a friend of mine, but he has gone beyond all bounds in trying me. I've got his measure now. He will be at Fotheringhay again by the end of the week and this time I shall not let him go. He shall cool his heels under lock and key for a while."

He rubbed his hands together with obvious satisfaction. Anne held her breath, not daring to look at Doctor Dee. What would he do? Would he give everything away by saying that he had seen Chris at Sulgrave, and even mention the trip to Woodstock? A moment later she reproached herself for imagining such a thing. Doctor Dee was not like that. She heard him offer sympathy to Sir Thomas on the difficulties of his task. Then he changed the subject. They began to talk about maps and about finding a new way to the Spice Islands.

She was relieved, but at the same time she was worried. What *was* Chris up to? How she wished that the boys would keep out of all this trouble. Father had warned them that they would bring danger not only to themselves but to their families.

Just at that moment Cousin Kit called her. "Anne, child, come to the nursery. Your father is going to see his longlost family."

Anne needed no second bidding. Chris and his problems were forgotten. She hurried after Father and Cousin Kit.

The nursery was at the far end of the house. She knew it well and loved it. It was a great high room, most of its space occupied by two huge curtained beds where the nurses slept with their charges. There were three windows, all carefully barred and very seldom opened and the room was warm and stuffy and cosy with the smell of wool, and babies, and goose feathers, and garlic, known as poor man's treacle, the remedy for every childish ailment from a cold in the head to a dog bite or a cat scratch. Added to all this homely perfume was the lingering aroma of the dried lavender stalks burned every night in the chimney place by Cousin Kit's orders, to keep the air sweet and healthy.

There was such a noise going on that at first none of the children inside heard the door open. A game of fox and geese was in progress, with nine-year-old John Spencer as fox. His sister Margaret and Ninnie, the eldest of The Tail, were hopping about with outstretched skirts, to protect their squealing broods of little ones. Then somebody looked round; there was a sudden

hush and lots of hurried bows and curtsies. But Ninnie did not
wait to be polite. With a scream of joy she hurled herself at her
father, and the rest of The Tail followed, dancing and tumbling
round his legs like a lot of puppies. The Spencers, not to be left
out, set upon their mother, and for a few minutes nobody could
make themselves heard.

The rest of The Tail dancing and tumbling round his legs

When the noise had died down a little Cousin Kit called out
that it was much too fine to be indoors. Ninnie and Anne linked
hands with Margaret and Bess and they all clattered down the
twisty wooden stairs and out through the courtyard to play in
the great field known as the Old Town.

The boys had escaped from Great-aunt Bath and were already there. The Old Town was a splendid place for games for it was full of grassy mounds where a whole village of cottages had been pulled down many years ago to make way for more sheep. There were still a few old walls, just the thing to dodge behind, and the hillocks were perfect for playing King-of-the-Castle. They chased one another up and down until they were unbearably hot. Then the boys went off with the shepherd and the girls retired to the kitchen garden to search for a few late raspberries. There was trouble because it came out that Ninnie had been down early in the morning and eaten every one. Margaret and Bess said a lot of home-truths about Ninnie's greed and Anne felt ashamed of her younger sister.

But Ninnie was quite unabashed. She led them to a sunny wall where some early apricocks were ripe. Master Tungston the steward came by and saw them and said that he would tell Sir John; but Ninnie coaxed him and he gave way. He said that he was just going to ring the bidding bell in the little belfry, to summon everybody to dinner; so they had best go and wash the tell-tale stains away.

Dinner at Wormleighton was very different from the homely meals at Sulgrave. The grown-ups sat at a long table on the dais and the boys waited on them, kneeling to offer the dishes. The rest of the children gathered round a lower table and the bigger ones helped to feed the little ones. It took a long time, but it was over at last; and when Cousin Spencer had said grace Cousin Kit told the children to go out and play in the Old Town again.

Anne hung behind. The grown-ups always went for a walk after dinner, to look at the gardens and the stables and the kennels and the mews. It wasn't very interesting but she decided that it was better than having to look after the babies all the time, or, worse still, keep Ninnie out of mischief. She saw Doctor Dee standing alone near the door; he *had* asked her not to leave him, so she tiptoed up behind him. He looked down at her.

"Well," he said softly, "and what has your ladyship been about all this time, may I ask?"

She suddenly remembered the talk with Sir Thomas Tresham.

"Sir," she whispered, "what about Chris? Is he going to get into trouble?"

He put his fingers to his lips. "Hush! Not a word to a soul. We must talk of that anon, you and I."

Anne sighed with pleasure. She felt suddenly very important. She shared a secret with Doctor Dee.

The tour round Wormleighton was duller than ever. Sir John led the way with Father and Sir Thomas Tresham, Great-aunt Bath with Anne and Doctor Dee followed a little way behind, while Cousin Kit hovered between, obviously nervous of what her mother might say or do.

The gardens were mostly neat square flower beds with trim hedges. To Anne's relief they did not go near the kitchen garden so the apricocks were not missed. They spent a lot of time in the stables, and from the stables they went to the mews, where Cousin Spencer insisted on showing off his hawks one by one and telling stories of how they could seize in mid air birds bigger than themselves or drop like a stone on to a rabbit. Anne shuddered, the hawks looked so fierce; and the smell of the mews was so strong that she wished she dared hold her nose. Great-aunt Bath was not so diffident. She said bluntly that the place stank and if they remained there she would vomit, so they moved on to look at the kennels.

This was the part of the tour that Anne really liked. The dogs were all kept in a walled yard in case they should go after the sheep, but they were friendly enough and she went inside with Cousin Spencer and Sir Thomas Tresham and enjoyed herself patting each dog in turn.

"I see you have no greyhounds, son Spencer," said Great-aunt Bath who had remained outside the fence for fear that her dress might be spoiled. "I suppose you fear for the sheep. That reminds me, I have not yet told you about the greyhounds that we bought for the Queen, and how the Earl of Pembroke stole them."

"*Stole* them? My lord of Pembroke?" Cousin Kit sounded truly shocked. "Surely Madam mother, you must be mistaken."

"Well, he or his man; it makes no matter. When my good

husband was in Devon he found a brace of fine young grey-hounds, the finest he had ever seen. So he bought them and sent them to me at Hampton Court, so that I could present them to the Queen. But on the way his messenger was waylaid on Bagshot Heath by a man of the Earl of Pembroke's, a fellow named Penruddock. The knave actually took the hounds, and refused to give them back. My husband's servant arrived empty-handed. Of course when I heard the story I wrote a letter to my Lord of Pembroke, a civil enough letter it was, but we have received neither the greyhounds nor heard any word at all."

"There *must* be some mistake, Madam," cried Sir Thomas Tresham turning back from the kennels. "The Earl of Pembroke is one of the Lords of the Council. He would never countenance highway robbery."

"I wish I shared your faith, sir," returned the Countess, tossing her head. "There seems to be no limit to what will be coun-tenanced nowadays, even by Lords of the Council. Pembroke is brother-in-law to your fine Sir William Parr. They are all tarred with the same brush. I would not trust a man of them."

"Perchance you will find a letter awaiting you when you get home to Hengrave," her daughter said quickly. "Will you come and see the sheep now, Sir Thomas, if it pleases you. There is a new Angora ram, a most fearsome beast. Sir John bought it to breed silkier fleeces, because Cousin Laurence puts the blame for falling prices on to coarse wool."

"And how about your twenty thousand?" inquired Great-aunt Bath maliciously. "When is the great supper to be?"

Anne held her breath. It was perfectly plain that Great-aunt Bath was itching to pick a quarrel.

"Not yet, my mother, I am sad to say." Cousin Kit was won-derfully patient. "There is murrain in the Sulgrave flock, and we are having a lot of trouble with the Old Town fields. The gates are always being broken down and the sheep driven out. One cannot set guards all the time. It is not our own people who do it, but it seems that there are vengeful knaves who roam the countryside."

" 'Tis the same all over England," snapped her mother. "You

sheep-masters have invited it with your greed for ever-greater flocks and your fencing of the best land. Look at the enclosing of your park at Althorp, son Spencer; and your Old Town with its wrecked houses. *My* sympathies are with the poor and outcast."

"That is a slander, Madam," cried Sir John hotly, his face as red as Sir Thomas's. "It was my grandfather who enclosed Althorp, and he was the most beloved of men. I tell you, he left a will to be read aloud in Northampton and Warwick and half a score of other great towns, in which he decreed that any man coming forward to swear that he was owed money or had suffered a wrong should be paid in full without further question. Yet even when this was read in the market places not a voice was raised against him. As for the Old Town fields, that was the work of the Copes fifty years ago, before my grandsire bought Worm-leighton."

He was obviously so angry that even Great-aunt Bath did not venture to say any more. They left the kennels in silence. Almost at once Father told Cousin Kit that he really must collect his family and call for the horses. What with the babies and the baggage, it would take some time to get ready and he had promised Mother that they would not be late.

"She sent a message which I must not forget," he said lightly, as though it was a relief to speak of something pleasant for a change. "As soon as she is quite recovered, she plans to have a party at Sulgrave for all the children. We hope, good Cousin Kit, that you and your family will come."

But Great-aunt Bath was not going to be so easily dismissed. Before her daughter could even accept the invitation she broke in again.

"Talking of Sulgrave, nephew, what shall you do if the Queen commands that all church land shall be given back? You will have to leave Sulgrave."

Leave Sulgrave? Anne stopped dead to stare at Great-aunt Bath, fear gripping her heart.

"On my life, Madam, the Queen will not command anything of the sort," cried Sir Thomas Tresham. "Parliament would never agree to it."

"You should ask yourself the same question, madam my mother," said Cousin Spencer in a dangerously quiet voice. "Was not Hengrave monastic land?"

"Nothing of the sort, sir," she snapped. "We bought it from the Duke of Buckingham before he went to the block. And about Sulgrave, I only asked a civil question. In countries abroad the Pope is excommunicating people who wrongfully hold church land; and what happens there may easily happen here."

"The case is different," persisted Tresham stubbornly. "No one dare apply such a law in England. It was bruited in the Council Chamber once, and my Lord Russell, the Earl of Bedford, went so far as to toss his rosary on to the fire, swearing that he loved his sweet abbey of Woburn better than any fatherly commands that could come from Rome."

"So far as Sulgrave is concerned I am doubly secure," said Father quietly. "I got the place from the monks of Northampton themselves some time before the monastery was destroyed. It was mortgaged to me and they defaulted on the debt, and so it became legally mine."

"What are you talking about?" cried his aunt. "You bought it from the King. I remember it perfectly. You paid the King three hundred and twenty pounds for it."

Laurence Washington laughed. "I commend you for your memory, Aunt. I did indeed pay the King three hundred and twenty pounds, but I paid him for what was already my own. It would have taken a braver man than I to refuse old King Hal what he claimed, however unjust that claim might be. But it was mine own land for all that."

"Well, I hope you will be able to prove it," replied Great-aunt Bath sourly. "It would be a thousand pities to lose so pretty a manor."

It was her parting shot. They had reached the door of the house. Cousin Kit hurriedly called to the steward to bring wine to the hall, so that the men might drink a stirrup cup before the guests started; at the same time she besought her mother's help in seeing that the children were properly dressed for the journey.

It took some time to get everybody mounted and the baggage

stowed away. Father himself carried baby Meg across his saddle-bow; Will had charge of three-year-old Moll; Barbara and Magdalen were old enough to ride pillion behind Robert and Laurie; Ninnie shared Meadowsweet with Francis, while Anne, to her great delight, was allocated the pillion seat behind Doctor Dee.

The entire Spencer family and their guests gathered in the courtyard. There was much chattering and laughter, and many cries of God Speed, and Thank You and Come Again Soon. Even Great-aunt Bath and Sir Thomas Tresham stood side by side without quarrelling. And so, with all bitterness forgotten, the Washington family started for home.

The arms of
SPENCER

The children's party

CHAPTER VI

King of the Castle

"Thank heaven we got out of that without bloodshed," sighed Father when they were well clear of the village. "My aunt Bath was always fond of ruling the roost and it seems that she grows no milder as she grows older."

Anne, holding on to Doctor Dee's belt, felt him quiver with laughter.

"She is a formidable dame," he said. "When she could get no other victim she set upon you with her stories about Church land."

"It did not disturb me. I am used to her. I have a deed in my possession which proves my right to Sulgrave. You see, when I was mayor of Northampton, twenty years ago, the monks of St. Andrew's priory were heavily in debt. To help them I gave them a mortgage on their manor of Sulgrave. You know without out my telling you what that means; I lent them a sum of money with Sulgrave as security. If they had repaid the money the

75

place would have remained theirs, but of course they did not repay. Debt and mismanagement were the charges on which they were dissolved. When the King seized the priory he invited me to buy Sulgrave, and I can promise you I valued my life too well to point out that it was already mine. It was wiser to pay what he asked and have done with it. But I kept the mortgage deed and I'm glad now that I did."

"I should not think you have any cause to worry," said Doctor Dee. "You heard what Sir Thomas Tresham said about the Earl of Bedford and his sweet abbey of Woburn."

"Nay, I do not worry. The lords of Parliament are most of them fat on church land and they are unlikely to pass any law that would endanger their own property. If it were not for that I should be sorry to rely on them. They turn their coats to suit every wind that blows. They've spent the last twenty years getting rid of the old religion, and now, I hear, they fall on their knees before the Queen and weep for joy to have it back again. How can one place one's trust in such men? They'll change again without a moment's hesitation if ever the Lady Elizabeth comes to the throne, which is not unlikely."

"Which, I can assure you, is far from unlikely," said Doctor Dee quietly.

Anne saw her father give him a quick glance. "How now? You speak as though you were very certain."

"I study the stars."

"Humph!" grunted Father. "If you take my advice, my friend, whatever you find in your studies you will keep to yourself."

Doctor Dee said no more and for a while there was silence. The horses jogged along. From her pillion seat Anne made funny faces to amuse baby Meg who was propped up in front of Father. Then the baby went to sleep and Anne settled down to her thoughts.

On the whole the day had been disappointing. The grown ups were quarrelsome; Ninnie was naughty and she was worried about Chris Hatton. If he was really in danger of trouble, as Sir Thomas Tresham had said, somebody ought to warn him. But she was frightened that if she told the boys it might start all that business of Woodstock over again. Perhaps Doctor Dee would help. After all, she had once heard him speak to Chris about Woodstock.

She sighed. It was funny to remember that only a short while ago she had felt so safe. Now in some strange way there seemed to be dangers creeping up round all the things she loved best. There was that new business about Sulgrave that Great-aunt Bath had spoken of. Of course Great-aunt Bath was just trying to be nasty, and Father had said that it was quite safe. But deep down in her heart Anne had an odd feeling that, whatever Father said, he wasn't really very happy about it.

Presently the two men began to talk again, but it was only about Antwerp and other places that they both knew, and not very interesting. Doctor Dee told some stories of Paris, and about a lecture that he had given at Paris University which was so crowded that students had even climbed the beams of the roof to hear him. The lecture was about Euclid. Anne could hardly believe it. Robert and Laurie learned Euclid; she'd peeped at their exercises and thought that never had she seen anything so dull. And how could he have made French people understand? She listened a little longer and found that he had lectured in Latin. She sighed again. He was dreadfully learned! Then she remembered his joke about the woolly lambs and chuckled to herself again. Thank goodness he wasn't learned all the time.

The horses were going uphill now, and their slow plodding made her sleepy. She closed her eyes and rested her head against Doctor Dee's back. When she woke up they were just turning into the gate at Sulgrave.

Mother had heard them coming a long way off. She was waiting for them with Marta and old Jake and the maidservants There was so much joy and so much excitement about the re-uniting of the family that everything else was forgotten. Anne ran in and out, taking in baggage, carrying the little ones upstairs, and now and again stopping to hug Mother, as if she, too, had been away for a long time.

She was helping to put The Tail to bed when, looking out of the window, she caught sight of Doctor Dee at the bottom of the garden in earnest conversation with Robert and Laurie. She knew at once that they were talking about Chris.

An hour later she and Ninnie went to the hall to say good night to Father. Robert was there ahead of them. He was asking permission to ride to-morrow to Holdenby.

Father frowned. "To-morrow? Mercy on us, boy; think of the horses. You have ridden close on twenty miles to-day. Holdenby and back would be another forty."

"It is of the horses that I *am* thinking, sir," said Robert dutifully. "You see I have Chris Hatton's Juno and he has my Betsy. 'Tis hardly right, sir, that I should be mounted on such a fine mare. I am in fear all the time that some harm may come to her. If I take her back to Holdenby to-morrow I shall be riding her only one way. I should return on Betsy."

"I agree that I do not care for you to be mounted beyond your purse," said Father. "In truth I did think to-day that she was too valuable to be a fair exchange for Betsy. Very well, my son, you can take her back to-morrow."

The matter was settled. But as she made her curtsey and came close to receive Father's kiss, Anne took a quick look at Robert. His cheeks were as red as a turkey cock. Father must be very blind if he did not suspect that there was more in to-morrow's ride than a mere exchange of horses.

She saw Robert go off very early leading Juno, but as soon as he had gone she forgot all about it. It was good for the Lizard to have its Tail again, as Father said when they all came down in the morning. But it made so much work that she really had no time to worry about the boys and their problems.

There were a thousand things to be done, and Mother depended on her eldest daughter in the most flattering way. There was fruit to be picked for Marta's preserves; herbs to be sought and gathered for the medicine chest; Ninnie was learning to spin, and was still at the stage where she broke the thread every few minutes, and Anne, who had learned last year, had to be constantly starting her off again.

Added to all this the little room over the porch was finished and Mother was getting it ready for Robert. It was very small, only big enough to hold his bed and a chest for his clothes, but it was to be his very own. Anne and Ninnie were to be promoted to the bed in the Inner Chamber, which had been his until now, and they were almost as excited as he was. The Inner Chamber was only a narrow strip over the screens passage of the hall. The Great Chamber, the nursery and the new porch room all opened out of it, and the linen closet took up much of the space; but it was a room to themselves and much better than sleeping with The Tail.

The days simply flew by. Presently Mother began to talk about

The little room over the porch

the promised party. They must not let the summer slip away, she said. Already the plums were ripe; soon it would be apple time and the days would be getting short. She began to count up on her fingers how many children could be invited.

First of all there were seven Spencers; then her own nephews and nieces, the five Pargiters from Greatworth and two Blencowes from Marston St. Lawrence; that made fourteen cousins to begin with. After that they could ask the two little Makepeaces from Chipping Warden and the Danvers family, all five of them, from Culworth. With their own ten that would make over thirty children. Of course some were mere babies, but there would be plenty of older ones to dance and play games and make the party a success.

So the invitations were sent. Marta and the maids worked hard to produce a grand array of cakes and confections and custards and jellies. Old Jake scythed the lawn anew, and The Tail did its part by praying for a fine day with such success that on the morning of the party the sun shone from a cloudless sky and Father declared that it was going to be almost too hot.

The Danvers from Culworth were the first to arrive, greatly to Anne's and Ninnie's disgust; for the three Danvers girls,

The Spencers in their chariot waggon

Temperance, Justice and Prudence were as dull as their names, and they had to be played with until the rest of the guests appeared. But soon a grinding of heavy iron-shod wheels announced the approach of the Spencers in their great red-wheeled chariot waggon. Cousin Kit herself sat enthroned on a pile of cushions under the scarlet tilt hood, with the children all packed in around her and Cousin Spencer riding alongside. By the time that they were all unloaded everybody else had arrived, including Chris Hatton and Tom Tresham, who, so far as Anne knew, had been invited only by the boys.

The party started with a feast in the hall for all the children, including the babies and their nurse-maids. The grown ups ate a collation in Father's parlour before they came to help feed the hungry multitude, as Father called it. When eating was done everybody went into the garden and there was music for the children to dance. Presently Mother said that it was too hot for dancing. She and Cousin Kit retired into the shade with all the little ones, and Marta brought out soapy water and straws for them to blow bubbles. The party began to divide up. Father and Cousin Spencer went off to look at sheep, the boys drifted away to try a new kind of cross bow that Tom Tresham had brought with him, and Anne found herself with more than a dozen guests to be entertained and only Ninnie to help her.

"What shall we play?" she asked, hoping to goodness that someone would suggest something.

"Hoodman Blind," cried Margaret Spencer. But Hoodman Blind was dreadfully hot and soon everybody was gasping.

"Mercy, no more of this," cried young John Spencer, dragging off his doublet. "Follow-the-Leader would be better, if we make a law that the Leader must keep always in the shade."

Follow-the-Leader-in-the-shade was a great success. They could have kept it up for a long time if Ninnie, as Leader, had not taken them all right through the foulest part of the pig stye. Their shoes were so covered with muck that Anne had to stop the game and take them back to the house to get clean.

It was gloriously cool in the hall. The servants had cleared away the remains of the feast and the place was quite deserted.

"Let's play Hide-and-Go-Seek all over the house," suggested Ninnie after they had all rinsed their feet in the horse trough and dried them on the hall rushes. "Everybody is out so it won't matter how much noise we make."

Hide-Go-Seek was the best game of all, and it went with a swing until Ninnie once more brought things to a standstill by disappearing so completely that she seemed to be lost. Anne was beginning to look anxiously at the well when Ninnie walked quietly out of the linen closet, declaring that she had been there all the time. Temperance said flatly that she was cheating; she and Justice had looked carefully in that closet and there was certainly nobody there. The others took sides and it seemed for a moment as if the party was going to end up with a fight.

Anne quickly took charge again. "Shall we play King of the Castle?" she cried. "We could play on the stairs. The people at the top can be holding the castle and the people downstairs be the besieging army."

The boys of the party started at once to pick sides. Robin Pargiter commanded the garrison upstairs and John Spencer led the attack. It was not long before Anne wished to goodness that she had never thought of it. The defenders made themselves secure by dragging Father's big oak coffer from the Great Chamber to the top of the stairs, and for a time the enemy was completely baffled. But the fighting grew hotter and hotter. The boys swarmed over the top of the barrier, and met in a hand to hand contest.

All of a sudden there was a deafening clatter. Father's coffer lurched over the top, bumped down several steps and came to rest, upside down, at the turn of the stairs, its lid open and its contents cascading higgledy piggledy to the bottom.

The noise brought Mother and Cousin Kit running from the garden. But though there were plenty of bruises and Bess Spencer's nose was spurting blood, nobody was really hurt. Cousin Kit led Bess away to the pump and Mother turned to examine the damage.

'What on earth were you doing with your father's coffer?" she cried. "See! The money bag is open; there is money everywhere. Pick it up quickly, every crown of it. If he comes in and finds it like this you'll all be sent to bed."

It was perfectly true that there was money everywhere. The contents of the coffer were not only all over the stairs, they had poured through into the hall. No one had ever seen so much money before. They all started gathering up gold pieces by the score and silver crowns by the hundred.

"How came the coffer to be open?" said Mother with a puzzled frown, when she had listened to the story of King-of-the-Castle.

"Try and see if you can lift it between you. It will be an ill business for all of you if Father finds it like this."

The bigger ones began to push at the chest. Then Robin and John pulled from the top. Their joint efforts succeeded. In a few minutes it was safely back in the Great Chamber.

Mother gathered up the few things still left in it. "Here is a list of the money that should be in the purse," she cried. "Count and see how much you have got. Perhaps if you can find every penny there will be no need to make a fuss about it."

There were still a few gold pieces and a few crowns missing, so they went back downstairs and turned everything upside down until they had really found it all. It was a marvel how far a crown could roll, cried young John Spencer as he dived for the last coin beneath the great table in the hall. Then they hastily collected a couple of bundles of old parchment and two big account books which had come loose, and Mother packed it all back into the coffer and shut down the lid.

"We won't say anything about this now," she whispered to Anne, who was standing anxiously by. "Your father would be very angry and it would only spoil the party. Leave it to me, child. If he has to be told, *I* will tell him."

Anne wanted to hug her there and then. Mother always stood between them and Father's anger whenever she could. But all she could do was breathe "Oh, *thank you* Madam" with all her heart, and follow her mother downstairs to the hall, where the others were standing about and comparing notes about their bruises.

Mistress Washington sniffed the air.

"What a dreadful smell!" she exclaimed. "Whatever have you children been doing? It smells like pig."

They all looked at one another guiltily.

"Have you been in the pig styes?" she demanded. "Let me see your shoes."

Everybody held up their feet for inspection. Though they had wiped them as clean as they could, the shoes still carried tell-tale traces.

"You naughty children!" cried Mistress Washington, making

a grimace. "It *is* pig. No wonder the place reeks of it. Ninnie, your feet are smeared all over. Where did you wipe them? On the *rushes*? That accounts for it. Upon my word will your mischief never end. You every one of you deserve a beating. Now these rushes must be cleared. John, go and fetch a wheel-barrow. Anne, get a rake. You can all set to work and gather up every rush in the hall. Don't touch them with your hands more than you can help. Throw them in a pile behind the stable in Madam's close. They are only fit to be burned. Bring in a fresh bundle, and some meadowsweet too. Unless we can rid the hall of this smell there will be no supper to-night."

The Party ended quietly. When the clearing up was finished they all went back to the garden and sat, very subdued, in the shade, singing songs to the accompaniment of Mother's lute. Then Cousin Spencer appeared from the fields and Cousin Kit asked for the chariot to be got ready. The children were all packed in, including the Danvers and the Makepeaces who could be dropped on the way. The Pargiters said good-bye, and last of all Tom Tresham rode off, calling out to Francis that he would be over again in the morning. Only Chris Hatton remained to stay the night.

"Well, that is done," said Mother with obvious relief. "The next thing is to get the little ones to bed."

But the little ones were tired and fractious. Ninnie had made herself ill with creamy custard and three-year-old Moll had lost her new red shoe in the long grass and would not stop yelling for it.

"Go and see if you can find it, Anne," sighed Mother. "I know 'tis foolish to give in to her whims, but if I smack her she will only cry herself sick."

Glad to be out of the nursery Anne ran down the garden. It was so quiet after all the excitement. There was nobody about except Chris, who was obligingly collecting cushions and platters from under the elms. He asked Anne what she was doing and came to help in the search. As they went slowly up and down, poking through every yard of the grass, an idea popped into Anne's head.

"Did it go well with you and Sir Thomas Tresham?" she asked eagerly. "He did not catch you, did he?" She saw his look of astonishment and took fright. "Your pardon, but I was there when he told Doctor Dee that he was going to catch you, and I saw Robert set off to take you warning."

Chris laughed. "'Pon my word, I am a dull fool. I did not know that you were in the secret. Robert saved me in the nick of time or I should have been taken. I was thankful, I can tell you. I have finished with Fotheringhay. It is too dangerous."

Anne nodded. "I'm glad," she said simply. "I have been frightened about it."

"I mean danger for the Lady, of course; that is what matters," he said hastily, as though she might think that he feared danger for himself. "Doctor Dee says there is danger for her in letting her name be linked with Courtenay's."

This was beyond Anne. She remembered that people had wanted Courtenay and Elizabeth to be king and queen, but she could not see where Doctor Dee came into it. She asked another question.

"Has Doctor Dee been to Woodstock yet? I know that you were going to take him."

"Heaven help us, you are a little Mistress Bright-eyes. And how did you learn *that*, I beg you?"

Anne's cheeks tingled. She did not know whether to take it for praise or blame.

"I heard Doctor Dee ask you," she said. "I was coming down the stairs and you were at the bottom. I couldn't help it." She saw that he looked upset so she added quickly, "No one else heard, and I haven't told a soul; not even Francis."

He grinned at her. "You are a good little maid. I can promise you I would rather trust myself to you than to your twin. Doctor Dee didn't go to Woodstock after all. We took letters to his kinsfolk for him. He decided to write instead of going to see them. The Parrys are his cousins, you know—Tom Parry, the Lady's treasurer and Mistress Blanche Parry, her woman of the bedchamber."

"Oh," said Anne blankly. That made it quite different. Doctor

Dee had only wanted to go and see his cousins; nothing to do with the Lady Elizabeth at all. But all the same Chris had used one word that made her prick up her ears again. He said "*we* took his letters——" That *we* let the cat out of the bag. She was certain it meant Robert and Laurie.

Just then Chris cried, "Here it is!" and held up the little red shoe. At the very same moment Marta called out across the garden to say that it was long past bedtime; Mistress Anne must give up hunting and come and say good night.

It was so late that the boys were also waiting to say good night. Anne took her place behind them at the door of the parlour where Father had taken refuge during the clearing up. She had to stand patiently while they dropped on one knee to receive his

The little red shoe

blessing, and listen while they asked permission for what they wanted to do the next day. Once more it was Robert who had a request to make.

"By your leave, sir, may I stay out the night to-morrow? Doctor Dee is teaching us about the stars. Chris would be with me, sir. He is learning about the stars too."

"What, Chris also?" exclaimed Father, highly amused. "Is he going to search for the Spice Islands too, or are we to have a Hatton marked on the map as well as a Washington? And how is it with Laurie? He's the stay-at-home, is he? That's odd. I thought it was Robert who loved his bed."

He was still laughing when it came to the twins' turn to say good night, and in such a good mood that he tickled Anne and made her squeal. But as she went up the stairs she grew thoughtful again. Out all night to watch the stars? Robert and Chris? So *that* was what they said.

When she reached the Inner Chamber Ninnie was already in bed but wide awake. The moment that Anne came near she began to talk in a loud whisper.

"There are scratches on the stairs. Have you seen them? There's one on the wainscot where the coffer hit the wall. Do you think Father will notice?"

Anne tiptoed back through the Great Chamber to the top of the stairs. It was true that there were tell-tale marks on almost every step, but luckily the scratch on the wall was not a deep one.

"It's getting dark. Nobody will see it to-night," she reported when she got back. "If we are up early and fetch a lump of beeswax from Marta's store I expect we can polish it till it doesn't show." She yawned. She was really very tired. But Ninnie was more lively than ever.

"Would you like to hear my secret," she invited. "Do you remember that I hid in the linen closet and nobody found me?"

"Um," said Anne, her clothes half over her head. "They swore that you were cheating. I did mean to ask you and then I forgot it."

She emerged from her shift to see Ninnie out of bed with her hand already on the closet door. Beckoning to Anne she opened it.

"Look!" she invited.

Anne peered inside the big dark cupboard. At first she could see nothing, then as Ninnie pointed upwards she noticed a thin slit of light at the top.

"There's a little door up there," whispered Ninnie. "The shelves are like steps and you can climb up to it. You wouldn't notice it because Mother's winter cloak is hanging in the way. I hid behind the cloak at first. That's how I found it."

"Where does it lead?"

"There's a little space in the roof. I think it is over Robert's porch room. It's a perfect place for Hide-and-Go-Seek. There's plenty of room to lie right down. Come up and look."

"Hush!" said Anne. "There's somebody coming."

They both made a dive for the bed. When their heads were beneath the bed-clothes Ninnie began to whisper again. "Don't forget that it is *my* find," she breathed into Anne's ear. "And whatever you do, don't tell Francis. You know he can't keep a secret."

The arms of
HATTON

Hawking

CHAPTER VII

The Locksmith

Though The Tail was cross and lie-a-bed the next morning, the older members of the family were awake betimes.

Robert and Chris were the first of the boys to be up and about; but early as they were, they nearly fell over Anne and Ninnie who for some unknown reason were kneeling on the stairs in their night shifts, busily polishing with lumps of beeswax. Anne stopped her work to watch the two of them as, their riding boots in their hands, they tiptoed downstairs. She heard them slip back the bar on the courtyard door and cross the yard to the stables.

"Where are they going?" whispered Ninnie.

"To Doctor Dee's," returned Anne briefly, hoping that neither Ninnie nor anyone else would stop to wonder why Chris and Robert should need horses to go to Stuchbery. They were very quiet out there. She took a peep from a window and saw that they were going out through the meadow to avoid the clatter of the cobbles. They had taken only Chris's horse. That was clever; no questions would be asked and Juno was strong enough to carry them both.

Up in the bedroom Laurie and Francis were not quite so hurried. Laurie got up first and went off to mass. He went every morning. He was devout by nature and had ambitions to become a priest. Francis went to mass on weekdays only when the fit seized him, and to-day his mind was full of other matters. After Laurie had gone he sat on the edge of the bed, his trunk hose half on, half off, and thought deeply.

Robert and Chris were on their way to Woodstock; he was certain of that. He guessed as soon as he heard Robert ask permission to stay out all night. That business of the stars was just bibble babble. It would need something much more exciting than stars to keep Robert from his bed.

Of course they had no idea that he knew; he took care of that. It was part of his plan about keeping secrets that nobody should guess what a lot he knew. He was collecting secrets as he had once collected seals and butterflies. He grinned to himself as he counted how many he had got.

First there was this one about the Woodstock business. He had suspected for some time that it was still going on, but now he was certain.. He was not sure about Laurie's part in it. Certainly Laurie *knew*; he and Robert and Chris all talked together, though they usually stopped when Francis came into the room. But apparently Laurie did not go to Woodstock with the others. Perhaps his conscience would not let him. Laurie was *good*; and though Father had not made them promise, nor even definitely forbidden it, it was certainly against his orders.

The second secret on his list was about Doctor Dee's map of Woodstock. He had never mentioned it to a soul, but he was sure that there was something fishy about it. Since that first afternoon the map had vanished. He was allowed to explore the little oak chest whenever he liked. It was still full of maps, but they were all of foreign parts. There were none of England.

His other secrets were his own private property and so not quite so exciting. There was the one about Jake and the old witch, which still puzzled him. He had been on the look out and he had several times seen Jake slip out with something hidden under his cloak. Probably it was just food, but if so why did he make such a mystery of it? Anyway it was a *secret* and therefore something to add to his collection.

The last secret was quite a small one. It was his discovery of the hiding place over the new porch room. One of the masons had told him about it a long time ago, and as soon as the building was finished he watched his chance to hunt for it. The excitement of finding it was rather spoilt because he was alone. He was sorely tempted to show Anne, especially as the entrance was in the linen closet close to her bed. But he resisted the temptation. After all he had his vow to think about.

As he sat day-dreaming a sudden uproar in the nursery brought him back to the present. The Tail was up and was being dressed and brushed and face-washed. He stood up and tied the points that kept his hose from falling down, said a hasty morning prayer and hurried downstairs, smoothing his hair with his hands as he went. He would swallow some breakfast and be off to Stuchbery before the children were running everywhere.

He was really interested in his lessons. Even dull geometry and arithmetic were not dull when they were part of what Doctor Dee called "mappery". Before Doctor Dee came Francis had never so much as seen a map. Now he was actually making one himself, a map of Sulgrave, with all the houses and the woods and fields, and even the strips in the fields where the villagers grew their crops.

Tom was helping with it. They went out together, taking with them Doctor Dee's *plane table*, a special board for making maps. It stood on three legs; a piece of paper was laid on it, and by peeping through two little holes in a bar like a ruler, landmarks like tall trees or churchtowers could be marked on the paper and the distances between them worked out by a sum. Even the sums were quite exciting when they proved that the landmarks had been marked in the right places.

When Francis reached Stuchbery Doctor Dee was alone in the little house, hard at work with his own elaborate instruments

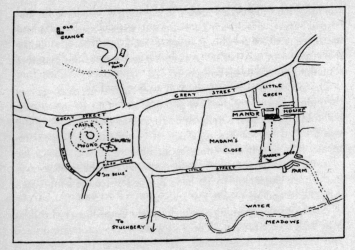

A map of Sulgrave

and the great globe on the table beside him. There was no sign
of Chris or Robert.

Francis made his bow and said "good morrow" politely. Then
curiosity became too much for him.

"Is Robert here, sir?" he asked. "I thought that he and Chris
came early?"

Doctor Dee glanced at him, then looked at his work again.

"They are out," he said briefly. "It is a lovely day. You and
Tom can go out too. You can take the plane table and go up
Barrow Hill. There are nine counties to be seen from the top.
If you can lay out a map from there, you are well on the way to
being finished map makers. Sit down and wait for Tom. And
don't talk; I'm busy."

Obediently Francis drew up a stool to the table. It would be
fun to go to Barrow Hill, but all the same he was quite certain
that he and Tom were being sent out so that they should not guess
that Chris and Robert had gone to Woodstock.

Before very long Laurie came in and sat down to work out
some problem of arithmetic. Tom was not long after him.

Directly he arrived Doctor Dee told him the plan that he and
Francis should have the day out. Tom was delighted. He said
that he had already been to Sulgrave. He carried a letter for
Master Washington from his cousin Parr. He was told there that
Master Washington had gone to see the shepherd at the sheep fold
by Culworth. That was on the way to Barrow Hill.

Doctor Dee nodded encouragement. "Go to it, my boy—
both of you. You can take your letter first and then enjoy your
outing. You need not come back here. Show me to-morrow
what you have done to-day."

Tom's horse was outside. Francis mounted behind Tom.

"We'd better take the letter first," said Tom. "I know what's
in it. It's an invitation for you all to come a-hawking at Greens
Norton; you and your father and Robert and Laurie. I've got to
take an answer, so we'd best find your father."

An invitation for hawking! Francis had never been invited
for a hawking party before. He agreed that it was most important
to find Father. So they started off for the sheep fold at Culworth.

When they got there the shepherd was alone.

"The master's been gone this half hour or more," he told
them. "You'll find him at home. He told me he would be
within doors till noon."

That was annoying. Culworth was half way to Barrow Hill,
and it seemed a pity to go back to Sulgrave again. But Tom was
firm about delivering the letter.

"You can go down across the pasture," the shepherd reminded
them. "There's no need to go all the way round by the road.
Keep to the left of the old ruins and you'll come out near the
church. You'll have to lead the horse, though; it's too rough for
the twain of you to ride."

Francis knew the way well enough, but he had hesitated to
suggest it because it took them within a bowshot of the ruined
grange. But he could think of no excuse to offer to Tom, so
they set out in single file, Tom in front leading the horse, and he
himself some yards behind.

From this vantage point he had a new view of the ruins. At
the back of them was an overgrown yard which he had never

seen before, closed in on three sides by crumbling walls. They passed so close that he could easily have thrown a stone into it. The hill was steep and as he followed Tom over a bump in the land he suddenly caught his breath. There in the yard, winding up a bucket from the well, stood the old witch.

Luckily she was facing the other way, and she did not seem to see them. She wore no black gown this time, but only a short ragged shift, revealing bony shoulders, a chest as flat as a board and a pair of long hairy legs. Francis let Tom get almost out of sight while he stood gaping, too startled even to be afraid. It was certainly the old witch. But *the old witch was a man.*

Tom called back, "What's to do? Are you coming?"

Francis took to his heels and raced downhill after Tom. When he had caught up he glanced back. The yard was empty. The old witch had gone.

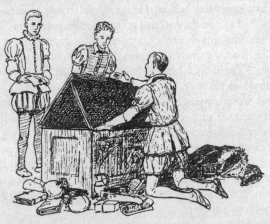

On his knees in front of the coffer

Back at Sulgrave they could not find Master Washington at first. He was not in the hall or in his parlour, but Marta told them that the Master had gone upstairs to look for something in his big coffer. "Let's go up," said Francis and led the way.

Master Washington was in the Great Chamber on his knees in

front of the coffer. The lid was propped open and the contents were spread on the floor all round him. He glanced up as the boys appeared from the stairs, his forehead puckered in a worried frown. He took no notice of them as he began methodically to put everything back again, examining each paper and parchment separately before he laid it away, Francis and Tom stood silently watching him until the floor was clear, and the heavy bag of money rested on all the documents. Then as he closed the lid, he looked up at the boys.

"Well," he said, still frowning. "What do you want?"

Tom drew the letter from his doublet and handed it to him with a respectful little bow.

As Master Washington read it his face cleared.

"This is very agreeable," he said. "Sir William Parr invites us all for a day's hawking on Holy Cross day. I will write an answer. Are you in a hurry, Tom, or can you wait till I have got this coffer locked? It is very troublesome."

Tom said that he could wait as long as Master Washington pleased. Father lowered the lid and endeavoured to make the key turn.

"This new coffer is not a success," he complained. "It is the first time I have had a lock cut into the wood, and I must say I prefer the old-fashioned padlock and staple. Francis, you are quite handy with your fingers. See what you can do with it while I answer Sir William Parr."

Francis dropped to his knees as his father got up. He was proud to be given so important a job. The lock was very stiff. He hurried downstairs to the stable and brought back some neat's-foot oil and a feather. He gave both lock and key a good dose, working them backwards and forwards many times until they moved quite easily. When Father returned he was delighted.

"You see, Tom, it is useful to have a locksmith in the family. Here is the letter. Can you keep it safely? I have told Sir William that we shall be happy to come."

By the time the lock was finished it was too late to go to Barrow Hill before dinner. Father was in excellent humour and told everyone in the hall how good Francis was with his fingers and how well he had mended the lock. Mother said at once that the tread of her spinning wheel needed attention, Ninnie was too rough with it. In the end Francis and Tom spent a whole long happy afternoon putting the spinning wheel to rights and refurbishing Father's old-fashioned crossbow.

"Will Doctor Dee be angry because we didn't go to Barrow Hill, do you think?" Tom suggested uneasily as he set off for home.

Francis laughed. "Set your heart at rest! I'd wager this crossbow to a pin that he never refers to it again."

Holy Cross day was a golden September morning. Father and the boys left Sulgrave early so that neither they nor the horses should arrive at Greens Norton hurried or untidy. The horses were groomed until they shone, and Father and Robert each had

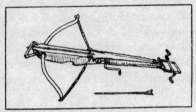

Father's old crossbow

a hawk upon his wrist while Laurie carried proudly the restored crossbow. Even Francis was promoted from Meadowsweet to a quiet little mare named Cherry Pie, kept as a rule for Mother's use.

Though Greens Norton was only eight miles away, Francis had never been there. Tom had not talked of it much, and he was surprised to find that it was a very old house, built half of stone and half of timber. A shield bearing the arms of the Greens, three bucks trippant, was still in place over the main gate.

"Small wonder that Sir William Parr is devoted to sport," chuckled Father, pointing it out; "he inherited Greens Norton from his mother, the last of the Greens."

Parr himself, with Tom at his heels, was waiting for them in the courtyard, wonderfully dressed in a velvet hunting suit of verderer's green with silver buttons and a silver hunting knife. He led them all indoors where wine was set out ready for them.

Tom was busy serving, so, as he sipped half a cup of light Gascon wine, ice cold from hanging all night in the well, Francis amused himself by looking at things in the hall. There were coats of arms everywhere, mostly the Green's bucks again; but on the centre of the oak table lay an engraved brass plate. He peered at it curiously. It was another coat of arms, with a crest and supporters and mantling and all the extras of a great nobleman. But the odd part was that the plate was broken clean in half and nobody had tried to mend it.

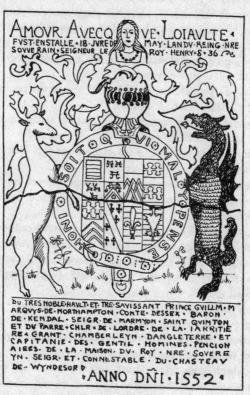

Sir William Parr saw him looking at it.

"Ah," he cried. "That is my Garter plate, boy. That plate

was over my stall in the chapel of the Most Noble Order of the Garter at Windsor. They broke it in two when they took mine honours from me. It was my good friend Master Secretary Cecil who managed to save the pieces for me. It is a witness that I was once a Knight of the Garter.' He sighed so deeply that Francis really wondered if he was going to weep.

"Let us hope that it will be restored one day," said Father, as gently as he could. "Fortunes change so quickly. 'Tis 'Up Jack' one day, and 'Down Jack Up Jill' the next.'

Parr shook his head. "I must not complain. At least I have my liberty. I live in my own house and am not like to be burned in my bed. You have heard of the fire at Woodstock?"

"Fire?" exclaimed Father "Nay, we have not heard. Tell us, I pray you. Was anybody hurt?"

"By God's providence, nobody. It was in the room beneath the Lady Elizabeth's bedchamber."

Everyone gasped with horror. "Great heavens!" cried Father. "It was an accident, of course?"

"Bedingfield says so and he is a man of honour. But I am consumed with anxiety for my niece."

"You know Woodstock, sir?" ventured Robert, his face very white. It was plain that, even in Father's presence, he just could not keep quiet.

"No, my boy, I have never been there, and I can assure you I am not likely to go. I have learned to value my neck. But we are wasting the day. Tom, go quickly and bid the cadger bring the hawks. May I fill your cup again, sir? Or shall we go forth in search of sport?"

Francis could not remember what a cadger was. His only experience of hawking was when Father took his goshawk, Bessie, round the fields to get a few rabbits or some pigeons for a pie. This was a vastly different business.

The cadger, who was waiting outside, turned out to be the falconer who carried the hawks on a sort of tray like a hurdle, slung from his neck; Sir William was taking out half a dozen hawks, each one with its head covered by a gay plumed hood. While his elders were preparing to mount, Francis ventured near enough to look at the hawks. Tom beside him whispered that they were peregrine falcons; the big ones were the females, and the smaller, the "tiercels", were the males. He had no time to ask why on earth the female should be so much better than the male, for Father called to them to hurry up. He mounted quickly and they all rode out of the courtyard in a long straggling line. Once outside the gate they paired off, Sir William leading the way with Father, Robert and Laurie next, and Francis and Tom following at the back.

At Greens Norton, apparently, Tom was very subdued, not a bit his usual confident self. He scarcely spoke at all, and Francis had time to notice that Robert and Laurie were talking only in whispers. They too were unlike themselves. It was clear that they were disturbed by the news from Woodstock.

As soon as they reached the open country Sir William halted the party and they all gathered round him.

"I thought we would first go across the stubble for partridge," he suggested. "Your goshawk sir, would do excellently there, unless you have a special fancy to stoop her at some other quarry?"

Father agreed politely. Bessie was ready to fly at partridge till she was tired. So they walked the horses further until they came to a field of golden stubble fringed on one side by a wood. At a nod from his host, Father loosed Bessie. Sir William watched her critically as she stretched her wings and took off from Father's gloved wrist.

"Very pretty," he said, shading his eyes as she swept upwards in widening circles. "I judge that she has reached her pitch, hasn't she? Then let the dogs go."

The dog keeper unleashed a couple of spaniels, who sped across the field, noses to the ground, tails waving. Very soon one of them flushed a covey of partridges which rose with a whirr of wings. Instantly the goshawk stooped, so fast that they hardly saw her go. But a partridge fell with a flurry of feathers and Father moved forward to retrieve his hawk.

Francis, sitting astride Cherry Pie near the edge of the wood, let out an Oh-h of excitement.

"Do you *like* hawking?" asked Tom suddenly.

Francis looked round at him in surprise. It was such a funny question. "Yes, I suppose so. I've never been out like this before. Do you?"

"No," said Tom unexpectedly. "I loathe it."

Francis stared. Tom had always bragged about his hawks and his hounds. "I thought you were mad about it," he said.

"I have to pretend to be," said Tom gloomily. "If my cousin Parr knew that I hated it I'd never hear the end of it and I believe my grandfather would beat the skin off me. Hawking's bad enough, but hunting's much worse. It's horrible when the hounds pull down a buck"—he looked round quickly to make sure that there was no one near—"and when they kill—*I'm sick*."

The last words were in a whisper. Francis continued to stare, but in a different way. This was quite a new Tom, one that he had not guessed existed. His heart warmed towards him. From now on they would be real friends. It wasn't until later that it occurred to him that he had acquired yet another secret.

Father came riding up. "What are you boys doing?" he cried. "Didn't you see that Robert's sparrow hawk has taken a woodcock? Phew! but it's hot in the sun. I must say that you have picked a nice shady spot for your wool gathering."

A minute later Sir William Parr joined them, a flask in his hand which he passed to Father.

"A good day's sport!" he exclaimed as Father drank. "There's no pleasure like it. I shall miss it sorely if I leave England."

"Leave England," Father repeated. "Are you really thinking of that?"

"Indeed I am. I have almost decided. Now that the Queen has married this Spaniard there is little chance that the good days of the last reign will ever return, whatever you may say about Up Jack, Down Jack. Many of my friends have gone already. Sir Anthony Cooke is at Strasbourg; Sir John Cheke, the young King's tutor, my very good friend, is gone to Padua. I could well live at Padua. It is a city of culture." He waved an expressive hand. "I have a mind to go and consult your Doctor Dee about it. He is a travelled man and a friend of Sir John Cheke's. It was Sir John who introduced him to Court."

"I'm sure he would be glad to be of any service," said Father, "though it would be a sad matter to lose you."

Francis wondered quickly what would happen to Tom if Sir William went away. Father might be sorry to lose Sir William, but he would be more sorry still to lose Tom. They kept close together at the back of the field all the day through.

In the afternoon they left the stubble and rode across open country so that Sir William could fly his finest peregrine falcon at a heron, which, he declared, was the finest sport of all.

Francis, sorry as he was for Tom, found it thrilling too. The heron was in the habit of crossing that particular hillside every day, on its way to the good fishing ground near the river, and the falconer had marked it for future sport. Sure enough they did not have long to wait before Parr cried, "here it comes", and every eye was strained to catch the first glimpse of the great bird as it sailed into view high over the tops of distant trees, its huge wings

The falcon above the heron

fanning lazily. The falcon was already in the air, loosed in good time against the certainty of the heron's coming. It was smaller than the heron but it had greater speed, and they watched it gain height as it circled faster and faster towards the clouds. The heron saw it too, and swept steeply upwards so as not to be taken from above.

The two birds were well matched; each knew the other's power. The heron's strength lay in his great wings and in the deadly spear-like beak which could kill at a single stroke. But if the falcon could climb quickly enough, circling up and up until it was overhead, then it could swoop upon the heron and grip with its talons, while keeping out of range of the heron's beak.

The battleground was the wide open sky; the white wings and the dark ones flew so swiftly that, led by Parr, everyone had to canter across mile after mile to keep in sight of them. At last the falcon reached its pitch, almost directly above the heron. It stooped, so swiftly that there was no time to take a breath before the two appeared to collide in mid air. Bound together in one pitching struggling mass, they dropped to the ground.

"Now, sir," said Parr, as they all rode slowly back from the gruesome triumph of the peregrine, "I have one more thing that I should like to show you before we go in to dine. I have at Greens Norton a couple of young greyhounds which are, I think, the noblest that I have ever seen."

"Indeed," said Father politely. "Were they bred in your own kennels?"

"Unfortunately not. I have no hounds to sire puppies of this shape. They were a present to me and one which I value greatly. They were sent by my brother-in-law, the Earl of Pembroke."

The Arms of the
GREENS

A bonfire in Madam's close

CHAPTER VIII

September the Seventh at Three in the Afternoon

On the ride home to Sulgrave the day's sport was scarcely mentioned. The boys would also have liked to discuss the fire at Woodstock and what it meant, but Father dismissed it almost at once and they did not dare to persist with the subject. He was in a state of excitement about the greyhounds, a brace of magnificent dogs of which Sir William Parr was properly proud. Great-aunt Bath's story of the greyhounds seized from her man by the Earl of Pembroke's man was new to the boys. They had none of them been present when she told it. They were dumbfounded.

"But surely," cried Robert, "the Earl of Pembroke wouldn't have *stolen* them?"

"Of a certainty he wouldn't, if he knew. Mark you we have no proof that these are the same hounds, though I admit that it is a startling coincidence. If they are the same there must be links in the story of which we know nothing. The man Penruddock, for instance, who took them from Aunt Bath's man; he might have *sold* them to my Lord of Pembroke."

"Or Great-aunt Bath's man himself might be dishonest," said Robert.

"Will you tell Great-aunt Bath that Sir William has these hounds?" inquired Francis.

"I suppose that I should have to do so, but luckily she has gone back to London," said Father with a laugh. "I should not at all have relished the task. I think I must mention it to Cousin Kit. She will be coming for the baby's christening and it would not be right deliberately to conceal it. Heaven be praised, she is more moderate than her mother."

In any case Mother and Anne had to be told about it when they got back to Sulgrave and were sitting comfortably over a supper of cakes and ale. Anne had been allowed to sit up to hear the adventures of the day, but the story of my Lord of Pembroke and the greyhounds was far more exciting than any news about hawks.

"Did you say anything to Sir William Parr?" asked Mother.

"What, tell him that his hounds had been seized from the husband of my Aunt Bath? Of course not, my dear. It would have been as good as accusing him of receiving stolen property."

"I only thought that he'll have to know sooner or later," said Mother gently, "and it would come more kindly from you than from your Aunt Bath. He might feel that you ought to have warned him, poor man."

"I won't be mixed up with it; that I vow. We will tell Cousin Kit and pray that she takes it all with good sense. Anyhow Cousin Spencer is not one to allow her to pick a quarrel."

The next few days were too filled with preparations for the christening for anyone to worry about greyhounds. They always seemed to be preparing for something nowadays, thought Anne, as on the morning of the great day she and Ninnie helped Marta to decorate the christening cake. That was a job greatly to Ninnie's liking; there were so many crumbs of sugar and almonds and candied cherries to be popped away without anybody making a fuss about it. Anne enjoyed it too, and she was almost cross when Mother called her to run an errand.

"Child, in all this bustle I've quite forgotten Doctor Dee," said

Mistress Washington wearily. "He has finished all the candles I sent him; he works so late at night. The worst is that what with the new baby and everything we've not made the year's supply yet. Will you run down to old Mother Compton, in the cottage by the rope walk; you know it. She dips candles for the chandler in Banbury. Doubtless she will let you have some, and you can take them straight to Stuchbery. Take Ninnie with you. I don't like you running about the village by yourself. And go quickly. I want you back when your Cousin Kit arrives."

Anne did not wait to be told twice. She would have left a dozen cakes for Doctor Dee. She and Ninnie trotted through the village as fast as they could go.

Old Mother Compton was a wrinkled old woman, not over clean, but her cottage was interesting when they peeped inside it. There were pans and shapes and moulds for dipping candles and rushlights lying about everywhere, but the place reeked of stale mutton fat, so they quickly drew back and waited outside till the old woman brought them the candles done up in a package.

There were no lessons that day. Robert and Laurie had ridden to meet Chris Hatton, who was to be the baby's godfather, and Francis had gone with Father to escort Cousin Kit. So Doctor Dee was all alone in his little house. He was sitting by the trestle table in the window, very intent over a sheet of paper on which was drawn a large circle ruled across with lines, which divided it into sections like an orange.

Anne looked at it curiously as she came to a halt at his side. Then she made him a little bobbing curtsey.

"Well," he said with his cheerful grin. "What does your ladyship here? Are you alone?"

"Ninnie is outside," she said. "She was too frightened to come in. I brought you——" She stopped as a new object on the table caught her eye. It was a globe very much like the other, but the painting on it looked different. "Is that another map?" she asked.

"Yes; but it's a map of the sky not of the earth."

"How can you have a map of the sky?"

"By observing the stars very carefully and calculating their distance from each other. It's a very complicated business."

"Did you invent it?"

He threw back his head and laughed.

"Indeed I did not. It is the accumulated wisdom of the ages, if you know what that means. Both these globes were made by a very great man, a friend of mine, Gerard Mercator. Remember the name; it will be famous. Look at it if you wish; there are pictures on it of the different groups of stars. See, here is Ursa Major, the Great Bear; and Ursa Minor, the Little Bear; and Taurus, the Bull; can you see them, painted on the globe?"

"Why do you want to know about the stars?"

"First of all because from the stars you can calculate the direction from place to place. They are man's only guide for exploring the world. But there are lots of other reasons too; most of man's understanding of the world we live in begins with a study of the stars."

An astrolabe

She nodded a little doubtfully. Then her eyes lighted on something else; a round brass thing rather like the face of a clock, with a ring to hang it up by. "What's that?" she demanded.

"That, Madam, is an astrolabe," he answered patiently. "It's an instrument for measuring the position of the stars, just as I have explained. It's the right hand of every astronomer and every map maker and navigator and even of ordinary people like you and me. If you know how to use the astrolabe you can calculate where you are by it, find your way by it, find out the date by it, or even tell the time by it. See, you hold it up by the ring and peep through the two little holes on that centre arm. It twiddles round so you can direct it as you want. Now are you any the wiser?"

She shook her head. It was too difficult. Her eyes were again on the paper in front of him.

"What's that you are doing?" she asked.

"Bless the child; she's as bad as the Inquisition. I'm drawing up a horoscope. You don't know what that is either, I suppose. Well, it's like making a map of a person's life. You find out what stars were in the sky at the hour they were born, and from that you work out how the stars may affect their lives."

She stared at the drawing, frowning a little.

"How can the stars affect anyone? I thought only God could do that."

He smiled at her again. "Foolish little maid; tell me, who made the stars?"

"God did, of course," she said simply and went on staring at the paper. " 'September the 7th 1533 between 3 and 4 o'clock in the afternoon'," she read aloud. "What's that? Is it the person's birthday?"

He pushed back his stool and stood up, sweeping the paper away with his hand.

"One always has to have a date to work from," he said quickly. "Let me see, what have you come for? Have you brought me something?"

"Some candles," she said, pushing forward the parcel. She felt that he was annoyed. She waited a little nervously while he undid it.

"What's this they are wrapped in?" He held up an old crumpled piece of parchment, turning it first one way then the other, as though it were something of great importance. "Tell me, where did you get this?"

"From old Mother Compton. I had to go there because our new candles aren't made yet."

"I must go and see Mother Compton to find out where she got her wrapping from. This is a page of Aristotle, handwritten on vellum. It must have come from the library of one of the old monasteries. The loss that learning has suffered by the destruction of the monasteries is just incalculable." He looked down and saw her puzzled face. "Do you think I'm talking nonsense? You see, until printing was invented the monks made most of the books, copying them all by hand. Their libraries were full of treasures, all lost now, that never can be replaced. I must look into this. Perhaps we may find other pages of Aristotle in cottage kitchens."

Just at that moment there was a stamping of horses' hoofs outside. Doctor Dee peeped out of the window.

"It's Robert with Chris Hatton," he said. "And there is Ninnie talking to them. You and I will be late for the christening if we are not careful."

Christopher Washington was baptised in the church of St. Nicholas at Sulgrave. Cousin Kit was his godmother and held him at the font, and he did his duty by yelling lustily when the water was poured over him; a sure sign, said old Marta cheerfully, that the devil had gone out. Afterwards they all went back to the manor, and Christopher's health was drunk and the christening cake cut. Cousin Kit, Chris Hatton and Doctor Dee were the only guests besides Tom Tresham, who always turned up for everything. After dinner they all sat under the trees, except the boys who as usual wandered off upon some interest of their own. Anne and Ninnie ran backwards and forwards carrying cushions for everyone to sit on. There had been a shower in the morning and Mother was afraid that the grass might be damp.

Doctor Dee, who wore even at the christening the funny old black gown from which he would never be parted, produced from somewhere inside it a piece of parchment which Anne recognised at once. He held it out to Father.

"That, sir," he said, "came to me as a wrapping for candles

bought in the village. Can you tell me what monastery it is likely to have come from?"

"Aristotle! By my faith, that's an odd thing to get from a chandler. I'm afraid I can't give you any help. This manor belonged to St. Andrew's, Northampton, a Cluniac priory, but it was only a grange—a farm, you know—for supplying the monks with corn. They would not have kept any books here."

Doctor Dee slowly shook his head. "Nobody yet realises what a disaster it is that all these things should perish. If I had the time I should like to make it my business to search them out and preserve them. I've even thought of petitioning the Queen to have them collected for a national library."

"How about Canons Ashby?" suggested Mother. "That was more than a farm. It was a priory of Austin Canons. And it is only three miles away. Things from there might easily have reached this village. Why don't you go and see Sir John Cope? He is making a fine house of it. Perhaps he could help you."

"A good idea," said Father. "If you like I will take you over there, sir."

"Speaking of monasteries," Cousin Kit intervened, "my mother writes that the Queen seems more set than ever on restoring the church lands. If she cannot pass a law she will at least set an example. The black monks are to go back to Westminster; and so far as her own possessions are concerned, even where the monasteries are too ruined to be any good, she is insisting that they should be used for some godly purpose. It seems to me that it will make it difficult for her subjects to turn a blind eye. You say you have a deed to prove your right to Sulgrave, Cousin Laurence?"

"Y-yes," said Father slowly. There was a shadow of doubt in his voice and Mother looked at him quickly. "Yes, I have a mortgage deed; at least I *had* one. At the moment I cannot for the life of me lay my hand on it, but I will look again."

"Is it not in your coffer?" said Mother anxiously.

Father shook his head. "I have looked. Doubtless I shall find it somewhere. You see, it all happened many years ago. I was in Northampton at the time."

Anne looked from one to the other. This was the old trouble back again.

"Supposing you cannot find it?" persisted Cousin Kit.

"Don't disturb yourself. We should get over it. Maybe I will go up to London and consult some of my legal friends at Grays Inn. 'Tis many years since I read law, but some of my old comrades are still there. Anyway I want to enter Laurie as a student. It would do no harm for me to go up and take both the boys with me. Then I should get the best advice."

"It would be a wise precaution," said Cousin Kit gravely. "You would not care to part with Sulgrave now."

Father rather pointedly changed the subject. "By the way, Cousin," he said, "I have a taste of gossip for you. We went a few days since for a day's hawking with Sir William Parr. He showed us a brace of greyhounds, very fine ones. My Lord of Pembroke had just sent them to him as a present."

"Greyhounds?" repeated Cousin Kit. "Greyhounds from my Lord of Pembroke? Surely it isn't possible. They can't be the stolen ones?"

"I agree," said Father lightly. "It isn't possible. But I thought that I couldn't do other than tell you."

It was Cousin Kit's turn to look worried. "It is very strange. Of course there may have been some knavery somewhere. We ought to get to the bottom of it. My Lord of Bath may have a dishonest man, or my Lord of Pembroke might have been hoodwinked. Could you not ask Sir William about it, Cousin?"

"Certainly I could not," replied Father warmly. "I am not going to tilt at his honesty; no, nor at my Lord of Pembroke's neither. Ask your husband, Cousin. The duty befits him if it befits any of us."

"He would never do it," said Cousin Kit with a little laugh. "He is a man of peace. I tell you what I will do. I will ask Sir Thomas Tresham. He is Parr's kinsman and our very good friend. He would be able to raise the question without offence. Yes, that is a good idea. I will ask him and I will let you know what happens. Now how goes the time, I wonder? I must not sit any longer in idleness. We are moving house from Wormleighton to Althorp this week, you know, and everything has to be packed up. We've lingered at Wormleighton most of the summer and it is high time the place was sweetened. Pray, good cousin, will you call for the horses."

"The boys and I will escort you part of the way," said Father. "Where have they got to, I wonder? Ninnie, child, run and look for them. Tell them to get ready. We are going to ride to Wormleighton."

"There's not such a great hurry, surely," said Mother. "Rest quietly anyway until Ninnie has found the boys. Anne, fetch some more 'gages. Doubtless these are not so good as your own, but they are refreshing."

A fresh supply of greengages kept the party together a little longer. Then Cousin Kit said she really must be going. Probably the boys were miles away. She would not wait for them. She had two grooms with her and it was daylight. She would come to no harm.

"Nonsense," said Father. "The boys have no business to run off like that. Anne, you go and look for them. You know their haunts better than Ninnie does."

Anne knew that Francis and Tom Tresham were celebrating the christening by having a bonfire of old rushes in Madam's close; she could see the clouds of smoke. But it was Robert and Laurie that Father wanted. She had seen them vanishing in the direction of the water meadows. She would look there first. Through the farmyard was the quickest way. But before she had even turned in at the farm gate she saw Ninnie running towards her, her face white and her eyes frightened.

"They're *fighting*," she cried. "Down there, in the big barn."

Anne raced across the yard. The latch of the barn door was jammed. As she struggled with it she heard Chris's voice ring out.

"If you would serve the Lady you must know how to fight for her. On guard!"

"She heard the clash of steel"

She got the door open at last. After the sunlight it was a few seconds before she could see anything, but her heart beat wildly as she heard the clash of steel. Chris and Robert were fighting with long slender swords in their right hands and daggers in their left. Chris was obviously getting the better of Robert for he was dancing round and round him, while Robert seemed to be able to do nothing but turn about, parrying the strokes.

Anne clapped her hand over her mouth, terrified to make a sound lest she should distract Robert. Then she noticed that Laurie was perched comfortably upon a pile of hay. He was *laughing*. Was he mad? She looked again at Chris and Robert and this time she saw that their swords were *sheathed*. She was so relieved that she gave a little cry. Chris heard her and glanced round. Robert promptly lunged at him. Chris's arm shot up and he dropped his sword.

"Well played," he cried as he picked it up again, "though it was Anne distracted me. But you'll make a fine swordsman yet. On guard!"

Anne remembered her message and tried to make herself heard. But they had started again. Before she could stop them the door flew open and Father strode in.

"Peace, you young fools," he cried. "Have you lost your senses?" Then he saw at once what had escaped Anne for so long. "Oh, you're fencing only. Ninnie came flying to say that you were killing each other. I thought that surely you couldn't be as mad as that, but I ran all the same. But——" There was a pause. Anne saw that he was frowning. "What's this? Fighting with knives? Great heavens! What are you? Savages?"

Both boys stood meekly with lowered points. Then Chris stepped forward with his usual charming smile.

"No, sir; this is not a knife. It is the poniard; for parrying the rapier thrust. 'Tis a new art, sir. Everyone is learning it. You use the poniard to engage the other's blade, which leaves your own free to lunge at him. You do not stand sideways, as one does with a single sword, but square on to him, using both hands."

"I know, I know," said Father testily. "You do not need to

teach me, boy. 'Tis one of those new vile fashions from France and Italy. If you are not swordsman enough to overcome your adversary with the blade of a gentleman you push your body up against him, as in some tavern brawl, and stab him in the back. Now that the Spaniards are at Court I suppose that anyone who draws a sword will have a knife in him before he can say the Holy Name. Understand I'll have none of it here. If you must fight, fight with the sword like honest men and leave the knife to foreign cut-throats."

"As you will, sir," said Chris easily. "I ask your pardon. I had been shown the art myself and I did but attempt to pass it on."

Father sighed. "You have a good heart, Chris, but you go too fast. Put your tackle away and let's forget it. I sent to fetch the boys for a ride to Wormleighton. Would you care to come with us? We shall be back before dark."

That night, when Mother came to tuck them up in bed Anne had two things to ask her.

"Madam," she said. "Can the stars affect peoples' lives?"

"Child, what a question," exclaimed her mother. " 'Twould take a wiser head than mine to answer it. Some people say they do. But you can be sure of this; not all the stars in the sky can make a thing happen unless God wills it; nor can the stars make you do wrong if you pray for grace to do right. Ninnie, you've got jam on your face again. Was there ever such a sticky little maid?"

Anne waited while Ninnie cleaned herself on a moistened corner of Mother's kerchief before she put the second question.

"Madam," she said again. "Who was born on September the seventh 1533 at three o'clock in the afternoon?"

"Bless my soul, Anne, what nonsense is this? How should I know? 1533? I was about your age then, and your father was older. It might have been Cousin Kit; no, I'm wrong; she would have been about five. Why do you want to know? Is it a game?"

"Not exactly," said Anne in a little voice. "I thought it was somebody's birthday, that's all."

"Well, I can't help you," said her mother, picking up Ninnie's shift from the floor and hanging it on the clothes horse in the corner of the room. But she went on pondering all the same. "Let's see, your Uncle Edward was older, and your Aunt Cicely wasn't born yet. I can't think of anyone who was born when I was your age—except the Lady Elizabeth."

The clothes horse

London from Holborn Hill

CHAPTER IX

"You are to go to London"

The next morning Father announced that he had decided to go to London and seek advice among his legal friends about the mortgage deed of Sulgrave.

"I am quite convinced that there is nothing to worry about," he said firmly. "But to ease your mother's mind it would be as well to go. You two older ones can come with me. I have long promised Robert a jaunt to London, and we can take the opportunity of entering Laurie's name for Grays Inn. How soon can they be ready, wife? To-morrow?"

Mistress Washington cried out at that. They must both have clean linen. She'd been so busy since the baby came that she'd had no time even to see to their hose. Could he not wait a day or so?

"Just like women's ways," groaned Father in mock despair. "First they tease a man until he consents to what they want, and then, behold, they are not ready. Make you a note of it, my sons. It will stand you in good stead for the future."

"Women's ways, forsooth!" cried Mistress Washington. "Your father has lost his deed and knows not where he has put it, and so he is impatient to be gone. You promised to take Doctor Dee to Sir John Cope's at Canons Ashby, sir. Surely you would not go to London until you have fulfilled your promise?"

Father shook his head at her, laughing heartily. "I' faith, wife, you would not be happy without the last word. Very well, then. I will take Doctor Dee to Canons Ashby. You boys had better go and tell him. No, I shall not take *you* to Canons Ashby. Your mother will be wanting to fit your finery. I will take Anne and Ninnie. It is time the little maidens had a treat. The boys must not have it all their own way."

Anne and Ninnie exchanged delighted glances. An outing was always an outing, even if it was only a little one. Anne, like Mother, had been worrying ever since Cousin Kit's talk yesterday, but, she concluded, there could not be very much wrong when Father and Mother were both joking. She and Ninnie drew lots for the honour of riding pillion behind Doctor Dee and Ninnie won. But in the end Anne was more than satisfied to be with Father, because then Doctor Dee could grin at her and she could smile back, whereas Ninnie, clinging to his belt, could see nothing at all.

"Sir John Cope's new house is nearly finished," said Father as they walked their horses up the long hill. "It is a fine place, though, mark you, he has plenty of material to hand in the old priory of the Austin Canons. I did hear that he has all the books of the priory in safe keeping; if so you will be in your element. But, by your leave, we won't stay too long to-day. The children can wait outside with the horses. They will give us a good excuse to get away betimes."

Being left outside with the horses was much better than being taken into a strange house to make their curtsies. And, it turned out, there *was* plenty to interest them. The great new house had brick walls, like Wormleighton, with stone at the corners, the doors and the windows. The stone came from the old priory buildings, just down the lane, and was pushed along in barrows by the workmen. Ninnie made friends with them at once, and was even allowed to trundle an empty barrow, but Anne stood and stared.

"They're pulling down the *church*," she gasped, in a shocked whisper. "Ninnie, don't you see? They're pulling down a church to build a house."

She watched open-mouthed, as the masons on ladders carefully detached the stones and handed them down to the labourers, one

Pulling down a church to build a house

at a time, to be wheeled along to the new building. It was a fine church, too, much finer and bigger than Sulgrave, with great window spaces from which all the glass had gone, and a tower and lots of little pinnacles. Already the altar end had vanished and they were now busy pulling down the chancel wall.

She made up her mind to ask Father about it on the way home. A church was God's house. How could it be right to use it for building an ordinary house?

But when they were mounted again Doctor Dee was so excited

about all he had seen that she could not get a word in edge-ways.

"Thank heaven that is one collection that is safe," he cried. "Sir John Cope seems to be a man of culture."

"It is a pity that he could not save the gold and silver as well as the books," said Father. "Canons Ashby had some wonderful altar plate. It was stolen, I believe, even before the King's men could lay hands on it. No one knows what happened to it. Not that it matters. It would all have been melted down in any case."

"A pity; but altar plate is not such a loss to mankind as the loss of rare books would be," insisted Doctor Dee. "Gold and silver can be replaced, but learning lost is lost for ever. Of course we know no more than we did to start with where that page of Aristotle came from. I think I must go and have a word with Mother Compton. She may have some other pages ready to wrap up her wares."

"I should go at once if I were you," said Father. "I would come with you but I must see about packing my saddle bags for the ride to London. Perhaps my daughters would like to help me, would they?"

Anne and Ninnie did not need to be asked twice. They ran up and down stairs all the evening fetching things for Father. The saddle bags were almost done when Mother came to find him. She looked worried.

"Robert has a sore throat," she said. "He has tried to conceal it all day but to-night I taxed him with it. It is red and he cannot swallow. I have given him a brew of knapweed freshly made, but I doubt if he will be fit to ride to-morrow."

"Certainly he must not ride to-morrow," said Father. "He might get ill on the road and then what should we do? It's a pity. The horses are all ready. Shall I take Francis instead? What say you, wife?"

Mother's first thought was for clothes. "Yes-s," she said doubtfully. "I think I could manage. There are those crimson hose which Laurie has outgrown. And he can use Laurie's old shirts too. Yes, let him go, by all means. He has been a good boy of late."

"Then bid him come here quickly. Do you know where he is, Anne?"

Anne did know. She had seen him go off with the crossbow that Tom had left behind him. He would be down in the water meadows, shooting at birds and searching for the bolts afterwards. She found him at once and called out the news as soon as she was within earshot.

"Robert is ill. You are to go to London."

It took him a moment to understand. Then he began to run.

"Find that bolt for me," he cried over his shoulder. "It fell somewhere in that patch of nettles."

They left very early in the morning, well stoked with ham pasty and warm ale. Mother saw to it that their saddlebags held packs of bread and cheese and that their water bottles were full. They were not setting out for the Indies, Father reminded her with a laugh, as she stuffed packets of raisins into all their pouches. There were plenty of alehouses on the road.

For Francis it might almost as well have been the Indies. He had only once been to Oxford, thirty miles away, and London was more than double the distance. The world was a wonderful place. He was riding Cherry Pie again and Mother had slipped a whole shilling into his pouch to spend in London. After he had dutifully kissed her hand, he hugged her with unusual warmth, and hugged Anne too, and even old Marta who came to the gate to see them off. He could afford to behave as a child to-day for he was going with Father to London like a grown man.

They rode single file along the narrow lanes until they reached the highway from Banbury to Buckingham which was a wide one, cut back thirty feet on either side in obedience to the law. From then onwards they could go three abreast, with Will behind them, leading a spare horse in case of accident.

Father began to outline his plans. They would have their dinner at Buckingham and rest the horses. If all went well they should easily reach Aylesbury by the night. It was just half way. It meant two long days in the saddle, but when they got to London the horses would be stabled all the time. The whole City only covered a mile, when all was said and done, and the streets were so narrow and so crowded that no one dreamed of riding if they could possibly walk.

"We will put up at the Saracen's Head outside Newgate," he said. "I usually stay at my Uncle Kytson's old house in Milk Street. The business still goes on, you know, both in London and in Antwerp. My brother, your Uncle Tom, is head of the Antwerp branch. But if we went to Milk Street now my Aunt Bath might get to hear of it; she is at Whitehall, in attendance on the Queen; and I think we will keep our own counsel until I know better where I stand about the mortgage."

"Is there really any danger, sir?" asked Laurie.

"About Sulgrave? No, I would not call it danger; but as your mother is not here I will admit to you that I shall be happier when I have taken some advice about it. I don't imagine for one moment that they will turn us out. But it is possible that possession of church land might not be considered what is called in law a 'good title'. For a good title to land you have to produce deeds that prove you have a just and legal claim to it; in fact, to show that you are *entitled* to it. My mortgage deed would prove it beyond all doubt, but unfortunately I cannot find the thing. I want Sulgrave to pass on to my children and to their children. If I cannot prove how I came by it, one day *your* title to it might be challenged."

They spent the night at the King's Head in Aylesbury, a pleasant country town, though they saw little of it, for Father insisted that they should go to bed at dusk so as to start again at dawn. He wanted to reach London early the following afternoon.

From Aylesbury onward there were more travellers on the road, most of them riding in company. Father said it was for fear of beggars; the country was alive with them. Most of them were harmless enough, poor wretches; they were the aged and the destitute and the cripples who had no homes, and no one to help them now that the monasteries were gone. All that the Council could do was to whip the ones who were strong enough to work and to give the others licences to beg. Of course they were supposed to stay in their own villages and beg from their

The country was alive with beggars

neighbours, but numbers of them collected into bands, and took to the highway and the towns. There was more money there.

He passed each of the boys a handful of small change, to give in alms, a farthing here or a penny there, where they could not avoid it. But they would have to harden their hearts or they would have no money left if they gave to every poor creature who begged of them.

They stopped at a simple alehouse at noon, drank ale and ate bread and cheese, and then pressed on. In half an hour more they came to a cross roads, posted all the four ways. TO EDGWARE. TO UXBRIDGE. TO WESTMINSTER. TO LONDON.

On a piece of open ground beside the crossways stood a gallows, mounted on a platform. It was deserted, but the grass around it was worn bare and littered with rags and bones and bits of orange peel. Father stopped his horse. "This is Tyburn," he said grimly.

Both the boys stared. They had imagined something more terrible and more stirring than this quiet country place with farm buildings in the background, a group of trees with an inviting patch of shade and a clear view of distant hills.

"Thank God there is no hanging to-day," said Father. "Many people treat it as an outing or an entertainment, but I have no stomach for it."

He turned to the left, along the way marked TO LONDON. It was still no more than a country road, but after a mile or two the houses began, most of them surrounded by gardens. It wasn't

until they had passed through a narrow village street which
Father said was the village of St. Giles in the Fields, that they
caught the first glimpse of a church spire so tall that it dwarfed
the houses, as the Sulgrave elms dwarfed the lavender hedge.
There was no doubt about that anyway, thought Francis, as
Cherry Pie clattered on the cobbled street. It must be St. Paul's.
They passed through a turn-pike gate which Father said was
Holborn Bar, then walked the horses down a long hill, over the
bridge across the Fleet river and up again on the other side. This,

TYBURN

thought Francis, *must* be the City. There was no break in the
houses on either side of the road. St. Paul's towered ahead of
them, and the noise of wheels on the cobbles, and people shouting
everywhere nearly deafened him. He was glad to turn aside
under an archway and come to a stop in the courtyard of an
inn.

Even here it was noisy enough. Everybody seemed to be in a
hurry. It was, Father told them, the Saracen's Head, one of the
finest and busiest inns in London, much frequented by well-to-do
merchants who had no London lodging of their own. The yard
itself was big enough to hold three or four waggons at the same

time. There were wooden galleries running right round it with numberless doors, each leading to a separate bedroom. You could actually have a room to yourself if you liked to pay for it, said Father. As there were three of them they would be quite certain not to have to share with strangers.

Francis and Laurie were both so stiff that they could hardly stand. Father prescribed a douche of cold water, a meal and then a walk. It was quite early still and it would do them good to feel the ground under their feet.

Their bedchamber was positively luxurious. It had two large beds in it, actually with feather bedding; there were fresh country rushes on the floor, and a basin and ewer with water for washing standing on a joint stool, so that they did not need to seek the pump. The lattice overlooked the road. Francis put his head out and kept it there while Father and Laurie made themselves tidy. The way ran steeply uphill. The houses were packed close together, the roofs showing over one another like a flight of steps. There was constant coming and going, men and women of every sort and size with a good sprinkling of lads in flat blue caps, whom even he knew to be apprentices. There were shops, too, with shopkeepers yelling their wares outside the doors, and a crowd gathered round a fallen horse which couldn't drag its waggon up the hill. He could have stayed for ever if Laurie had not pushed him aside in order to empty the washing water out of the window.

He should be honoured with some clean, Father said with a laugh. After the two of them had washed it would really put on more dirt than it took off.

They ate in the dining hall where a meal seemed to be going on all the time and then he followed the others outside, completely forgetting that he had ever been tired.

They were on Snow Hill, Father announced. Newgate lay just at the top of the street. Did they realize that they weren't really in the City of London yet? But they wouldn't go that way to-night. There was plenty to be seen outside the wall. So they went down the hill to Holborn Bridge to look at the basin of the Fleet river. It was really nothing but a dirty ditch blocked with barges of sea coal. The smell of it nearly made Francis sick. He was glad when they turned back, up the hill again, and branched off to their left at the top, through a network of streets so narrow that there was hardly room to walk three abreast. At last they emerged on to a wide imposing road with a water standard in the middle of it.

"Here is Fleet Street," said Father, "and this is the conduit that gives you water carried in pipes all the way from Tyburn brook. I brought you to see it because shortly the bells should ring. That carved figure on the top of the little tower is St. Christopher and if you look at the angels, the stone ones, down the sides, you will see that they each carry a bell. There is clock-work inside the tower and at six o'clock they will ring a little tune. I wonder what the time is now? One of you go and ask that woman standing at her door. Fleet Street citizens are prosperous. 'Tis probable they all have clocks."

Laurie returned in a moment to say that it still lacked a quarter to six.

"Then we will stroll along and come back again. Come here, into the middle of the road, where you can see both ways. Look towards the City. You can just see Ludgate, halfway up the hill past the Fleet bridge. Now look the other way. That is Temple Bar across the road in the distance. Both of them are gates into London, the outer gate and the inner gate. You should be specially interested in this spot because it is where Wyatt's rebellion met its end six months or so ago. I am sorry that Robert and Chris Hatton are not here. It would be of interest to them too."

He looked from one to the other of his sons with a little smile. When he saw that they were both listening with all their ears he went on.

"Wyatt stormed Temple Bar with some of his followers. They broke through it and poured along here, along Fleet Street, cock-a-hoop because they felt they had captured the City. But they had walked into a trap. Ludgate was fast closed against them. They had to retreat and face Temple Bar once more, in order to get out again. The few who managed to fight their way through were taken by the Queen's men directly they reached the outside of the gate."

The boys stared, open-mouthed. It was hard to realize that all this had happened here, where they were standing, only a few months ago. Father looked at them, pleased that he had driven the lesson home.

"You have seen Tyburn," he remarked as a final stroke. "Dozens were executed there, and on gibbets all over the City, too. But that's enough of horrors for to-night. It must be just about time for the angels to ring their little bells."

They were all in bed before it was really dark. Francis thought at first that he would never get to sleep; the noise on the hill went on so late and the church bells never seemed to stop. If there was a moment's peace a watchman came round crying at the top of his voice that it was a quiet night and all was well. But he found to his astonishment that he must have been asleep, for he woke to find Father and Laurie nearly dressed and just about to start for Mass at St. Sepulchre's church a few yards further up the hill.

"We will go to Grays Inn this morning," Father announced later, as they were breaking their fast. "Likely enough I shall not be long this first time, and then we will go into the City and amuse ourselves. We must buy fairings to take home to Mother and the children, and we might have our dinner at a tavern."

Grays Inn was up Holborn hill and quite a long walk along High Holborn at the top, a fine wide road with great houses on either side. Father drew their attention to several as they passed. There was Furnivalls Inn and Scrope's Inn and Staple Inn, all of them Inns of Chancery.

"The Inns of Chancery are the smaller Inns, and are like nurseries for the greater Inns of Court. The students begin their studies at an Inn of Chancery and from there move up, if they are good enough," explained Father. "If I enter Laurie at Grays Inn he will likely enough go to Staple Inn across the road for the first year or two. They will teach you manners and accomplishments there, my boy, as well as the rudiments of the law. So you had better brush up your lute-playing and learn to dance a galliard. It will stand you in good stead."

Francis stole a surreptitious glance at his brother. He could picture Robert as a gallant, but not the sober, pious, pains-taking Laurie.

"This on our right, with the great garden, is Ely Place, the London house of the Bishop of Ely." Father pointed to a long garden wall and a magnificent stone gatehouse. "It is noted for its strawberries, so noted that in King Hal's reign the good bishop could hardly call his home his own. It was a dangerous business to have something that the King coveted. He was lucky not to lose his house altogether. Now we go out through Holborn Bars again. Grays Inn, you see, is just outside the London boundary."

He turned to the right as he spoke, under an arched entrance and into a paved square with a chapel on one side and ancient houses all round it. It was a quiet place; the noise of London seemed far away. It reminded Francis a little of one of the colleges he had seen at Oxford. At first he was quite interested to look about him. A new hall was being built, and for a while he watched the workmen. Then he explored and found the gardens in which there was a windmill, an unexpected interest. There was also a fine view to some wooded hills to the north. But he soon got tired of it and went back to the gateway where an aged porter told him lurid stories of prisoners dragged along Holborn at the cart's tail to the gallows at Tyburn. He was glad when Father and Laurie reappeared. It seemed to him that London was full of horrors. But Father was in good spirits. He clapped Francis on the back and asked him if he was weary of waiting.

"You've been a good patient lad," he said. "And now we will go and enjoy ourselves."

They wasted no more time sight-seeing in Holborn, but walked briskly back the way they had come, straight past the Saracen's Head and St. Sepulchre's Church, and for the first time saw Newgate straight ahead of them.

"Now you really are in the City," announced Father when

they had pushed their way through the archway among a line of carts waiting to pay the toll. "We'll go straight on to Cheapside and see the goldsmiths' and the mercers' shops, and later on we'll find our way to the Bridge. You've not set eyes on the river yet. After we've had our dinner we might go and look for a waterman to take us out for a row."

The streets inside Newgate were as narrow as ever and even more crowded, and Francis dodged along at his father's heels unable to look at anything for fear of getting lost. And then all

NEWGATE

at once they emerged into a great wide road with houses standing far back, three or four or sometimes even five stories high, all wonderfully carved up the front and glittering with numberless panes of glass. This great wide place seemed to stretch for miles down the centre of the town. A church with a fine square tower jutted out half way along; and in the middle a great tall cross, all pinnacles and carved figures, stood on the top of a flight of steps. Francis drew a deep breath. There was no need for his father to tell him that this was the heart of London, the famous Cheap.

Now that they had arrived Father no longer hurried. They

pottered slowly along, sticking their heads into the open shop fronts to look at the wares inside. Francis could not believe that they were shops at all. They were more like rich parlours hung with carpets and tapestries and lengths of wonderful silks, and sometimes there were tables covered with goblets and dishes and flagons all made of silver or gold.

Father actually went inside one of these goldsmith's shops to look at a brooch of silver and enamel which he thought would be just the thing to take to Mother. Laurie and Francis waited outside, watching him across the counter board. Suddenly a hand was laid upon Laurie's arm.

"How now, young Washington! It *is* young Washington, isn't it? Don't say that you don't remember me."

A tall young man, elegantly dressed, stood behind them, regarding Laurie with a friendly grin.

Laurie went suddenly red up to the roots of his hair. He glanced at Father who was watching across the shop counter.

"Ye-es," he stammered. "Of course I remember you. I'm here with my father." He looked round again. There was no help for it, Father was obviously waiting to know who it was he was talking to. "Sir," he began, "this is—I mean, may I present Master Francis Verney."

Francis looked at the stranger with interest. So this was the famous Verney. He had expected to find him about Chris and Robert's age, but he was a great deal older. In fact he was a grown man, not very much younger than Doctor Dee.

Master Verney swept a bow. Father acknowledged it.

"I am very glad to meet you," he said pleasantly, leaning across the shop window and extending his hand. "I knew your father many years ago. Is your brother Edmund well? I heard that you had both been confined to your house with some—er—indisposition. Is it a thing of the past?"

Master Verney threw back his head and laughed. "You heard correctly, sir. They kept us prisoned in our own house till they decided whether we were traitors or not. Now, apparently, they are satisfied, for we are free again. Have you come to London to see the Spaniards? The new King brought a whole shipload of them to his wedding. The Londoners longed to cut their throats at first, but now they have found that their pockets are full of gold, so they have decided to bleed them slowly instead. I hear the City is doing very nicely on it."

Father obviously enjoyed the joke, but the shopkeeper was waiting at his elbow with the brooch and he turned away.

Francis Verney looked at Laurie.

"What has happened to you of late?" he inquired in a low voice. "Your brother often comes to see us but you have not been since that first time."

Laurie shook his head. "No," he said softly, "I cannot come, but my will is with you just the same."

"A pity," said Verney briefly. "We could do with more than your will. I go back to-morrow. Tell your brother so." He looked round and saw that Father was still paying for his purchase. He bent to Laurie's ear. "Things are speeding up, I think. Tell Robert to come soon."

Father emerged from the shop.

"Have you dined, Master Verney?" he asked. "We are just going to find a tavern. Will you join us? No? Well, it is pleasant to have seen you. Do not fail to come to Sulgrave if ever you are riding that way."

The Arms of
VERNEY

The Traitors' Gate

CHAPTER X

"Those Plaguey Greyhounds"

After the excitement of four whole days in London, the ride home seemed as dull as ditchwater. Francis, jogging along at Father's side, paid little attention to the country. He was far too busy living through every day over again, and remembering it all in the right order, so as to be able to tell Anne all about it, or, more important still, to be able to tell Tom. He hugged himself at the thought of telling Tom. Never again would he mind if Tom bragged. *Tom had never been to London.*

They seemed to have done so much in the time. There was Cheap, with its shops, and St. Paul's, and London Bridge with all the houses built on it. He'd been to the Tower, and because Father had a friend who was captain of the yeoman guard, he'd actually been across the drawbridge as far as the Lion Tower, to see the wild animals which were kept there. He was ready to wager that Tom had never seen a live lion. Then on another day they had seen the royal palace at Whitehall. Of course they did not go inside, and it was a little disappointing that they had not caught even a glimpse of the Queen, or her new husband. But at Westminster Abbey they had seen the chair that she sat on at her Coronation.

But best of all was the day that they went on the river. Father did not come with them. They were to shoot the rapids under London Bridge and Father said that he preferred a dry skin. So he put them in charge of a reliable waterman and waited for them on the wharf. Shooting the Bridge was tremendously exciting, and when they got to the other side they rowed about among all the great ships anchored below Bridge. After that the waterman took them down river as far as the Tower to show them the Watergate, where important prisoners went in, many of them never to come out again. It was known as Traitors' Gate.

"Is that the way they took the Lady Elizabeth?" inquired Laurie boldly.

"Aye, that's it. They say she sat on the steps and wept, poor lady, remembering how her mother went that way before her," said the waterman shaking his head.

"But *she* did come out," said Laurie eagerly. "She's at Woodstock now, not many miles from where we live."

The waterman was interested. He wanted to know if they ever saw the Lady. "She's got a way with her," he said. "There's many a London man that keeps a warm corner in his heart for her. You can tell her that when you see her. And like enough there'll be more that feel that way if we get too much of this Spanish trumpery."

Francis hugged himself as he remembered it. That would interest Robert and, what was more, he'd enjoy telling Robert about it. And there was that meeting with Francis Verney, too. It was fun to think that though Robert had kept him out of the Woodstock business, Francis Verney had let him in. They wouldn't be able to keep him out of it any more.

Suddenly he heard his own name. Father was talking to Laurie about the everlasting question of the lost deed.

"You see," he was saying, "the lock *was* bad until Francis

mended it. For a long time the coffer often wasn't locked at all. But still, all my money was in it and I have never missed a penny. I cannot believe that anyone would help themselves to a deed and leave the money behind. There is no one to whom it would be of any value. All the same it is worrying. I shall put a good face on it to your mother, but I will admit to you that at Grays Inn they thought that my position would be much stronger if I could produce a mortgage deed."

"Is there nowhere else it could be?" inquired Laurie sympathetically. Whatever Father might say to the contrary, it was clear that he was worried.

"I will go to Northampton and look there. I was Mayor when the deed was drawn up. But I could take my oath that I put it in the coffer at Sulgrave."

Francis gasped. An idea suddenly shot into his head. "Sir," he said. "If the Queen took Sulgrave away from us who would she give it to? Would she give it back to the monks?"

"Why, boy, what a question," cried Father. "She might like to, but the monks have pretty well vanished. There are none of them left. The Prior, for instance, is now Dean of Peterborough. I doubt if he would care to return to his monastery."

Francis persisted. "But if the monks could get hold of the deed it might be valuable to them?"

Father looked round in surprise. "Bless my soul, Francis is taking to the law now. Are you trying to suggest that the monks have stolen the deed from my coffer? Where are your wits, boy? You're talking nonsense. There are no monks at Sulgrave."

"There's old Jake."

Father threw back his head and roared with laughter. "Jake? Old Jake? He would not know a deed if he saw one. Besides Jake was not a monk of Northampton. Sulgrave never belonged to his monastery. He came from Canons Ashby."

Francis said no more. He rode on with his face red and his mouth firmly set. He was quite unconvinced. Father might laugh at him, but Father would probably sing a different song if he knew that Jake was hand in glove with the old witch and that the old witch was really a man. Jake was a monk, so quite likely the old witch was a monk too. That was an idea that had just occurred to him. He didn't see how it mattered that they came from Canons Ashby. They might have their eye on Sulgrave just the same. There must be something crooked behind it or why should they make all this mystery? It was a pity that Father wouldn't listen to him, but he would hunt out the matter himself. He would have to screw up his courage but he would do it. The old witch went out sometimes. He had seen her creeping round the cottages collecting the broken bread that the villagers left outside their gates by way of alms. He might take the chance to slip in and search the ruins. What a triumph it would be if he found the deed hidden there.

He was awakened from his daydream by Father's voice again.

"How now? Who is this coming? Someone is waving to us. Great heavens, I hope there is nothing wrong."

Francis stared ahead. Two horsemen were coming towards them and one was certainly waving his arm. Thoughts of highway robbers flashed through his mind and he glanced right and left at the bushes beside the road. Could there be others in hiding?

But as they came near he could see that they were not robbers. Laurie was the first to recognize them.

"They are Cousin Spencer's men," he cried. "It is Master Tungston the steward and one of the grooms."

"Then there *is* something wrong," said Father, and slowed his horse down as though to prepare himself for a shock. But Master Tungston rode up smiling.

"Good day to you, sir," he said cheerfully. "I hope you did not think there was something amiss? We are riding to London as you come away from it, that is all."

"Then you might have waited until you met us before you made such a to-do about it," Father was indignant. "We thought you must be bringing some direful tidings."

"I am sorry indeed. I thought to reassure you, but I would have done better to have made no sign at all. His mastership, Sir John, said that we should likely meet you and we were to stop and tell you the news."

"The news? Then something has happened. Stop beating about the bush, man. Can't you see we're on tenterhooks?"

"It is those hounds of Sir William Parr's," said the steward shaking his head. "They have broken into Althorp Park and worried countless of the master's sheep. He has lost at least a hundred."

"Into Althorp? But that is miles from Greens Norton."

"Nevertheless it is true. My lady cried out at first that it must have been done on purpose; someone must have led them there. But of course greyhounds like that will cover a great distance when they run wild. It is just ill fortune that they chose Althorp for their outrage."

"But it is shocking," said Father. "I suppose somebody has told Sir William Parr?"

"Indeed, sir, yes. My lady herself told him. The family had only just arrived at Althorp from Wormleighton, and as soon as the damage was discovered my lady rode straight over to Greens Norton. She saw Sir William Parr. I understand that there were high words between them."

Father clicked his tongue with dismay. "A plague on it. Surely Parr did not argue. He is liable for the damage."

"He did not argue, sir; he said he would pay in full. But that did not satisfy my lady. She told him the hounds were stolen and he had no right to them; she said they were stolen from her mother and her stepfather, my Lord of Bath, by Sir William Parr's kinsman, my Lord of Pembroke. He denied it hotly; he would have done better to have taken it with a good grace, for there is no denying that he had them from my Lord of Pembroke. My lady was very angry, and as you know, sir, when my lady is angry she does not mince matters."

Francis and Laurie looked at one another behind Father's back. They could hardly restrain their laughter. Not for nothing was Cousin Kit the daughter of Great-aunt Bath.

Father heaved a sigh, as if it was all too much for him. "And what now? Why are you riding to London?"

"To find my Lord of Bath, sir. I have a letter to him begging that he will send back with me the dog keeper who had charge of the stolen hounds. He is to see them to identify them."

"Upon my soul," cried Father aghast, "have they gone mad? I wish I had been there. I might have poured oil upon troubled waters. If Sir William Parr is ready to pay for the damage surely it could rest so without raking up all this mud. Did Sir John send you on this wild goose chase or was it only my lady?"

"It was Sir John, sir. He was powerfully moved about the sheep and my lady went to Sir Thomas Tresham. He is Sheriff, sir, and he said we must get the keeper to give evidence."

"I suppose there is no help for it if Sir Thomas Tresham is in it too. I wish you joy, good Master Tungston. My advice to you is to get my Lord of Bath to talk with my Lord of Pembroke, man to man. They could settle it all between them. If they can keep the women out of it there is hope."

They parted in friendly fashion. The steward rode off towards London, leaving behind him plenty for Father and the boys to talk about. They spent the night at Aylesbury, as before, and after an early start the next morning made so good a pace that they actually reached home while the sun was still high in the heavens.

Anne and the younger children were on the lookout for them. They were spotted in the distance even before they crossed the water meadows, and by the time they reached Sulgrave the whole family was outside to greet them, including Robert and Chris Hatton.

"Well, wife, I've brought your fledglings safely home again," cried Father as he drew rein at the door. "Is all well here? Robert has recovered, eh? Chris, I'm glad to see you. We're all surpassing weary. We'll have a wash and a cup of wine before we even begin to tell all about it."

Anne was allowed to stay, but The Tail was banished to the nursery. The travellers rested and quenched their thirst, while Mother recounted everything that had happened at home since they went away. Ninnie had made herself ill with green apples, the little glutton, and baby Christopher was bursting out of his swaddling bands. As for Robert, his throat had recovered almost at once, and he was so upset at losing his jaunt to London that she had invited Chris to bear him company. They had spent a couple of nights with Doctor Dee, for their star-gazing madness, and now he was quite set up again.

When the home news was finished the saddle-bags were opened and presents produced. There was something for everyone; the brooch for Mother, a curled feather for Robert's cap, a silver thimble for Anne, and, for the younger ones, ribbons and a wooden mannikin on a string that moved its arms and legs.

The presents from London

After that all the week's adventures had to be told. Father sat back in his chair and sipped his wine, while Laurie and Francis did the telling. He put in only a word or two here and there, though when they were describing vividly the scene inside Temple Bar, where Wyatt and his followers had been defeated, he insisted that they should also describe the Tyburn gallows.

Mistress Washington shivered. "Upon my soul, sir, must we have all these horrors at this time o' night? We shall all be dreaming of them."

"Better to dream of them, wife, than to forget them altogether. But I have a story for you now which will make you laugh instead of shudder." He took another pull at his wine and then launched forth upon the story of the greyhounds.

"Preserve us," cried Mother. "What has come to Cousin Kit? She is not usually so peppery."

"It sounds perilously like her mother. Anyhow they have sent to my Lord of Bath for the keeper who can identify the dogs, and the fat is in the fire. You have seen nothing of Sir William Parr, I suppose?"

Mother shook her head. "He has not been here. Neither, now I come to think of it, has Tom Tresham. I imagined that he did not come because Francis was away, but of course he did not know that Francis was going; it was only arranged at the last moment. Do you think that Sir William has kept him away of a purpose?"

"I should think that it is more than likely. We are the Spencers' kinsfolk. It's a pity. I should be sorry to fall out with Parr, and Francis would certainly miss Tom's company."

"We must all say a prayer that it may be settled in peace," said Mother. "And really it is high time that the boys went bed-

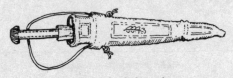

A sheath knife for Robert

ward. As for Anne, it is shameful for a little maid to be up so late."

Francis went upstairs slowly and thoughtfully. It had never dawned on him that the quarrels of their elders might affect him and Tom. It was horrible to think that Tom might not come any more. He sat on the edge of his bed until Laurie came in. Then he remembered that he had not given Robert the present that he had brought for him. He'd spent his whole shilling on a sheath knife, a beauty, to make up to Robert for having taken his place on the jaunt to London. He'd not given it downstairs, with the other presents, because he thought it might be a chance of getting back into Robert's good graces. He could tell Robert about Francis Verney at the same time, and perhaps, in return, Robert might let him into the secrets of Woodstock.

Anne sat up as soon as she saw him

He stood up, and saying to Laurie that he was going to take the knife to Robert, he crept across the empty Great Chamber, and softly opened the door of the Inner Chamber, to get to Robert's Porch room.

Anne and Ninnie were in bed. Ninnie, next to the wall, was fast asleep, but Anne sat up as soon as she saw him.

"Francis," she whispered. "Has Father found his deed?"

"I think not," he whispered back, taken by surprise.

"Then maybe we shall have to leave Sulgrave. And Robert's been to Woodstock again, while you were away. Oh Francis, I'm sorely frightened. You know what Father said."

"Yes," said Francis, almost roughly. The last thing he wanted just then was to be reminded of what Father said.

"Francis, shall I tell you something?" she began again.

"No," he said firmly and turned away. He wouldn't be tangled with a lot of new secrets. He had enough already. Then, fearing he had been unkind, he said gently: "Set your heart at rest and go to sleep. I'll tell you all about London to-morrow. God keep you."

"God keep you," she answered obediently, and slipped down between the sheets.

Robert too was sitting on the edge of his bed. He received the knife with astonishment and obvious delight, and Francis watched joyfully while he slipped it in and out of the sheath and tested its sharp cutting edge.

"It'll serve for peeling apples," Francis said modestly. "Or the cutler said that it was strong enough to turn against footpads. You might find it of use when you go to Woodstock."

He held his breath. Robert looked up quickly. He said nothing, so Francis went on.

"I know you go to Woodstock. I've known it all along, and I've kept it as close as an oyster. We met Francis Verney in Cheap. *He* talked in front of me, so you needn't be afraid. He said that things are speeding up."

"Did he let *you* hear that?" exclaimed Robert with withering astonishment. "I would not speak you harshly, Francis, but these matters are not peppercorns, you know." He began fastening the sheath to his belt. "This knife is a beauty. You should not have spent your money on it. You're a good fellow. Go on keeping your mouth shut and one of these days you may be opening it to some fine tune."

Arms of the
Earl of BATH

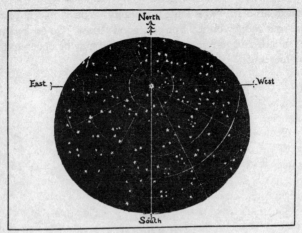

A chart of the stars

CHAPTER XI

All gone up in Smoke

When Francis woke in the morning his first thought was not of Robert and Woodstock, nor of London, nor of the mortgage deed, nor even of Anne and her fears. He thought of Tom. How dreadful if Tom did not come any more. He and Tom were hand and glove. He'd hate to lose him now.

Mother had said Pray, so when Laurie got up to go to Mass he got up too and followed him. The keen morning air was like a tonic after the foul smells of the London streets. Before he so much as reached the church he stopped worrying. Of course Tom would come back. People couldn't keep up silly quarrels indefinitely.

Even without Tom he was looking forward to a piece of work which he'd started before the London adventure was thought of.

It was a chart of the stars, copied from Doctor Dee's big globe, and he was longing to get back to it.

When Mass was over he went outside and waited for Laurie in the churchyard. The sun was up by now and after the cold church the air was warm and smelt good. From where he stood he looked over the roofs of a row of thatched cottages and over the lane that sloped down to the mill pond, to a sunny hillside dotted with sheep. He could see the tree where he had sat the morning he made his vow. He glanced casually at the ruins of the grange, from this point almost hidden in greenery. As he looked, history repeated itself. Old Jake, wrapped in his cloak, hurried across the corner of the field, just as he had done on that first morning, and vanished round an ivy-covered wall.

Even that distant glimpse of him revived all Francis's suspicions. He looked back into the church; it was empty; Laurie must have gone out with the parson by the other door. In that case he would go and have a look at the old grange. Perhaps he would confront Jake as he came out again, and ask him what he was doing there. He didn't feel frightened any more. The old witch was only a man in disguise, and he was certain that something was going on which Father ought to know. If he could get some definite story perhaps Father would listen to him.

Feeling exceedingly brave he ran down the churchyard, dropped into the village street and slipped unnoticed down the path towards the mill pond. Halfway up the slope on the other side he stopped in the shadow of a hedge.

From there he could watch the cellar door, so Jake could not leave without being seen. He waited for what seemed an age. There was no sign of life. He wished that Jake would hurry up; he was hungry, and standing there for so long doing nothing sapped his courage. He had almost made up his mind to give it up and go home when a movement in the cellar doorway caught his eye. Somebody was coming out.

He strained his eyes to make out which of the old men it would be. But it was only the dog. That was worse. The dog might get wind of him. But the beast did not come any further than the top of the steps. It stopped, threw back its head and howled.

It was an unearthly sound. Francis stood rooted to the spot, a cold shiver running down his spine. Never had he heard a dog cry like that. All his mortal fear of the old witch came surging back again. He just could not stand it. He turned, dodged through the hedge, and, pursued by the desolate howling, pelted down the hill on the other side.

By the time he got home he felt thoroughly ashamed. Thank goodness nobody need know anything about it. At the house the whole place was in a bustle. Father was eating his breakfast in the hall and at the same time talking to Robert. Old Marta hurried in with Father's travelling cloak, the London dust all brushed away, and hurried out again with his riding boots to be

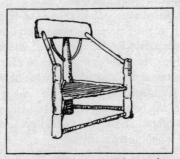

The tiny chair that had belonged to each of them in turn

cleaned. Anne, sitting on the tiny chair that had belonged to each of them in turn, sewed a button on his best doublet. Mother hovered over him, pouring more ale, cutting another slice of pasty, and stopping in between whiles to peep at the swaddled baby lying in a basket on the window seat.

Clearly something was afoot. Francis inquired from Anne and learned that Father was off to Northampton. It was about the deed again.

Francis took his ale and his bread and cheese into the garden, to think quietly by himself. What ought he to do? Father had laughed at the idea that Jake might have something to do with the lost deed, but then Father had only heard half the story. Ought he to let him go off to Northampton without trying once more to make him listen? After all what did it matter if Father did call him a little fool?

His breakfast finished he went back into the house, his mind made up. He was ashamed that he had run away from his search because of a dog howling, but he wouldn't be a coward again. This time he would make Father listen to the whole story.

Father had left the hall. Anne said he had gone through into his parlour. With beating heart Francis knocked at the door.

The parlour was a cheerful room with a tapestry on the wall, a shelf of books, plenty of bright cushions and a carpet on the table. Father was standing by the window reading a letter. He looked at Francis inquiringly.

Francis drew a deep breath. "It is about the deed, sir," he began. "Do you know the old witch who lives in the cellar at the grange?"

Father laid down his letter and looked at Francis with sudden attention. "Old witch?" he repeated, and smiled. "Yes, boy; I know who you mean. Proceed."

"Well, sir, old Jake goes there. I've seen him go, cloaked and secretly. And, sir"—he lowered his voice—"the old witch is a man."

To his great disappointment Father did not look astonished, but only amused.

"And even if that be true what has it to do with the deed?"

Francis knew that his face was red. He did think that Father might help him out instead of laughing at him.

"You see, sir, Jake is a monk and I thought the old witch might be a monk too, and they might have got the deed and be hoping to get Sulgrave back, even if it didn't belong to them before." He stopped for lack of breath.

"In other words you fancy that Jake might have stolen the deed in order to turn us out? I'm afraid you are something wide of the mark, my boy. To begin with, you imagine that Jake's visits to the grange and the old man who lives there, are news to me. That is where you are mistaken. I know all about it."

Francis stared. It had never occurred to him that Father might be in the secret.

"Don't look so crest-fallen; I am glad to find that you are so vigilant. I think you deserve to be in my confidence. You were quite right in some of your hazards. The old man *was* a monk. He was at Canons Ashby with Jake. When the monastery was undone he found no honest work anywhere. He fell on ill days and did something for which he might have ended on a gibbet. That part I will not tell you; it is not my story. Jake found him ill and starving. They were brothers in religion, so Jake hid him in the ruins and tended him. Then he came to me and begged me to let him stay there. He was a broken man and in peril of his life. That is all. But of one thing I am certain; Jake would cut off his own hand before he would rob me. Now do you understand?"

Francis nodded. It took him time to absorb the story. "But the old witch, sir? How came it that people thought he was a witch?"

Father laughed. "I do not inquire," he said. "I daresay Jake invented it to keep the village folk away. But remember, Francis, all this is strictly betwixt the two of us. The old man is in our hands."

Francis said "Yes, sir." His eye was very bright. It pleased him to think that in addition to all the others, he now shared a secret with Father. He turned to go and Father picked up the letter again. But as he laid his hand on the latch, there came a knock on the door. He opened it and Old Jake burst in. He wore his cloak with the hood thrown back; his hair was rough and his eyes wild.

"He's gone, sir," he cried. "When I got there this forenoon, he was bad, and now he's gone. He'd been a-coughing for days past, but I thought yesternight that he was mending. But this morning he had a spasm and died. I came to you, master. What must I do?"

Francis stood rooted to the spot. He thought of the dog creeping outside to howl. Father laid a hand on the old man's arm.

"God rest his soul," he said. "It is the best for him. You must not fret. You were a true brother to him. Calm yourself, and let us think. The parson must be told. It can do no harm now. You know my view that he should have been told before."

Old Jake shook his head. "We did not trust him, sir. God knows whether he is a true priest or not. But I have more to tell, sir. You know not all the story." He glanced over his shoulder, caught sight of Francis and stopped.

"Do not concern yourself," said Father. "You can speak in front of the young master. He came to me just now because he had seen you at the grange, and he thought that things were afoot that I ought to know."

"He was right," said Jake. "You should know all." He looked quickly over his shoulder again and spoke in a whisper. "Master, in that cellar is hidden the treasure of Canons Ashby."

The treasure of Canons Ashby

Taken aback, Father stared at him. "Treasure? What treasure? Do you mean the altar plate?"

"Aye, master; the vessels that were used on the great feast days. Some of them are pure gold. We swore the King's men should not have it, so we took it and buried it before they seized the church. They took the silver plate, but they never found the gold."

"But what did you expect to do with it? Why didn't you give it up when the Queen came to the throne and the Mass was restored?"

"Who should we give it to? I told you, sir, we did not trust the parson. For years he followed the new religion. I came to ask you what I am to do now."

Laurence Washington stroked his chin. "That is a poser, my

good Jake. 'Tis certain that it cannot stay there unguarded, and I am not willing to have to answer for it. I have a thought. How would you like to send it to the Queen herself? She is the champion of the old faith. Nay, don't answer at once. Go to the pantry and have a cup of good ale, and think it over while you drink. I will be with you soon."

There was silence when he left the room. Then Father sighed. "Poor Jake," he said. "He has been a faithful friend. God send me such a one when I am in need. As for you, Francis, it seems that when you sniffed out something odd your nose did not deceive you. But, alas! it does not help me towards the deed. And what is more it delays my starting for Northampton. I must see to this matter before I go." He stood gazing out of the window deep in thought. Then he turned round and saw Francis still standing there. "By the way, what are you doing here this morning? You should be back at work. You've had nearly a week of idleness. Be off with you. Doctor Dee will think you are playing truant."

Reluctantly Francis collected his books. He had lost his zest for work. Even the star map could not charm him now. And there was no Tom. He would like to have stayed and seen the gold plate, but he knew it was useless to argue with Father. Robert and Laurie had gone hours ago. He said a reluctant and dutiful good-bye to Mother, who was busy with Marta in the still-room over some problem about preserves. She gave him her cheek to kiss with a preoccupied "God bless you", and he dawdled across the fields feeling thoroughly unsettled.

But as he neared the little house he saw that a couple of horses were standing outside. There was a groom with them and he quickened his step as he recognised the blue and white and black of the livery colours of the Parrs. Perhaps it might be Tom after all. But no; it wasn't Tom's horse that the man was holding, but the tall chestnut belonging to Sir William Parr himself.

It occurred to him at once that if Parr was inside there might be some news, so he went round to the back of the house and slipped quietly in by the buttery door.

Sir William Parr stood in the hall talking to Doctor Dee. It looked as if he were just taking his leave. Laurie sat at the end of the long table buried in his books. Francis stole across the room, pulled out his star map and sat down at Laurie's side.

"You would advise me to go by Ipswich, then?" Parr was saying. "I have always crossed the Channel by way of Sandwich. But I can see the advantage of Ipswich when one starts from here; it saves a journey to London. You are sure that I can get a ship direct from there to Antwerp?"

"Quite sure, sir. I travelled to Antwerp that way myself when I went from Cambridge. There is a constant traffic in ships carrying English cloth and leather. Sometimes you can pick up a passage in a German ship belonging to the Hanse merchants. Your mind is made up about leaving England?"

"Yes, I have quite decided. I am sick of living like a prisoner with none but boors or country bumpkins to consort with— saving your presence, sir, of course. Would you believe it, a certain dame arrived the other day and accused me of stealing her greyhounds. *Stealing* them, I ask you! 'Tis ludicrous, but it is enraging. For some time I have considered going abroad; so many of my friends have gone. Some are living in Strasbourg, some in Basle or Padua. I was uncertain about it, but this ridiculous insult has decided me. I shall go as soon as it can be arranged."

"If you like I can make some inquiries for you," suggested Doctor Dee. "I have friends in Ipswich and the messenger who takes my work to Cambridge could easily ride a little further. We could have an answer in a few days."

"That is uncommonly kind of you, sir. If you can find a ship that is due to sail I could be ready to start at any time. Good Master Washington told me that you would give me good counsel, and indeed he spoke no more than the truth. Commend me to him, if you please. I will not call on him at present. The fools who accuse me are his kinsfolk and it might be an embarrassment. It is all just women's nonsense and it will blow over, I have no doubt."

Francis and Laurie exchanged glances, They were both

Doctor Dee came striding back

remembering that messenger riding to London, and they were not so sure about the blowing over.

Doctor Dee accompanied his visitor to the horses and stood while he mounted. "I will let you know directly I hear of a ship from Ipswich," he repeated. "It may be short notice, so I should advise you to be ready."

"I will start my preparations at once," Parr reassured him. "And once more, sir, be assured of my profoundest gratitude."

Doctor Dee watched him ride away. Then he came striding back to the house, his gown flying out behind him.

"Where is Robert? Where is Chris?" he demanded.

"You sent them out, sir," said Laurie, "but I'll wager they are not far off."

"Then find them quickly." He started to pace restlessly up and down the room, his eyes on the ground, his brow puckered with thought. Laurie hurried out, and Francis sat without moving a finger. He didn't want to be sent away.

The three boys returned almost at once. Doctor Dee faced them.

"Has Laurie told you?" he demanded. "Sir William Parr is to cross the Channel. This is exactly what you have been waiting for. You must act without a moment's lag. The first thing is a messenger to Ipswich to arrange a ship. Somebody must undertake that. Where is Francis Verney? Did you say he was in London?"

Laurie frowned. "I think he said he was going back in a few days," he answered. "Do you remember, Francis?"

Doctor Dee swung round. "Francis?" he exclaimed. "I didn't realise you were here. When did you come?"

"A few minutes since," said Francis, purposely vague. "My father sent me. He said I had had holiday enough."

"Then you must tell your father I am too busy to-day. And look you, Francis, not a word of anything you may have heard. Sir William Parr's business is his own. Do you understand?"

"Yes, sir, I understand. I'll be as mute as the grave if only you'll let me stay."

"Be as mute as the grave in any case, and be off with you. I tell you I have no time to-day. You can take your star map with you and get on with it at home." He watched in silence as Francis gathered up his things; but as he was going out of the door he called after him. "And, Francis, say that the boys will not be home for dinner. They can have it here with me."

Francis went off grumbling to himself. Surely they must realise that he knew half their precious secrets already. They might just as well have allowed him to stay and share the rest.

True that all this business about Sir William Parr puzzled him. Why should it be so important to find him a ship? But he was really only interested in Parr because of Tom. What would happen to Tom if Parr went away? It would be hateful if Tom really did not come any more.

Playing backgammon with Anne

His wounded pride was salved a little when he got home, for Father took him aside to tell him what had happened during the morning about Jake.

"I've seen the parson," he said; "he will arrange all the sad business for the old man, for I must be on my way to Northampton directly after dinner. The treasure is to be lodged safely until I come back and can send it to the Queen. Keep your mouth shut, Francis, and if anybody asks you questions just act the simpleton."

The afternoon was dull. Francis divided the time between his star map and Tom's cross-bow. Anne came with him when he went shooting; he was quite glad to have her. She picked up the bolts for him and by way of reward he allowed her to try her hand with the cross-bow.

When they got home Robert and Laurie were back. Chris had taken leave of Mother and gone. Francis rather pointedly took no notice of them. He preferred to spend the evening playing backgammon with Anne.

The next three days passed without excitement. He went to Stuchbery as usual. Doctor Dee set him enough sums to keep him busy for weeks, as well as showing him fresh groups of stars to be added to the map. Laurie was there working peacefully, but Robert was in and out like a will o' the wisp, full of mystery and self-importance.

Sunday came round and Father was not back. Mother, very worried, told them she had received a letter to say that he would be away for some days longer. He had not found the deed in Northampton, and had decided to go on to Peterborough. The Dean of the cathedral used to be Prior of St. Andrew's, Northampton, and perhaps he might be able to make some helpful suggestion.

"What did the deed look like?" inquired Anne suddenly. She and Francis were keeping Mother company under the elms on Sunday afternoon.

"Look like? Upon my word I can't tell you, child," sighed Mother. "It can't have been very big for Father was so sure that it was in his coffer. Why do you ask?"

"I wondered," said Anne nervously. "whether it could by chance have fallen out of the coffer that day."

Her mother looked at her quickly. "Fallen out? What day?"

"The day of the party; when the coffer was upset upon the stairs. Don't you remember?"

Mistress Washington clapped her hands to her cheeks. "Saints in heaven! I had forgotten all about it. Why didn't you remind me before?"

"I thought you knew," faltered Anne. "You told us not to mention it. You said that if Father had to be told you would tell him."

"What happened?" demanded Francis. "How could the coffer upset? I didn't hear about it."

His mother cut him short. "It's so long since the party, and so much has happened; upon my word I can scarce remember. Anne, you helped to pick the things up. Are you certain that nothing was left behind?"

Anne nodded vigorously. "Quite certain, madam. You see, the money rolled everywhere and we had to root about among the rushes to find it."

"The rushes!" cried Mother. "I remember now. They smelt and you had to take them all out. Where did you put them?"

"In Madam's close behind the stable. That is where you bid us put them."

"I don't know what I bid you," wailed Mistress Washington, holding her head wearily. "Anyway we must go and look. Come you, quickly now."

Anne held her ground. "It is no use, Mother. They're burnt."

"Burnt?" Mistress Washington nearly shrieked. "When were they burnt?"

"At the baby's christening," said Anne. "Francis and Tom made a bonfire."

"I beg you, wait a minute," cried Francis. "I have heard nothing of all this."

Anne told him briefly about playing King of the Castle on the stairs and somebody pushing up Father's coffer as a wall at the top. Mother began to cry. "Lack-a-day," she wailed. "There is your father riding across the country looking for his deed and all the time you children have burned it."

Francis started to protest but she wouldn't listen. He turned to Anne. "The ashes may be there still," he said, "I doubt if parchment would burn away to nothing. Come and look."

They all poked about with sticks in the field called Madam's close. But there were no bits of curled-up parchment among the few charred remains of the rushes. Mother was in despair.

"I believe it would burn quicker than anything else," she cried. "Of course this explains all. Your father was quite certain that it was in his coffer. What he will say only heaven knows. And I suppose now there is nothing to prevent us from being turned out of Sulgrave."

They tried in vain to comfort her, reminding her of what Father had said, that it was not at all likely that they would be turned out. It was no use. She would not be consoled. When she and Anne had vanished into the house, Francis went back to the field again. Of course it was not his fault if he had burned the deed, since he had known nothing about the upset coffer. All the same it was a terrible thought, and he could not help remembering how, on the day of the christening, he and Tom had piled on dry grass and twigs and fir cones and anything else they could find to make a really good blaze.

The rest of the day was wretched. Robert and Laurie were at Doctor Dee's. Anne stayed all the time with Mother. He wandered about miserably by himself and was quite glad when it was time to go to bed.

He was still lying awake when he heard the boys coming upstairs. To his surprise it was Robert and not Laurie who came into the room. There was something odd about his manner. He looked carefully outside before he closed the door. Then he crossed the room and sat down on Francis's bed.

"I'm going to ask you a question," he said mysteriously. "But be sure that you answer quietly, Would you like to come with me to Woodstock to-morrow?"

Francis sat up with a jerk. "You can wager I would!"

"Then listen," said Robert softly. "We shall start in the morning, just the two of us. Doctor Dee will ask Mother for you. He will say that he has some work for you to do, *and that is true*. Nay, don't ask me now what it is. You'll hear in good time. Father won't be back for another three days and we shall only be away one night."

It was on the tip of Francis's tongue to say "Forget not that you thought that last time," but he stopped himself. After all the great thing was that he was to be taken to Woodstock. He was not to be left out any more. Compared to that the chance of being caught and beaten was a small matter.

"Take some spare clothes," whispered Robert. "They must

be old and dark. You had a pair of dark hose you used to wear in the winter, and your old leather jerkin would do finely. Get them early in the morning, before anyone is up. Roll them in a bundle and hide them outside somewhere, where you can pick them up without attracting notice. Now get to sleep. You'll want all your wits about you to-morrow."

He left Francis wide awake and tingling with excitement. Laurie came to bed but did not speak to him. Francis thought that he would never go to sleep but suddenly to his surprise he found Robert shaking him. The sky through the window was grey with the dawn. He had slept after all.

He slipped out of bed and dressed himself. In the nursery the little ones were chattering but in the rest of the house there seemed to be nobody awake. He found the dark clothes, rolled them up, on Robert's instructions, with a spare pair of shoes, and hid them in the hedge at the bottom of the lane.

"Shall I take Meadowsweet?" he inquired from Robert who was waiting for him in the garden.

"No, you won't want a horse. I've got Juno from Chris; she will carry us both. Bring a pouch with some lesson books. We're both to be scholars on our way to Oxford. Doctor Dee will fit you up with a gown."

This was more and more exciting. Francis could scarcely swallow his breakfast, and it was difficult to be calm and ordinary with Anne who looked at him queerly. He avoided her eye. He supposed she had spotted his excitement. That was the worst of Anne. She saw too much.

They had barely finished when Doctor Dee arrived to get Mother's permission for the boys to be out all night. It was ordinary enough for Robert, but it was the first time that he had asked for Francis. Mistress Washington raised no difficulty.

"If you have work for them to do, sir, then I suppose they must stay," she said a little grudgingly. "But it is a pity that one cannot observe the stars by day. Francis is young to be out of his bed all night. I beg you to see that he does not catch cold. Have you heard the new disaster about the mortgage deed?"

Doctor Dee settled down to listen. He made signs to the boys not to wait for him, so they slipped out of the garden gate, picked up the bundle of clothes and set off across the fields to Stuchbery.

They were only half way there when Doctor Dee caught them up.

"Well," he said cheerfully, "and how is the new knight errant? Does he know yet what is needed of him?"

Robert shook his head. "I have told him nothing yet, sir, except where he is going."

"And he is ready to follow you blindly, eh? I think he deserves better than that. Listen here, Francis. You are needed as a locksmith."

Francis looked blank. "A locksmith?" he repeated.

"Yea. A pick-lock if you like it better. There is a certain door in a certain private garden which has not been opened for years. The lock is on the inside of the door and the garden is enclosed with a high wall topped with a palisade of spikes, impossible to climb. Now there is a stream that runs through the garden. It comes out by a channel under the wall, quite a big channel, but unfortunately the opening is covered by an iron grating. Now, Francis, we need to find someone who is small enough to slip through the bars of the grating and get into the garden that way. But he must be someone who is a clever locksmith and can undo the door in the wall. What say you?"

Francis drew a deep breath. "I will try, sir. But I don't know whether I'm a good enough hand at picking locks."

"But you see, my boy, this is not truly lock picking. *We have a key.* But it is old and rusty. The door, as I told you, has not been opened for years. If you should have a flask of oil with you, and a supply of feathers, think you not that it would be possible?"

"If the lock is not broken——" said Francis hopefully.

"I'll wager it is not broken. By the way I suppose you have guessed already what is the house and garden we speak of. The house is the Gatehouse of the Manor of Woodstock, and the garden is the privy garden of the Lady Elizabeth."

The old Palace of Woodstock

CHAPTER XII

Woodstock

They left just before noon, fortified by a good dinner. Francis was surprised to find that Doctor Dee was not coming too, but he asked no questions till he and Robert were both comfortably mounted on Chris's horse, Juno, and were well away down the narrow bridle lane that led south from Stuchbery.

"Oh, he never comes," said Robert lightly. "He vows that he has no interest in state matters—just like Father. But he sends endless letters, mostly to the Parrys. They are his kinsfolk, you know."

"Who are the Parrys? I've heard of them but I know not what they do."

"Oh, they are very important at Woodstock. Master Thomas

158

Parry is the Lady's steward; he has charge of all her household concerns. He lives at the Bull because Sir Henry Bedingfield, her jailer, won't allow him to live at the palace. His sister, Mistress Blanche, is the Lady's closest friend, woman of the bedchamber is what they call her, I think. She actually lives inside, but she can come out and visit her brother, and he can go in; so you may imagine they are very useful."

"Useful for what?"

"For getting at the Lady, of course. Though *she* can't get out, they can carry letters in. Nobody is supposed to be able to see her without Bedingfield being there, but the Parrys can usually work it. They seem to be able to manage almost anything."

"What does Doctor Dee write about if he isn't interested in state matters?" inquired Francis incredulously.

"I think it's about the stars. I believe the Lady is interested in them too, and I know that Mistress Blanche is. I tell you what, Francis; Doctor Dee has been working out the Lady's horoscope, telling her future, you know." He lowered his voice to a whisper, though they were riding across a field and there was nobody but the sheep to hear. "I'm not certain, but I believe that he's found out that she'll be queen someday."

Francis was startled. For a few minutes he said nothing.

"Why have I got to open that door?" he asked at last. "Is it for the Lady to escape?"

"For goodness sake don't talk so loud," said Robert nervously. "I can't tell you because I don't know. Francis Verney and the Parrys arrange everything, and there are others of her household there too. Chris and I only do what we are told."

"Where's Chris? Isn't he coming with us?"

"He's there already. He took the news about Sir William Parr so that a ship could be arranged."

"What news?" Then the idea came, as clear as day. "Robert, is the Lady going to cross the Channel with Sir William Parr?"

"I don't know," said Robert again. "Chris took the message but there's been no time for an answer. But Francis Verney has said all along that she'd try and escape if there were anywhere for her to go. Well, Sir William Parr might be just the right person to take her. She's fond of him, and his sister, Queen Katharine was kind to her when she was a child. Don't you remember how he talked about 'my honest uncle' the first night he came to Sulgrave?"

"What does he say about it?"

"He doesn't know anything about it yet. It would be silly to let him into the secret until the Lady has said whether she would go with him or not."

Francis sat still again. There was such a lot to think about. They were riding through country which he did not know at all. Instead of following a highway Robert was sticking to bridle paths and narrow green lanes which seemed to avoid the towns and villages.

"Where are we going?" he asked at last. "I thought Woodstock was on the way to Oxford."

"We always go by a roundabout route so as not to attract notice. Presently we shall come out on the road from Chipping Norton and we'll go into Woodstock as though we came from the north west, which is the way most travellers come. If anyone asks questions we are scholars on our way to Oxford."

They jogged along for what seemed to Francis an age. Once when they stopped at an alehouse for a long cool drink they changed places for a while, Francis riding in front with Robert perched up behind him.

"What's the palace like?" Francis inquired presently.

"You mean the Manor. The people of Woodstock call it the Manor, not the palace. It's a great ramshackle place, nothing but towers and battlements all crumbling to pieces. The Lady is in the Gatehouse, which stands outside the rest, almost like a separate castle. Henry VII, her grandfather, made it into a proper house, with rooms and windows and chimneys, because the old palace was so vast and ruinous. It stands in the middle of a great deer park surrounded by a stone wall seven miles round. The town of Woodstock is outside the wall and the Bull Inn is in the centre of the town. We're not far away from the main road now, so keep your eyes open for Chris. He is to meet us before we leave the shelter of the lane."

The Gatehouse

Sure enough before they had covered more than another half mile they saw Chris lounging in the shade of a hedgerow tree. He hailed them cheerfully.

"So ho!" he cried. "You've brought Francis. I've always told you that he was the man for us. Well done, my boy, and good fortune to all of us. Dismount and rest awhile. You'll have to walk from here while I go ahead on the horse. It will attract less notice if you arrive at the Inn on foot."

"How fares it?" inquired Robert eagerly. "What says the Lady? Will she go?"

"Yea, she'll go gladly enough under the protection of Parr. That has been the trouble all through. She would not trust herself to us. But she is quite content at the idea of crossing the seas with Parr. We have not been idle I promise you. A messenger went post haste to Ipswich to make sure that there will be a ship waiting for them."

"Who will come with her?" asked Robert. "I suppose she will not be alone."

"She is to bring Mistress Blanche, her bedchamber woman, Parry's sister. They will pass as farmers' wives, with the Lady as Mistress Blanche's daughter. 'Tis strange this last week how everything has happened to incline her to the plan. There's gossip from the Court that the Queen is going to have a baby. That would mean a new heir to the throne, only a quarter English, its father Philip of Spain and its grandmother Katharine of Aragon. What would life be like for the Lady then? She would never be anything but Anne Bullen's daughter and pass her life in captivity. To make matters worse, a fire broke out in the Gatehouse last week, in the room beneath her bedchamber, and she is sure that it was no accident. So she is ready enough to chance her fortune with Parr. By the way, have you a letter from Doctor Dee?"

Robert opened his doublet and produced a pair of doeskin gloves. "As usual," he said and passed them over.

Chris slipped them away quickly. "That's good," he said. "She is eager to know if the stars are favourable. She relies upon Dee."

"What is the plan?" inquired Robert. "We dare not stay more than one night away in case Father should come home."

"One night will be enough now that we have got Francis," said Chris lightly. "Verney has charge of all that business and he has it worked out to the last inch. The moon is just right. It rises late, so they will be able to get across the park in darkness and yet there will be light for Francis to see what he is doing. Now I must be off. Give me time to get away before you emerge from the lane. The landlord of the Bull is expecting you. You know him of course; he is a good fellow. If anybody is on the watch he will treat you as students going to Oxford."

He mounted Juno and rode away, leaving them to follow slowly. By the time they reached the highway he was out of sight. Francis wanted to ask questions; Chris had raised him to a fever of suspense. But Robert refused to talk any more. There were travellers coming and going in both directions; a party of gentlemen on horseback, with their servants; a train of pack-horses with a couple of drovers; a tinker with his tackle flung over an ancient mule; a farm cart or two, and a stream of noisy children running home from school.

The road was bordered on one side by a high stone wall, which continued in both directions as far as the eye could see. Within the wall were the trees of a great forest. Robert nodded towards it and said briefly, "The deer park."

Soon the way began to run down hill with cottages on either side, but even behind the cottages the wall was unbroken and forbidding. At the bottom of the hill they crossed a small bridge, and stopped to look at the water gushing underneath it. It was only a narrow river but it made the most of itself as it churned noisily through a water mill and passed in a spate of bubbling foam through some arches into the park.

The road now climbed again, and they plodded steadily up, Robert with his nose ostentatiously buried in a book. Francis looked about him. The town itself seemed to be at the top of the hill, but there were houses all the way up, and he was reminded that Woodstock was famous for its gloves, for outside every cottage a row of soft skins hung drying on the line, while groups of women sat in the doorways gossiping as they stitched at their craft.

The Bull Inn stood in the middle of the town, close to the market cross. Compared with the Saracen's Head in London it was a small place, but it was solidly built of stone and the pattern of it was the same, for they went under an archway into a cobbled yard where an outside staircase ran up to the upper floors.

Robert turned into a low doorway with the air of one who was on familiar ground. In a long room so low that even Francis could touch the ceiling they found the landlord, a burly man with warts on his face, who was obviously expecting them. With no more than a friendly word to ask if they had travelled comfortably, he led them upstairs to a loft among the rafters where, as poor scholars, they would be expected to sleep, and there he left them. Robert unloaded his bundle on to one of the several beds. Thank goodness, he remarked, that as there were two of them, they would not have to share a bed with strangers.

After a wash at the pump Robert led the way into the common room, a large place with benches and trestle boards against the walls and a bright fire burning on the hearth at the far end .

In the corner nearest the fire sat Chris with a man whom Francis recognised at once as Verney, though he was not dressed elegantly as he had been that day in Cheap. He looked up and saw them, and promptly called to them in a voice obviously intended for the benefit of the strangers in the room.

"Hey, you two lads, methinks I have seen you before. Aren't you the students of astronomy I talked with a few weeks ago? Come you over here and tell us how your studies go."

Francis had a strong desire to laugh as he followed Robert across the room. It seemed more like a game of play-acting than a matter of deadly earnest, possibly with people's lives at stake.

They sat down opposite Verney and Chris and ate slices of brawned pork washed down by cans of excellent ale. All the time Verney kept up a flow of chatter about lectures and colleges and tutors, enough to convince any casual listener that they were a party of scholars. He ended, as he got up to leave the board, by inviting them to come up to his room and see the notes that he had made in Oxford last year.

Supper finished Robert said loudly to Francis that they might as well go and see what the gentleman had to show, and they both climbed the stairs in the direction that Verney and Chris had gone. Verney's room was on the first floor. It was large and comfortable and furnished with his own four-poster bed, his own table and armchair and cushions, and several stools.

There were two strangers in the room and Francis felt suddenly shy, as he realised that they were scrutinising him closely. The first was a round-faced ruddy man who spoke to Robert and asked after his "good cousin Jack Dee". Then there was a swarthy, bearded foreigner with a long name that Francis could not understand. But before very long both these two got up to go, the first bidding Master Verney "a *very* good night," with a warmth and a twinkle which gave the words a special meaning.

"That was Master Parry," said Verney when they had gone. "He has managed the Lady's household since she was a mere child. They put him in the Tower once because he would not betray her secrets. The other was Castiglione, her Italian tutor, who is her devoted slave. He is a man of many talents and at present they are all directed to one end, which is to bait the wretched Bedingfield and keep him hopping about like a popinjay on a perch. If I had time I could tell you a dozen stories of his pranks, but they must wait for another season."

He led Francis to the table, pulling up a stool for him. "It's not very long since you and I met in Cheapside," he remarked genially. "We are much-travelled people, both of us. Now, you must be on tenterhooks to know what we want of you. First of all, as it will be dark when we set out, here is a map to help you understand."

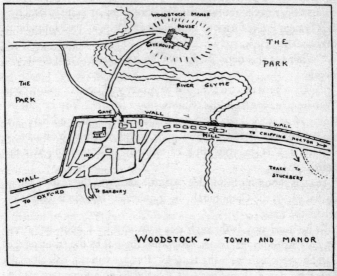

WOODSTOCK ~ TOWN AND MANOR

"Here is a map to help you"

The very word *map* made Francis feel at home. This one was very simple. Doctor Dee would scarcely have called it a map at all. Verney bent over it, pointing out the places as he mentioned them.

"Here's the town," he said, "and here is the Bull, where we are at this moment. There is a gate to the park at the end of the street here, by the house that they call Chaucer's house, but that need not interest us for the present. The little river Glyme runs through the park on its way to join the Evenlode and the Thames;

you crossed it when you came into the town to-day. Do you remember? Well, the river forms a marshy valley round the foot of a little hill, on which stands Woodstock Manor. The Manor, you know, includes both the old Palace and the Gatehouse, and it is the Gatehouse that we are aiming at. Now do you see this little stream marked close to the wall of the Gatehouse? It once filled the moat. Now it serves the fishponds inside the privy garden, and comes out again through a gulley in the garden wall before it flows into the river."

His finger rested on the spot. He looked up at Francis, smiling, and Francis looked back at him. Doctor Dee had told him about that stream. He knew what it meant.

"Where is the door in the wall?" he asked. "Is it near the stream?"

"Only a yard or two away. The moon will light it up for you. You are screened from the windows by a fig tree. You cannot be seen. Here is the key; we have cleaned it up well; and here is a phial of oil, some feathers and some pieces of wire. You have a knife, I see. Can you think of anything else that might help you?"

Francis shook his head. He was still staring at the map. "How do we get to the Gatehouse?" he inquired. "It looks a long way across the park."

"The usual way is through this gate, and by a built-up cause-way across the river marsh. It climbs the hill to the front of the Gatehouse, which is on the far side. But we will not risk all that. There are guards at the gate. It is better to go a long way round and approach the Gatehouse from behind. Did you notice the mill as you came into Woodstock? That is where we shall enter the park."

Francis looked puzzled. He had not noticed a gate by the mill.

"There is the mill race," said Verney, reading his thoughts. Then as Francis pictured the churning bubbling water he went on. "You need not worry. I am coming with you, and it will be calm enough when we get there. The wheel stops sometimes, you know. If it is stopped conveniently, you need not question how or why. Come, you had better rest until it is time to go. Chris,

166

bring the sherry sack. A mouthful for Francis will help to keep his spirits up, but we must not make him tipsy until he is back again."

There was not a light to be seen anywhere when they left the Bull, but Verney seemed to know his way like a cat. Keeping to the grass at the side of the road he led unfalteringly down the hill until, by the sound of running water, Francis knew that they had reached the river. But the roaring and gushing of the mill had stopped. Francis's eyes had by this time grown used to the dark and he could see that where the mill race had boiled up against the park wall, there was now no more than a sluggish stream trickling through the arches. Verney took his hand as they groped their way down into the water. It was only about ankle deep, and though they had to crouch like frogs, there was just room to squeeze through. Once inside the wall they scrambled out on the far bank and began without delay to climb a long grass slope.

Already it was not so dark as it had been when they left the inn, and they made for a belt of woodland which stood out black against the sky. When they reached the shelter of the trees they turned and looked back. There was enough light now to show the winding of the river down in the valley. The wood seemed to be full of little noises. A breath of wind rustled the leaves so that Francis's heart pounded within him. An owl hooted, and close to them a pheasant rose with a whirr and a cock-cock-up. Verney swore softly, and waited motionless. It would be enough to give them away if there should be anyone near. In the distance a dog barked. Francis wondered nervously if there were watch-dogs at the Gatehouse.

After a few minutes of listening Verney moved on again, hugging the edge of the wood. The moon would soon be up. Already Francis could see the shapes of the hills and valleys in front of him. Then suddenly he became aware of a black mass of buildings not very far ahead. Verney began to work down the hill towards it, crouching and dodging from one piece of cover to another. Francis found himself at last pressed up against a stone wall that towered over him. The shadow was pitch black.

Verney laid a hand on him and they both stayed without moving for what seemed an age, until the moon, on the other side of the Gatehouse, lit up the hillside, leaving them in the black cast shadow of the wall.

Then at last Verney began to move, feeling his way along inch by inch. The wall seemed to be endless, but when they finally got to the corner the moonlight was so bright that Francis almost blinked. Cautiously they rounded it and saw the valley and the river bathed in a light almost as clear as day, and at their feet a tiny stream which gushed out, glittering like diamonds where the moon caught it.

The stream poured through

Francis held his breath. This must be the place. He dropped to the ground beside Verney and took stock. There was the opening into the garden where the stream poured through a grid of iron bars. The moon was shining on the inside, silhouetting their criss-cross pattern. Could he possibly squeeze through that tiny space? And where was the door? He peered along the wall, seeing no sign of it. Then he realised that their backs were actually against it. He felt it, a small heavy door, iron-studded, with a heavy iron ring for handle. The hinges were rough with rust. He had better oil them on the outside as well as on the in. He fumbled for his oil and his feathers. When both lock and hinges had been dosed freely, he gave the things into Verney's hands, to pass to him, when he was safely inside.

Now that he was busy he did not feel frightened any more. He felt the water. It was cold but the stream was several inches deep. So much the better. His best plan would be to lie down in it and try to creep underneath the bars.

His head and shoulders went through quite easily. He wriggled on, very confident, until his hips stuck firmly and he could not move either forward or back. Repressing a wave of panic, he worked away with his hands, digging at the bed of the stream underneath him. Luckily the wind was rustling the leaves loudly enough to cover the sound. At last he found that he could move again. He pulled himself cautiously through, and lay for a moment, half in and half out of the water, getting his breath. The moonlight on the inside of the wall was dappled with a moving pattern of black and white. It was difficult to see the door, but by the same token, it would be almost impossible for anyone to see him. Inch by inch he got up. Verney's hand through the grid held out to him his oil and feathers. He took them and went to work.

The door certainly had not been opened for years. There were strands of ivy growing across it. After he had oiled the lock and left it to soak, he sliced the ivy neatly all the way round the rim of the door, leaving it clinging to the surface. With luck the strands might remain green until after the door had been used. Then he tried the key in the oiled lock. His heart sank. It would not yield at all. He gave it more oil and prodded about in the inside. Then an idea struck him. He could see Verney's face peering at him through the bars. He crept back and whispered "Pull".

There was a tiny sound as Verney took hold of the iron ring. Francis put his shoulder to the door and pressed hard on the key. It moved and with a grating noise that seemed to echo through the night the lock turned.

He waited for a moment, his heart hammering; but there was

no sign of life from the Gatehouse. Thank heaven no one had heard. The door was open an inch or two. He pulled it wide enough for Verney to slip through. Together they set to work with oil and knife to scrape the lock clean. Afterwards they patched up the broken ivy, scattered dust over the fresh oil marks, raked up their footprints and then squeezed out again. Now for the test! They closed the door behind them. The key turned easily and noiselessly.

The moon by this time was high in the heavens. The Gatehouse towered above them. The shadows were black, but there was one stretch of hillside to be crossed where it seemed that every blade of grass was visible. Verney lay down flat and Francis copied him. They reached the shelter of the trees in safety and there turned to look back.

The old palace lay below them, the plan of its straggling walls and towers cut out sharply in the moonlight. Francis looked for the Gatehouse and saw it standing by itself, a massive pile, beyond the largest and most ruinous courtyard. A light flickered suddenly in one of the upper windows. He heard Verney catch his breath. They both stood motionless watching until after only a few seconds it went out again. They waited anxiously but there was no further sign of life. Apparently it was but the flash of a tinder box. Someone up there was restless, yet not restless enough to light a candle.

Verney heaved a sigh of relief. "Come along," he whispered. "It's time you were in bed."

Chris and Robert were waiting up for them, anxious for news, but Verney would allow none until Francis had been stripped of his wet clothes and tucked into the big bed. Then they gave him sherry sack until he was all a-glow, and his eyes would not stay open, not even while they heard the story.

He woke in the morning to find Robert shaking him. There was nobody else in the room.

"Where are the others?" he asked.

"We shall see them later. Don't talk now. Get dressed. We have to walk as if we were bound for Oxford."

When they were once more rigged out as sober scholars, their

him. After all he had done was he to be left out? "Sir," he cried, "can't I be in it? I would give my ears to see the Lady."

Verney grinned at him. "You will see her, lad; never fear. Don't you realise that she is coming to visit your Doctor Dee?"

Francis gasped. He could hardly believe his ears.

"She will come straight there by your little bridle track. There could not be a place safer or more remote. She can rest there till dusk before she goes on to Greens Norton. Anyway she herself insists upon it. She has great faith in Doctor Dee. He has cast her horoscope and she cannot be content until she has consulted him about her future."

A weather cock

CHAPTER XIII

Jam-Pots

Chris rode back with Robert and Francis, using the same quiet bridle tracks by which they had come, and talking only in undertones for fear that the very hedges might have ears.

They went straight to Stuchbery where Doctor Dee was watching anxiously for them. Laurie was there too, eager to hear everything. But best of all there was a great hotch potch of meat and vegetables and dumplings bubbling in the cauldron, and they were hungry. Doctor Dee himself ladled it into bowls, while they sat round the table and divided their attention between the stew and the story. It took a long time to tell everything, but he listened without missing a word.

"Well," he said briskly. "You are all deserving of a good rest. As for Francis he has done magnificently. Now I shall ride to Greens Norton, at once, without wasting a moment. Sir William Parr is a fish who may need a little playing."

It was decided that Chris and Robert should wait at Stuchbery until he returned so as to hear the result of the visit. Francis in the meanwhile could go home. This time Francis made no objections. He was really dead beat.

As he walked back across the water meadows he had to remind himself that he had only been away for one night. It felt like a week at the very least.

Indoors he plunged straight into the middle of a family scene. Mother and Anne and old Marta were all gathered in the hall in a ring round Ninnie, who stood in the midst of them in floods of tears. It must be something serious, thought Francis, for never in his life had he seen Mother so angry. It took him a little while to grasp that Ninnie had been caught helping herself to Marta's new plum preserve, taking a little bit from every single pot in the still room, and replacing the covers carefully so that it should not be missed.

Francis barely repressed a titter. After the excitement of the past twenty-four hours, all this to-do about a child stealing jam seemed just ridiculous.

His mother saw his face and rounded on him.

"And what are you laughing at, sir, I would like to know? Upon my word I am ashamed of my children. Have you no sense of right and wrong? Here is this little glutton caught red-handed, stealing with the most shameless and cunning deceit, and you can stand and laugh. A pretty story I shall have to tell your father when he comes home to-morrow. She will have to be whipped for it. Such wickedness must be beaten out of her."

Francis stood meekly with his eyes cast down. Mistress Washington looked at him more closely.

"What ails you, boy? You look as glum as an owl. Oh, of course, it is this staying up all night to watch the stars. I must have been crazed to allow it. You had better go to your bed at once. No; don't argue. I don't care if it *is* still broad daylight. Go when I tell you. Marta will give you some milk; and before you sleep, say a prayer that you may wake in a better mood, and that your sister may be cured of her gluttony."

Francis submitted quietly. He was so tired that really he was quite glad to go to bed. He saw Anne watching him with a curious expression, but he couldn't be bothered to find out why. Almost as soon as his head touched the pillow he was asleep.

He woke in the morning with one thought in his head; he must get to Stuchbery quickly and hear the latest news. He helped himself to ale and bread and cheese and started off at once, without waiting for anybody.

He was climbing over the stile to cross the Helmdon road when he heard Anne's voice behind him. She was running up the hill, and he sat down on the stile to wait for her. It was some seconds before she had enough breath to get out her words.

"Tell me—about—Woodstock," she gasped.

He stared at her. "How did you know?"

She laughed, still a little breathless but triumphant. "I didn't know. I only guessed. But now you've told me."

He grunted with annoyance. She had caught him out perfectly. To give himself time, he said, "What made you suspect?"

From the folds of her dress she produced his star map. "You were going to study stars but you left your map behind. I brought it after you to Doctor Dee's, and I saw you ride away with Robert. Nobody noticed me, and so I came home again. I've guessed for a long time that Robert still went there. He stays over at Stuchbery so often. And once I heard Doctor Dee talking to Chris about Woodstock. Is it the first time you've been?"

Francis sighed. Anne was much too sharp. He would have to be very careful now. "Yes," he said cautiously. "It's the first time."

"Did you see the Lady?"

"Nay, I didn't see her. We spent the night with Francis Verney at the Bull, and I saw the palace, but——"

"Stop!" she said quickly. She was looking past him with startled eyes. He turned. There in the lane behind them sat Tom Tresham astride his horse.

"Saints preserve us!" cried Francis, "how long have you been there?"

Tom dismounted and hitched his horse to the stile. "I was riding on the grass," he said dully. "I suppose you didn't hear me."

It was not an answer to the question, but Francis did not notice that. He was too taken up staring at Tom. Whatever had happened to him? All the jauntiness seemed to have gone out of him. He was very white and his eyes had dark circles round them as if he had been crying.

"Where have you been all this time?" asked Francis.

"My cousin Parr would not let me come because of those accursed hounds. I'd like to poison them." He looked at Francis. "I heard you say you'd been to Woodstock. I would that I could have come with you."

Francis looked round for Anne, but she had tiptoed off and

A ship for him at Ipswich

left him to deal with the situation. He frowned. Whatever was he to say to Tom?

"Did you see the Lady?" Tom inquired. It was the usual question and Francis just grunted. Tom continued without waiting; "You can set your mind at rest. I shall not tell. In all likelihood I shan't be coming here any more."

That brought Francis back with a jerk. "Why not?" he said. though he already knew the answer.

"My cousin Parr is going away. He's setting forth to Italy or some such place, and I'm to go back to my grandfather." His voice broke. A fat tear actually rolled down the side of his nose.

"The plague take it!" cried Francis. "Isn't there anything we can do?"

Tom shook his head. "Doctor Dee came yesterday. He's got

the journey all arranged and my cousin Parr is overjoyed. There's a ship waiting for him at Ipswich, and Doctor Dee has promised to ride with him and put him on board. He starts three days from now."

Three days from now! That was news anyway. But Francis was filled with misery for Tom.

"I begged him to let me go too," Tom went on, "but he said that he would need no page out there. I'm to go back to my grandfather's so 'tis likely that I shall never come here again. Rushton is too far and my grandfather is a bear. I tell you, I wish I were dead and buried."

He gave way to a real sob. Francis too had a lump in his throat. He racked his brain for some way to help. It occurred to him that perhaps Father would consent to having Tom at Sulgrave. That would be better than anything. He began at once to think deeply about it. It might be wise to get round Mother before approaching Father.

Tom in the meanwhile went rambling on. "I did think that I might run away and go as a ship's boy to the Indies. But since I heard you talking a new thought has come. If only the Lady Elizabeth would beg my cousin Parr to stay in England! That would keep him at home for certain. *You* go to Woodstock; I dare swear you're hail-fellow-well-met with all of them. Couldn't you contrive it? If *she* asked him not to go it would solve everything."

With only half his mind on what Tom said, Francis frowned at him. Tom was a want-wit; he never grasped things properly. "How *can* she ask him when she's going too?" he said impatiently.

There was a silence that seemed like eternity. Francis felt himself sinking in a cold sea.

"I'm mad!" he cried desperately. "What shall I do? Oh, saints in heaven, *what* shall I do? I've told what I was pledged never to tell."

"Comfort yourself," said Tom calmly. "You are safe with me. No one shall ever know that you told me."

Francis pulled himself together. That wasn't enough. Tom must be made to understand that Parr was not in the secret yet.

But how could he do it? He couldn't very well say "they don't trust him"

"For pity's sake be careful with your cousin Parr," he began. "You see, they have not told him yet that the Lady is going with him. They think that it is safer that way."

Tom was really astonished this time. "But how can he take her without knowing? Upon my word, Francis, I don't understand. What is to happen? I've no wish to pry, I promise you; but as I know so much surely it would be safer for me to know every-thing, so that I do not blunder and do harm."

Francis gave an enormous sigh. He did not know whether he was on his head or his heels. What Tom said was perfectly true; for him to know a little was worse than anything. Rather shakily he explained that the Lady was to come to Doctor Dee's; Chris and Robert and Verney were to bring her. She was to wait there until Parr was ready to start. *Then* they would take her to Greens Norton and escort the two of them in safety to the ship. "You see," he ended, "when she is actually there he can't refuse to go with her, can he? After all he loves to say that he is her uncle."

"No," Tom repeated a little doubtfully, "I suppose he can't refuse to go with her."

Francis suddenly went cold with fright. "Tom, in heaven's name be careful. If they should find that I have told you I should die of shame."

"Keep your heart up," said Tom cheerfully. "I'll warrant that I can keep a secret as well as you can." He caught sight of Francis's face and grinned at him. "Your pardon; I did not mean it as a gibe. I'll be careful. I swear I will. And hark you, I've just had another thought. This means that he *will* want a page. I'll be able to go with them. He can't take *her* with nobody to wait on them."

Francis took fright again. "But you can't speak of it," he pro-tested. "How can you plead to be taken without giving it away?"

"Oh, I shall manage it," said Tom loftily, "I shall prepare and then when the time comes I can just say, 'good cousin, I am ready'." He swung himself into the saddle. All his old cockiness had returned. "Never fear, Francis; I'll be on my guard."

He trotted away down the Helmdon road a very different Tom from the one that arrived. Sick at heart Francis watched him go. Then he picked up his star map and continued on his way to Stuchbery. It was his turn to be miserable now. He could easily have thrown himself down in the grass and cried his heart out. He knew now for certain that he was no good. In spite of his vow, in spite of all his joy in being trusted, in spite of the desperate secrecy of the whole matter he had done the same thing all over again; he had just blurted everything out. Of course Tom would be careful. He had made Tom understand how serious it was, and Tom was a great deal more fit to be trusted than he was. But for all that it was he, Francis, who had once more given the secret away.

Ought he to tell Doctor Dee what he had done? At the very thought he turned sick again. It was not only telling Doctor Dee, it was telling Robert and Chris and Laurie and all of them. He just could not face it. The shame was too much to bear. He would never be allowed to forget it, as long as he lived. And perhaps they would cancel the whole plan and then everybody would have to know, Parry and all the people at Woodstock, and Francis Verney who had praised him so much; and the Lady would have to know too. And perhaps because of him she wouldn't be able to escape at all, and there might be another fire under her room——

He went on working himself up until he just could not bear any more, and jerked himself round the other way. Of course it was all right. Tom had promised. And what Tom said was true; it might be a good thing for him to know. If anything went wrong he could bring them warning.

Anyway he could not face telling anyone what he had done. The only thing he could do was to pray and pray and pray. It must go right; it *must*. Surely God wouldn't make everyone suffer just because he couldn't hold his tongue.

At last he brought himself to the point of tapping on the door of the little house. To his great relief Doctor Dee was alone, working at his table as quietly as if he had not a secret in the world. He looked round with a cheerful grin as Francis came in.

"Well, and how is the young locksmith this morning? Robert and Laurie are not here. Your mother sent a message that your father was expected and she could not spare them. Why, you look a washed-out rag. What ails you? I suppose you are tired still. Your mother will be wanting to know what you have been at. Did she ask any questions last night?"

"She said I looked as glum as an owl and she blamed the stars." It was a relief to tell the story of Ninnie and the jam and make Doctor Dee laugh.

"I suppose you are agog to hear the latest news," Doctor Dee went on. "You will be glad to know that everything is arranged. Parr is delighted with me. He says I am the best courier in the world; and when I said that I must go to Cambridge and would ride with him, his joy was unbounded. Whether he will be quite so pleased with me three days hence remains to be seen; but anyway, in three days from now we start. Chris has already gone back to Woodstock to carry the news."

"And the Lady?" Francis scarcely dared to ask.

"The Lady is coming here. She does me the honour of wishing to see me, to understand more fully the horoscope I drew for her. She will have her lady with her, Blanche Parry, who is a kinswoman of mine. I shall ride out from here to meet them with Robert. If you want to, you may come. And now, my boy, we have another task in hand." He ran his finger along the dusty table and held it up for Francis to see. "Look there. We cannot bring the Lady to a dirty house, but I don't want some local Goody poking her nose about. If we could borrow some brushes and brooms from Marta, maybe we could do it ourselves. What say you?"

Francis jumped up. He was ready to get to work immediately. He was glad to be busy at something.

They started off at once for Sulgrave. Marta quite certainly would give them what they wanted. The difficulty would be to stop her from coming to do the work herself.

But as soon as they put their noses inside the house they realised that something was very wrong. Anne, her face all blotted with tears, met them as they came in by the porch, and told them what had happened.

Father, it seemed, had arrived from Northampton tired and dispirited; and before he had even taken off his riding boots, Mother, unable to contain herself any longer, had poured out to him all her worries, beginning with Ninnie and the preserves and ending with the burning of the mortgage deed on a bonfire of dirty rushes.

At first Father was struck dumb. Then he broke into a storm of rage. Ninnie and Anne and even Mother herself were reduced to tears. Anne had never known his anger last for so long. He had now just gone off to cool himself at the pump.

"He said that if we were all turned out on to the highway it would be our own fault and not his," repeated Anne tearfully. "I shouldn't let him see you, Francis. He'll only ask you questions about the bonfire, and that will start it off all over again."

But even as she spoke Father reappeared through the courtyard door and caught sight of them. He seemed to have washed away most of his anger, for he took no notice of Francis but called out quite briskly to Doctor Dee.

"Some brushes and brooms"

"A good day to you, sir. I am mighty glad to see you. Will you stay and have dinner? I've had such a flood of tribulations ever since I set foot in the house that it will do me good to talk to you. Have you heard about it all? First there's Ninnie's thieving, the little baggage; and then the wicked lunacy of these young ruffians who've burst open my coffer and burned my mortgage deed. Yes, actually burned it, if you please. Here have I been riding half over England searching, while all the time they had made a bonfire of it. Great heavens, man, what would *you* do with such a family? I warrant you'd beat them until you were weary."

"I confess that I should want to," said Doctor Dee poking with his beard. "But if no amount of beating would bring back the deed, I doubt if I should count it worth an aching arm."

Father actually laughed. He took him by the elbow. "You are a practical man. I'm not sure that you are not right. Tell me your news. How are the stars? By the way I have some booty for you, spoils of the monasteries, like your Aristotle. You have started me on the craze and wherever I go now I have my eyes open. There are several good finds stowed in my saddle-bags. I'll show them to you as soon as we have finished dinner."

Dinner itself was something of an ordeal. Father himself had recovered. He talked to Doctor Dee quite happily, but Mother was almost over-anxious to see that everything went well and that none of the children angered their father again. Not a single member of the family dared to speak, except the smallest ones of The Tail who banged their spoons and chattered and were promptly hushed by the bigger ones.

"I suppose there is no more news about the greyhound business?" Father inquired, washing his fingers in the bowl that Francis brought to him, after a more-than-usually rich helping of roasted duck. "Did Sir William Parr ever come to see you about going abroad? He said some weeks ago that he wanted your advice, but perhaps all this trouble has stopped him."

Doctor Dee also wiped his fingers and his beard before answering. He took rather a long time about it.

"As it happens he came a day or two ago," he replied casually. "He said little or nothing about the greyhounds except, I think, that all this unpleasantness does not incline him to remain at Greens Norton."

"And small wonder. I really must go over to Althorp and see if I can't do something to patch up peace. Is there any sign of young Tom?"

Doctor Dee shook his head. "I've not set eyes on him since the trouble started."

"It is hard on him," said Father. "He must feel lonely now that he has got used to being with other children." He changed the subject. "Have you ever visited Peterborough? You should go and see it. The new building of the Abbey Church—nay, I should say the *Cathedral*, I always forget that it is an abbey no longer; what was I saying? Oh, the new building has a fan roof as lovely as your chapel at King's College, Cambridge; indeed I believe the same mason designed it; and the north choir is lit day and night by tall candles. Queen Katharine of Aragon lies there, you know. Poor lady, she had so little honour when she died that our present Queen would make up for it now. They say she idolised her mother."

Francis hovering with the copper bowl of water and the towel almost sighed aloud with relief that they had got on to a harmless subject of conversation. His heart had stood still while Father was asking questions about Sir William Parr. But now they were talking about abbeys being turned into cathedrals and abbots into deans and bishops, and books and parchments which had been thrown out and scattered about the country.

"As I told you I have had several finds," said Father with an air of satisfaction. "At Peterborough the library is still safe, but in Northampton every shop-keeper seems to cast up his accounts on pages torn from monkish books. Francis, go and fetch my saddlebag; not the cloak bag, mark you; that is full of clothes; but the leather one, strapped on the saddle itself."

Thankful to get out of the house Francis took a few minutes to undo the buckle and carry in the bag. During his absence all the children had left the hall with Mother, and Robert and Laurie were clearing away the dishes.

"Take the bag into the parlour," Father ordered. "Come, sir; we shall be more comfortable in the next room."

While they were pushing back their chairs Francis went ahead. He opened the parlour door, then stopped taken aback. On Father's writing-table stood half a dozen pots of preserves, all neatly covered and arranged in a row. And beside the table, her face the colour of the parchment tops, stood Ninnie, on the verge of tears.

"Go on, boy; you're blocking the way," said Father from behind him. "How now, what's all this? Oh—oh, I see! 'Tis the little glutton, and this I suppose is the evidence of the crime.

Doctor Dee, I blush for shame that you should see my daughter thus. Have you heard the dreadful story? She has been stealing jam."

"What?" cried Doctor Dee, in mock horror. "All that jam? Six pots? Where does she find room for it?"

"Ah, that just makes it worse; she's a cunning thief. She just takes a little from each pot. Look at them and you'll see." He turned back to Ninnie. "Who sent you here with all these jars? Your mother? No? It was Marta, eh? I might have guessed as much. You'll get no mercy from Marta. And what am I supposed to do with you? What is your punishment to be? A whipping?"

Ninnie stood looking at him, her mouth drawn down at the corners, her eyes brimming.

Suddenly Doctor Dee, who was looking at the jam-pots, gave a funny little cry. Father glanced at him. "What is it?" he inquired.

Doctor Dee stood with one of the parchment covers in his hand, turning it this way and that.

"What have you found?" said Father again. "Some more Aristotle?"

"Not Aristotle. Something that will be of interest to you. There is only a fragment, but I can read a few words. '—*do hereby assign—the manor of Sulgrave*'."

Father sprang forward and seized the piece of parchment from his hand.

"Great heavens," he cried. "It *is*—it *IS*, a bit of the deed. Is there any more?"

Already Doctor Dee was pulling the covers from the other pots. The two men bent over them excitedly, flattening them out on the table and piecing them together.

" 'Tis nearly all here," exclaimed Father. "Ninnie, go and find Marta. If she has any more preserves like this, tell her to bring them here. Quickly now!"

Ninnie did not need to be told twice. Father caught sight of Francis. "Fetch your mother," he cried. "Tell her the mortgage deed is found."

The news spread like wild-fire. Mother came running with

"She takes a little from each pot. Look at them"

Anne at her heels. Laurie came from the garden and Robert from the stable. Marta and Ninnie brought more and more pots of preserves, till Mother warned them that it was only those made within the last few weeks that were wanted. Father and Doctor Dee went on fitting the pieces together, in spite of the family pressing round them. At last Father called out that it was complete, except for one torn corner which really did not matter. Here and there the ink was washed out and faded, but it was still readable.

The problem was how had it come to be cut into covers for the jam pots? Marta gave the answer quite simply. She had found what seemed to her an old piece of parchment stretched across a window in the pig stye to keep the rain off a farrowing sow. It was just what she wanted for her preserve jars, and a piece of oiled rag would cover the window just as well. But how had the deed got to the pig stye? Old Jake was fetched to clear up that point. He came, twiddling his hat in his hand and looking frightened. Oh, yes, he remembered using the old parchment for the pig stye. He didn't mean any harm. He'd found it on the rubbish heap in the field, all among the rushes waiting to be burned.

CHAPTER XIV

Snake in the Grass

From the eldest to the youngest it seemed as though a great weight had been lifted. Even the tail end of The Tail, who were too young to understand anything about it, seemed to feel that the world round them was different. The nursery was full of laughing children instead of crying ones. Mother beamed on them all and Marta, for a few days, forgot to be cross. Even Ninnie, who walked on air, was as good as gold, as if to show that it was possible to learn a lesson without the help of a whipping.

Only Anne was a little ill at ease. At first of course she was off her head with joy. She had felt so guilty about the coffer that her sense of relief was greater than anyone's. But when the excitement died down she noticed that Francis was not happy. He had kindled the bonfire, so he ought to have been almost as overjoyed as she was. She was certain that he had something on his mind, and of course that something was bound to be Woodstock.

188

Several things made her suspicious. As soon as the excitement about the deed was over, Doctor Dee and Francis asked Marta for brooms to clean the little house. Doctor Dee was a favourite with Marta and she promptly offered to come and do it for him, but he firmly refused. So when they set out for Stuchbery, brooms in hand, Anne herself ran after them, begging to be allowed to help. Doctor Dee shook his head.

"Hark at her, Francis," he laughed. "She's a small size, but he's true woman. No woman can ever believe that a man can do her work as well as she can. Nay, my poppet, we are going to do it all ourselves. Why can't you come? Well, child, I would not trust any woman with my precious instruments. A little later on, when it is all finished, you shall come and see that we have done it properly."

Anne returned home unconvinced. For some reason they did not want her there. For the next day or two she said nothing, but she kept her eyes open. Francis did not go to Woodstock again; she was certain of that because he could not get there and back in the day and he did not sleep away from home. But he was as restless as the manikin on a stick which they had brought to the children from London. If he was spoken to suddenly he jumped and quivered all over, just as if someone had pulled a string.

All the boys were up and away each morning as soon as it was light. Even Father remarked on it, saying that John Dee was a wonderful tutor to make them all so keen on work.

On the third day Anne was sitting under the elm trees with some of the little ones, trying to teach them their alphabet, when she heard a horse trotting along the lane. She wondered which of the boys it would be, for she had noticed that they had all taken horses when they went out. Through the hedge she saw the rider dismount in a great hurry. He opened the garden gate and started to run towards her. To her astonishment it was not any of her brothers, but Tom.

"Where's Francis?" he demanded in an urgent whisper.

"He's at Doctor Dee's."

Tom shook his head. "I've been there. The house is empty."

"Well, he's not here," she said. "He went to Stuchbery. They all three went. They took horses."

Tom gave a sort of groan. "*What* shall I do? I must find them, either Francis or Robert or one of them."

He started running back to the gate. Anne scrambled to her feet and raced after him. She caught him just as he unhitched his horse.

"Tell me what it is," she urged. "I may be able to help."

Tom paused, one foot in the stirrup. He hesitated only for a second. "The Lady Elizabeth is escaping from Woodstock. They are bringing her to Stuchbery. And now my grandfather Tresham has found out and he's coming to catch them."

For an instant Anne was speechless. The Lady Elizabeth at Stuchbery! Then as Tom swung himself into the saddle she caught at his foot.

"Help me up. I'm coming with you. We must find them. Quick, Tom! Help me up."

She jumped on to the mounting block by the gate and with a wild leap flung herself across the front of Tom's saddle. He caught her and held her until she wriggled into a sitting position, then they started off at a brisk trot.

"Tell me what's happened," she demanded breathlessly as they bumped down the hill and over the little bridge.

"Well, you see, my cousin Parr was going abroad somewhere. Doctor Dee had arranged it. They intended him to take the Lady Elizabeth with him, but they hadn't told him that part yet. They were going to bring her to Greens Norton to-night, as a sort of surprise, so that they could start off to-morrow. But last night he"—Tom gulped, as if the words wouldn't come—"last night he found out."

"How did he find out?" demanded Anne. She saw at once that Tom had told him, but she was determined to make him say so.

"He got it out of me. I wanted to go with them. He'd have to have a page if *she* was going. But he was too sharp for me. Before I knew where I was, he'd guessed. Then he said that he wouldn't risk his neck again, so he packed in a hurry and went off to London before it was light. I wasn't to say that he knew about her coming."

Anne snorted; already he had said it. So much for Tom! "But your grandfather? You said he found out too."

"He came this morning about the greyhounds, and found my cousin Parr gone. Something made him suspicious, and he beat me and said he'd go on beating till I told him everything. Then he locked me up while he went to fetch some men, but I got out of the window and rode here like mad."

She longed to tell him what she thought of him, but it wasn't worth while. He was a poor sort of boy. No one would ever get things out of Francis by beating. And yet, when she came to think of it, it must have been Francis who had told Tom in the first place. He trusted Tom where he wouldn't trust her and this was what he got for it.

She swallowed her indignation and set herself grimly to tackle the consequences.

They had reached the corner of the lane to Stuchbery and Tom paused to look both ways.

"We'd better go on to Doctor Dee's," she said; "but keep under cover of the trees so that we can see without being seen."

Obediently he turned off on to the grass and walked his horse through the fringe of a copse.

"Look!" she whispered suddenly. "There are horses outside the little house. Someone's arrived. Is it your grandfather? Can you see?"

Tom screwed up his eyes. "I can see people moving, but it's not Grandfather. His horses are trapped with green and white, his livery colours."

"Wait here then," she commanded. "I'll go round by the back and get in by the buttery door."

She slipped to the ground, picked up her skirts and ran, dodging among the shadows of the trees. Tom stayed where he was. But he had been noticed. Some figures detached themselves from the group outside the door and hurried towards him. The two foremost were Chris and Francis. Tom rode to meet them.

"You can't come here," cried Chris as soon as they were within earshot. "Doctor Dee is busy. You'd better go home."

Tom looked past him at Francis whose eyes were wide with fear. Robert had come running up now and another fellow who he thought must be Verney. "I came to tell you that my cousin Parr has gone," he said. "He went away last night to London."

"Gone!" cried Chris in consternation. "How can he have gone? Verney! Verney, did you hear that? Tom Tresham says that Parr has gone."

Verney swore forcibly. "It can't be true. In heaven's name what could make him go off like that? Are you certain, boy?"

Tom nodded, his eye on Francis. "And my grandfather, Sir Thomas Tresham, is coming here with his men. He must be on his way by now."

They stared at one another, too appalled to ask him any more questions.

"Tresham is Sheriff, isn't he?" cried Verney. "Quick, Chris, get back to the house and break the news. Francis, you know which way they'll come. Go with Tom and keep a lookout and give us all the warning you can."

He turned and ran after Chris and Robert. Francis and Tom were left together. Without a word Francis scrambled up behind Tom.

"Go to those trees at the top of the hill," he directed. "From there we shall see them coming down the Helmdon road."

Anne reached the buttery door, opened it without knocking and went straight in. A lady was sitting at the table. Doctor Dee was bending over her. Both of them were intent upon a paper which Anne recognised as the horoscope.

Doctor Dee looked up. His eyes blazed with anger. "How dare you come bursting in," he cried. "Go out at once. I'm busy."

Anne stood her ground. "Sir, Tom Tresham is here. He says Sir William Parr has gone away. He rode to London last night. And Tom's grandfather is coming."

"Coming where?"

"Coming here." She drew a breath and said timidly. "He's looking for the Lady."

Dee strode to the door. "Your pardon, Madam," he cried. "I must find out the truth of this."

Left alone with the Lady Elizabeth, Anne dared for the first time to look at her. She wore a big grey home-spun cloak like a farm woman. The hood was pushed back, showing her vivid red-gold hair. Her face was very white, her mouth pursed up and her brows raised a little. She sat very still but her eyes darted brightly, like the eyes of a robin. Obviously she was thinking

"The lady was a royal Princess"

hard. Anne was uncertain whether it would be proper just to curtsey; after all the lady was a royal Princess; so instead she dropped on to one knee.

The Lady looked down at her. "Who are you, little maid?"

"Please Madam, I'm Francis's sister, Anne Washington."

"Francis? Francis Verney? No, of course, the little locksmith. I remember now. This Tom Somebody who brought the news, who is he?"

"Tom Tresham, Madam. He's page to Sir William Parr. He rode from Greens Norton."

The Lady frowned. "He must be wrong, unless there is some mischief somewhere. Parr could not have gone without me; he would never leave me thus." She turned to Anne again. "Get up, child. Don't kneel to me. It seems that you know me, but we must not publish it. Tell me, where do you live?"

"At Sulgrave Manor, Madam. It is quite close."

The Lady nodded. She seemed about to say something more, but the door flew open and Doctor Dee came in, followed by an older woman who hurried to her mistress's side.

"It seems to be true, Madam," Dee cried. "Parr has gone, though we know not why, and Tresham, the sheriff, is on the way. We must get you to safety. You must go from here."

"Go," she repeated. "Where am I to go to? Where is my uncle Parr. Why did he not wait for me? He knew that I was coming."

"No, Madam, we resolved not to tell him until you arrived. It was for safety, Madam."

Elizabeth sprang up. Her chair crashed to the ground.

"You did not tell him?" she cried. "You have the face to say that you did not tell him? Then in heaven's name what did you expect? Was he to know by magic? Never have I met such crack-brain fools. Is this what you call safety? Thanks to you I'll be in the Tower again for this. Where is Verney? Where are all my fine gallants?" She banged the table with her fist. "I'll not wait here like a lamb to be slaughtered. Where can I find shelter?"

Anne looked from the angry princess to the door, where the boys were all crowded together. An idea came suddenly into her head. She pushed her way to Robert. As she whispered to him his face brightened. He stepped forward.

"There is a hiding place at Sulgrave, a secret place over the porch. There is room to lie in comfort."

Doctor Dee looked from Robert to the Lady. "A secret place," he repeated. "Sulgrave is the home of Master Washington, the father of these boys. Will you go, Madam, or would you rather trust to the woods?"

"And be chased like a deer with hounds?" she retorted. "Nay, I'll go with them. My good Blanche can come too?"

Robert shook his head. "I fear that there is but bare room for one."

Mistress Blanche, an elderly woman with a round good-tempered face, gave a short laugh. "Give me an apron and put me in your kitchen, sir," she said to Dee. "I will be your cook-maid; they will never know me."

At that moment Francis pushed his way into the room. "They are coming," he cried without ceremony. "We have seen their colours in the distance along the Helmdon road."

The Lady Elizabeth pulled the hood over her hair. "We must be quick. Show me the way."

While Mistress Parry wrapped her in the cloak, Doctor Dee issued orders.

"Robert, take the Lady by the fields. I must stay here to answer questions. Stay hidden among the trees until Tresham has gone by. Anne, you go with them, and Francis too. The rest of you, get the horses away quickly. Don't rest for a mile or more, not till you're sure they can't be seen or heard. Hurry now; there's not a second to lose. Francis, is the coast clear?"

Francis went outside to listen. He beckoned. Without another word the Lady Elizabeth slipped out of the buttery door, and between Robert and Anne, across the little orchard into the copse the way that Anne had come with Tom only a short while ago. Francis, scouting ahead, signalled them to stop before they reached the Helmdon road. They could hear the sound of voices and the drumming of horses' hoofs. Hidden with the Lady behind a clump of bushes, Anne caught a glimpse of green and white trappings as a party of horsemen rode by. They slowed down and she held her breath. She could see them clearly. There were six or seven of them. But they did not even glance at the copse. They went a few yards further, then turned along the lane to Stuchbery.

As the last one vanished Francis beckoned again. In another minute they were all running down the field towards the water meadows.

A party of horsemen rode by

Robert pulled Anne to one side. "Go in front and get everyone out of the way," he whispered. "Be ill or anything. I don't care how you do it, but leave the hall and the stairway clear."

Anne nodded and darted ahead. She had not the least idea what she could do, but before she reached the home farm the inspiration came. Luckily the garden was deserted. She dodged round to the back of the house and into the meadow at the far side; it was called Little Green and it was where Marta hung out her washing to dry. There she flung herself panting against a tree. Tearing down her short hose she flicked her bare leg over and over again with a stinging nettle, regardless of the hurt. Then she began to scream.

Never in her life had she screamed so. She had not known that she could make so much noise. Her shrieks echoed round the meadow. She thought to herself as she screamed that the Lady and Robert would probably hear it and they would guess the reason.

Marta was the first to appear, running from the house; then Ninnie, terrified. Then came Mother, then Father, then the wenches from the kitchen and the men from the stable. And still Anne screamed. It was becoming easier every moment. All the pent-up excitement of the day took hold of her and soon she was shrieking because she could not help it. When they came near her she clung desperately to the tree and kicked at the long grass crying "Snake! Snake!" between the screams.

"She has been bitten," cried Mother. "Marta, let me see her leg. Heaven protect us, it is scarlet."

Father pushed about in the grass with the toe of his boot. "Keep your distance all of you," he said. "It may still be here. We had better take the child indoors." He tried to pick Anne up but she clutched the tree with all her might and redoubled her screams.

"Let her alone, let her alone," cried Mother. "She is crazed with terror. Let me try and soothe her."

Under Mother's loving touch Anne quietened a little. She was tired out with screaming. But still she would not let go of the tree, even when Mother tried to loosen her hands. She felt like a traitor, for all the time that her head was resting in the hollow of Mother's shoulder she was trying to listen. Could they have got upstairs yet? Was the hiding safely done? Surely it would be all right for her to stop now.

Then Father grew angry. "This is silly," he said. "The maid is just stubborn. Let me see her leg. Hum! It is red, but there are no traces of a bite. I have never seen a snake here in my life. She is touched with some ague I should say. Let me have her, wife. I will make her let go."

One by one he loosened Anne's fingers. She fought him and

it hurt. She began to cry in real earnest. She had been playing a part. Now with fright and anxiety it became true. She did not have to force the tears. They came in a torrent.

Father picked her up in his arms and carried her indoors, Mother and Marta and Ninnie all following anxiously behind. As they went into the hall Anne checked her tears enough to peep over Father's shoulder. She almost began crying again with sheer relief. Robert and Francis were both in the hall, inno-cently engaged upon whittling a stick.

Father carried her indoors That must mean that the Lady was safely in the hiding hole. Robert's face was the colour of a beetroot; Francis's was deadly white. Nobody must notice them, thought Anne, and began to sob anew.

"Your sister is ill," declared Father. "She is seized with some ague or other." He looked round at Mother. "She had better go to bed, I think; shall I carry her up?"

To bed! That was best of all, thought Anne. Her bed was just outside the door of the linen closet. She would be on guard.

But before they reached the bottom of the stairs she heard the clatter of horses outside. Father heard it too and paused to listen.

There came a rapping at the door. Robert laid down his knife and went to answer it. He came back with his face redder than ever.

"Sir Thomas Tresham to see you, sir. He says it is urgent."

The Arms of
TRESHAM

"Little Ease"

CHAPTER XV

"Little Ease"

Father stood in doubt at the bottom of the stairs. Then as Tom's grandfather strode into the hall, he carried Anne to the cushioned window seat and laid her down, signing to Mother to see to her.

Mother came and bent tenderly over her. "Can you walk upstairs, sweetheart," she whispered.

Anne shook her head and lay back. "Let me stay here," she pleaded softly. "I'll be very quiet." As Mother tiptoed away to get a cloak to put over her, she raised her head and looked round. Both the boys had vanished. The only people in the hall were her father and Sir Thomas Tresham.

"I am sorry to disturb you, sir," Tresham was saying. "But I have come in the course of my duty as Sheriff to ask some questions. I have reason to believe that the Lady Elizabeth has escaped from Woodstock and is in hiding round here."

"Escaped from Woodstock?" repeated Father. "That is news

200

that will cause a stir indeed. But why should she come in this direction? She has no friends here."

"You have forgotten. Parr calls himself her uncle. It is from Greens Norton that I have the news. You will grant me pardon if I ask you straitly if she is in this house, or if you have heard aught of it?"

Father shook his head. "She is neither here, nor has she been here, and I know nothing of the matter; I pledge you my word. As it happens I have seen nothing of Sir William Parr for some weeks. There is trouble between him and the Spencers about some greyhounds, and it seems that I am involved."

Tresham nodded. "I have good reason to know about that. It was actually the matter of the greyhounds that took me to Greens Norton to-day. I had the dog-keeper with me, the man who had charge of the Earl of Bath's hounds before they were stolen. The Spencers sent for him from London and I took him to Greens Norton to identify the animals. When I got there I found everything in confusion. Sir William Parr had gone off in the night at a moment's notice. Even his servants did not know he was going. It seems that for some time he has been planning a flight to the continent, and the Lady Elizabeth was to go with him. She was to join him to-day. But for some reason he took fright at the last moment and went without her. So she will have broken out of Woodstock to find herself deserted." He paused to chuckle. "'Tis not a case of 'Put not your trust in princes', but of 'Princess, put not your trust in William Parr'." He shook with enjoyment of his own joke.

Father looked shocked. "But do you really mean that he has left her in the lurch?"

"So I understand. I have reason to believe that the rendezvous was at the house of Doctor Dee. I went there and made a search. He was alone working at a map. There was nobody at all in the house except his cook-maid. There were fresh traces of horses by the door. I asked him for an explanation and he said that your boys were always there with their horses."

"That is true enough. They seem to spend more time there than they do at home."

Tresham shook his head. "I am not satisfied. There is so much coming and going between your house and his that I fear I must beg you to allow me to search. You have given me your word and I would not cast doubt upon it, but in my duty I must leave no stone unturned."

Father stood up stiffly. "You are welcome to search, sir. Go into every room. Nay, I will take you myself. I see you have your men with you. Will you bring them too?"

"That is not necessary. I have told them to make a search outside." He turned and bowed to Mother. "I must ask your pardon for this intrusion, Madam. I trust that I do not inconvenience you."

Mother stood beside Anne clasping and unclasping her hands in trepidation, but she managed to answer Sir Thomas civilly and the two men started upon their tour of the house. Under the cloak Anne lay trembling. She closed her eyes and prayed more intensely than she had ever prayed before. They did not take very long to go through the downstairs rooms and with her heart thumping she heard them go slowly upstairs. Their footsteps sounded overhead in the Great Chamber. She tried to follow where they had got to, and every time a door opened or closed she caught her breath. Was it the door of the linen closet? Would Father think of the hiding hole, or would Sir Thomas find it?

It seemed a lifetime before she heard them coming down again. They were talking in the most friendly way.

"Of course it may be all a false alarm," Tresham was saying. "Mark you I have had no official tidings from Woodstock that she is missing. All I have learned comes from Greens Norton. Tom, my grandson, was my principal informant."

"*Tom!*" exclaimed Father. "Do you really mean, sir, that you have taken all this on the word of young Tom Tresham?"

Sir Thomas wagged his head. "Ah, but he didn't *tell* me. That is to say he did not tell me willingly. I had to beat it out of him. I could see that there was some mystery. I know William Parr too well. He is first cousin to my wife, you know. I found ample to show that he had been planning to slip out of the country

202

by some back-stair route, the port of Ipswich, I think it was. Doctor Dee had helped him. Tom knew all about it. It took me the best part of an hour to get the story out of him, but when I got it there was no doubt. The Lady Elizabeth must have left Woodstock before dawn to-day, only an hour or so after Parr took to his heels. There would have been no time to stop her."

Father laughed gently. " 'Tis not for me to question your conclusions, sir, but I would wager heavily that you have disturbed yourself for nothing if you have your information only from Tom. If I may be so bold as to advise you on your own grandson, the boy is a wind-bag, overfull of his own importance. He will make a mountain out of any molehill. We see a good deal of him here, you know."

"Indeed, sir, I know. I have been wanting to see you to thank you for all that you have done for him. He has improved beyond measure since he has been in the company of your children. I should be thankful if I could persuade you to have him in your household now that his cousin Parr has gone."

Father looked astonished. "Have him here? That must be a question for my wife, sir. For my part I should be glad enough, and my boys would be delighted. Tom is a good lad at heart. We are all fond of him."

They both looked at Mother who said without any hesitation that she would be happy to welcome Tom.

"Well, that is a weight off my mind." Sir Thomas rubbed his hands with satisfaction. "And I am beginning to wonder with you whether I have not been hasty in jumping to conclusions. As you say, Tom's story is scant evidence to rest on. I think I shall go back and wait for some official notice of her escape."

"I think you are wise," smiled Father. "A beating might quite well have inspired him to tell you any story that would stay your arm. That, to my mind, is the weakness of torture as a means of getting information. They can make a man speak, but they can never be sure that what he says is not just moonshine. But you must have a cup of wine before you go. Where are those boys? They were here a moment since."

He went to the door and clapped his hands, but no boy appeared. Mother herself hurried away to the buttery and in a few moments old Marta appeared bearing a tray with a flagon of wine and the best Venetian goblets.

Anne, lying without moving a finger, wished to goodness that Sir Thomas would go. And yet, when he went there would be a fresh problem to face. The Lady was upstairs in the hiding hole, and how were they to get her down again without anybody seeing; and when she was down what was to happen to her then?

At last Tresham refused to have his goblet filled again. He

really must be off, he said. His men were waiting outside and for very shame he must look round the neighbourhood a little on his way home, or they would think that he had brought them on a wild goose chase. "Though," he added smiling waggishly, "wild goose chase it really is. You have convinced me of that."

"By the way, we haven't heard yet about the greyhounds," said Father, as he held open the door. "You told us that you took the keeper over to Greens Norton. What did he say?"

Old Marta bearing a tray

Sir Thomas paused on the threshold. "I quite forgot. That too I fear has been a great to-do about nothing. The keeper was in no doubt about his verdict. They are not the stolen hounds at all."

Anne could hear Father laughing as he escorted Tresham across the yard. He was still laughing when he came back.

"Well, wife," he said as he poured himself some more wine. "It looks as if poor Cousin Kit will have to eat a morsel of humble pie, which she is not likely to enjoy. Perhaps it is just as well that Parr has gone away."

"That is a strange story about the Lady Elizabeth," said Mother. "Do you suppose there is any truth in it?"

Father sipped his wine. "I know not, my dear. I made light of it to Tresham, but there is no smoke without fire. I'd like to see the boys and ask them a few questions. I've never told you that I had trouble with them before, about mixing themselves up with affairs at Woodstock, when you were abed with the new baby. Where are they, by the way? They vanished when Sir Thomas was here."

Mother did not know, so Father's eyes lighted on Anne. "And how is the snake bite, eh? Gone, I warrant. A sorry tantrum you treated us to, mistress; I hope you are ashamed of yourself. There's no need to lie there as though you were plague-stricken. Go and find your brothers. Tell them I want to speak to them."

Thankful to have got off so lightly, Anne went outside. She knew that they would not be far and she found them in the stable yard, watching the door of the house. Chris and Verney and Doctor Dee were all somewhere about, they told her, keeping an eye on everyone who came and went. They had seen Tresham and his men ride off; that was one danger past anyway. Now the problem was how to get the Lady safely away.

"Father was splendid in making Tresham think that it was all moonshine, but I think he is suspicious," Anne warned them. "What are you going to do?"

"We may have to tell him," said Robert. "Tresham has gone and I don't believe he would hand the Lady over. Doctor Dee says we must feel our way."

They followed Anne into the hall and stood in a row like a party of schoolboys awaiting a beating; Robert, with his head held high, Laurie looking ill-at-ease, and Francis, his face so white and worn that he scarcely looked like Francis at all. Anne, determined at all costs not to be sent away, crept to where Mother sat looking worried and anxious, and hid herself behind Mother's chair.

Laurence Washington spoke slowly and solemnly. "I have sent for you because Sir Thomas Tresham has told me a most strange story, which, so he says, he had from Tom. It concerns the Lady Elizabeth and a plot to free her from Woodstock. I have persuaded Sir Thomas to pay no more attention to it until he hears it from a more reliable source. But for all that I am not satisfied. I am going to tell you what he said, and I insist on the truth from you as far as you know it."

He paused, looking intently at each one in turn. Then he told them slowly all that they already knew, just as he had heard it from Tresham.

"Well?" he said at the end. "What have you to say?"

Robert looked him straight in the face. "It is true, sir."

"True? How mean you 'true'? Tell me exactly what is true."

"It is true that the Lady has escaped from Woodstock, sir. She was to leave England with her Uncle Parr, but something went wrong and he did not wait for her."

Laurence Washington stared at them, half angry, half horrified. "She has actually left Woodstock? Then in heaven's name where is she now?"

"She is here, sir," said Robert simply.

"*Here?* What do you mean by *here?* Be quick, boy."

"Here in this house, sir. She is hidden upstairs, in the little place over the porch room."

Mother gave a gasp. For a moment Father was speechless.

"Great heavens," he cried at last. "She was actually there all the time I was taking Tresham round. It makes my blood run cold to think of it. You blockheads, don't you realise the peril of it? You will end on the scaffold and take your princess with you. And what is all this madcap story about Parr? You had better tell me the truth now, if truth is a word which has any meaning for you. Was she going to join Parr, and if so how comes it that he has gone off without her?"

Robert pulled himself together enough to explain that Parr had not been told he was to take the Lady with him, because he was untrustworthy. But he had found out somehow, they knew not how, and he had taken to his heels and deserted her.

"Ungallant maybe, but upon my soul I cannot blame him," Father commented grimly. "You had all just marked him for the scaffold without so much as a by-your-leave. And now what is to happen to the Lady Elizabeth?"

"I think Francis Verney has a plan," said Robert. "He is outside with Chris. Shall I call them in?"

"Certainly not," said Laurence Washington firmly. "I will

have no hand in their conspiracies. By the grace of God I was in good faith when I told Tresham that she was not here, and I pray that he does not return to ask me again. In the meanwhile she is a woman in peril, the daughter of the King in whose reign I grew up. It is my duty to afford her protection while she is in my house, but I will have no dealings with anyone outside, be it Francis Verney, or Chris Hatton or any other conspirator. Is that beyond your understanding?"

Suddenly Mother broke in.

"While you are talking," she cried, "the Princess is lying in a tiny loft. Isn't it safe to bring her out? It seems to me that she may have something to say about what is to happen to her. And it is long past dinner time, you know. She must have some food."

Father tossed his head impatiently. "Yes, I suppose we must bring her out, but it is full of peril, for her and for all of us. Can't you take her some food up there? The servants must have nothing to babble about."

"The servants can stay in the kitchen," said his wife quite firmly. "The boys will serve the dinner; they do so often enough, so there is nothing odd in it. I will tell Marta you have a headache, and must not be disturbed. For double safety the Princess can be served in the parlour. None can go there save through the hall. 'Tis safer far than taking food upstairs." Mother actually smiled. "For your headache, sir, it would be wise to draw the curtains and keep out the light. Is there aught else that you can think off?"

Laurence Washington spread his hands, sighing deeply. "I leave it to you, wife. Arrange it as you will, but for the love of heaven remember all that hangs on it."

"I will remember," she said tranquilly. "Robert, you had better go and warn your friends outside and bid them keep their watch. When that is done, slip the bolts in the doors so that none can come in unannounced. Set the dinner in here as usual, but lay a cover in the parlour with the gilt mazer and dish and the finest linen. Anne, fill a bowl with rose-water for her fingers. There is no time for new rushes, but strew some lavender and rosemary to freshen them. I must go to the kitchen."

Anne hurried to carry out her instructions, feeling that a great weight had been lifted. She noticed that Father and the boys were drawing curtains, moving chairs, setting the table, fetching the best silver and opening the best wine, all without arguing any more. However bad things were, when Mother started to arrange them they never seemed to be so bad after all. By the time that Mother reappeared from the buttery door everything was done as she had said.

"That is very good," she approved, changing the cushion of

She went up the stairs

the best stool and poking away a muddy clump of rushes with her toe. "The maids understand that we must not be disturbed and Marta is keeping the children to the nursery, because their father is ailing. Praise heaven, I had ordered roasted pheasants for dinner. Now I will go and free the Princess from her captivity. As soon as she is safely in the parlour the boys can fetch the dishes."

Whatever anyone else was feeling, it was clear that Mother was enjoying herself. She turned and, lifting her skirt, went up the stairs with no more concern than if she were going to fetch her needlework.

To the others waiting below it seemed that she was away an age. But just as Father was beginning to say that something must be wrong, they heard the sound of whispering at the top of the stairs. They all stood up expectantly, gazing in the same direction.

Mother was the first to appear. She led the way downstairs as carefully as if she were shepherding one of the little ones. When she reached the bottom she turned and sank into a deep curtsey. Laurence Washington bowed almost to the ground and his sons dropped on to one knee. Anne, while she copied Mother's curtsey, did not bow her head, but raised her eyes to the slim, graceful girlish figure of the Lady Elizabeth.

When she had seen her at Stuchbery, Anne had not realised how young the Lady was. She paused in the entrance of the hall, looking round quickly and nervously. She wore a simple green dress buttoned from throat to hem with little silver buttons. At her neck a fine lawn shift was gathered into a tiny ruff. She wore no jewel. The only brightness about her was the shimmering coppery gold of her hair.

"Madam," said Father in his best manner, "you do me honour by allowing me to welcome you under my roof."

His words broke the spell. The Lady Elizabeth looked at all of them in turn, a smile twitching the corners of her mouth. "Sir," she answered, "let me assure you that never have I known a roof under which I was more glad to lie. I feel that every rafter is a lifelong friend."

Everybody laughed, and Father led her through to the parlour where his great chair, furnished with the best cushion, was drawn up ready for her.

"I fear you must have been very cramped," he said. "Could I have guessed the company to be entertained I should have made the guest room a little bigger."

"Nay, sir; it is admirable for its purpose. It made me muse upon the charms of Little Ease. You will have heard of Little Ease, but perhaps your sons have not. It is a dungeon in the Tower so cramped that a man cannot lie stretched out in it."

"The lady Elizabeth paused in the entrance"

"I hope that none of them will ever know it personally," said Father with a glance at his family who had all crowded in through the parlour door.

"Amen to that, sir. When I heard you bring Tresham round I feared that I should be brought to know it for myself. What is the position? Is he still scouring the country with armed men to find one helpless lady and a handful of boys?"

"I hope that he has gone home, Madam. I did my best to persuade him to it. But I fear that his suspicions are aroused. 'Tis certain that you would be ill advised to go on to Greens Norton when you leave here. Tresham has his eye on it, and, as you doubtless know, Sir William Parr has taken himself off."

The Lady Elizabeth sat very still. Anne, watching her, remembered how, in the little house, she had stormed and raged. Now she was as unruffled as though she were listening to a sermon in church. When Father had finished, she looked at him with an expression of amused surprise, her chin held high, her eyebrows raised.

"Greens Norton? Sir William Parr?" she said coolly. "I know not why everyone should be talking to me of Sir William Parr. The last I heard of him he was planning a journey to Italy, but that is no concern of mine. I am returning to Woodstock tonight. Did you not know, sir? Except for Tresham's zeal I should have been almost there by now. The way by which I came will, I trust, suffice for my return. I only rode out from there to visit Doctor Dee." She gave a demure little laugh. " 'Tis almost unbecoming to confess it, sir, but I craved to have my fortune told—like a silly maid at a fair."

CHAPTER XVI

"I suppose we shall never know"

The Lady Elizabeth left Sulgrave after a hasty meal; too hasty for the liking of Mistress Washington, who grieved that the pheasants were barely tasted. Wrapped in her grey cloak, she was smuggled out almost as secretly as she had been smuggled in, and she went back to Stuchbery on foot, as she had come, across the fields and through the little copse. There Verney and Chris Hatton waited to escort her, with Blanche Parry and with fresh horses. It was calculated that they would reach Woodstock soon after dusk. If her luck held, and the women of the bedchamber, whom she had left behind, had played their part successfully in claiming that she was ill, her absence might not have been missed yet, and she could be safely back indoors before the appointed hour when they were to raise the hue and cry.

As she said good-bye, the Lady promised to come back to Sulgrave some day, and at the same time she wrung from Father an undertaking that there should be no beatings or punishments for anybody.

Francis and Anne were permitted to go with her as far as the stile, that fatal stile, where Tom had overheard the talk about Woodstock. There she kissed Anne on the cheek and gave Francis her own hand to kiss. They stood watching as she crossed the road and vanished among the trees, escorted by Robert on one side and Laurie on the other. When there was no longer even a shadow of her to be seen, Anne turned to go home.

She had not got far when she discovered that Francis was not with her. She looked back just in time to see him vanish towards the water meadows. His head was bent and his shoulders slumped. Anne frowned. Francis only looked like that when he was in trouble.

She found him propped against an old crooked willow over the stream. His face was buried in his folded arms. She was pretty sure that he was crying. She stood beside him in silence for a while. Then she said softly, "Francie."

He stiffened, but after a moment he raised his head and looked at her.

"It was me that gave it away," he said miserably. "I'm no good, Anne. I always spoil everything."

"It was Tom," she said indignantly. "He let it out to Parr because he wanted to go with them as a page, and he told his grandfather because his grandfather beat him." Her voice was full of contempt.

He shook his head. "It was my fault. They trusted me and I gave it away to Tom. Now she's had to go back to prison and perhaps they'll put her in the Tower again, and it's all because I can't keep a secret."

"Tom was worse than you," she said stubbornly. "You only told him. He told Parr and his grandfather, and he knew what he'd done, because he came to warn us."

He paid no attention. "And I've broken my vow too," he went on. "I'd made a vow to hold my tongue about things, and that makes it worse than ever."

"A vow? When did you make a vow? You didn't tell me."

"No, of course not; that was part of it. It was after I'd given

213

them away about Woodstock. I made a vow that I'd never tell anyone anything again. Not even you."

"*Not even you.*" Anne's heart jumped. A cloud had suddenly rolled away. A vow! *That* was why he had been so different. And she had been blaming Tom. As if to make amends, she said suddenly, "Did you know that Tom was coming to live here?"

He stared at her, startled out of his misery. "To live *here*? At Sulgrave? How do you know?"

Francis and Anne took their places beside their brothers

"His grandfather asked Father this morning, and Father said Yes. I was there."

Francis stood up straight. "Goodness, I am glad. Poor Tom, he was so miserable. I say, Anne, I'm hungry. Let's go home."

For one moment a little stab of the old jealousy caught her, but another thought crowded it out.

"Francis, when I told the lady that I was your sister she said, 'Oh, the little locksmith'. What did she mean?"

He broke into a delighted grin. "Did she really say that? She meant——" He stopped dead. "No," he said firmly. "I can't tell you. It's a secret."

When they reached the house they found that Robert and Laurie had got home before them. Mother was waiting at the door. She warned them with a grave face that Father wanted them in the hall. They looked at one another with frightened eyes. Clearly the day of reckoning had come.

Father was sitting in his big chair, as grave as a judge, with Robert and Laurie in front of him. He waited until Francis and Anne took their places beside their brothers.

"Well," he said at last; "I hope you are satisfied with the results of your meddling. You have done your best to put your princess in danger of her life; you have made me pledge my honour to a lie; you have risked your home and your mother, never to mention your own precious necks. It seems that you are all in it, up to the hilt—even Anne with her snake bite, the little baggage. There is nothing I should like better than to beat the lot of you as you have never been beaten before."

"It is Doctor Dee that I blame the most," Mother broke in. "It is he who has led them all astray."

Though she was on the point of tears Anne almost smiled. That was, as ever, Mother's way, to stand between them and Father at any cost. But this time she did not succeed.

"Stuff and nonsense, my lady," said Father firmly. "As I told you an hour or so since, I caught them coming back from Woodstock the very day that Doctor Dee arrived. 'Tis plain that he has a part in it, a great part I fancy, but what it is I do not ask. He is leaving us and returning to London. Did you know that? He told me a day or two ago that his work here was finished. I regretted it then but now I am content that he should go."

"I thank God for it," said Mother fervently.

Father shook his head at her. "There is more than that to thank God for," he said. "It makes me shake to think of the peril we have all been in, but the greatest peril of all was for our guest. Fortunately for her, she has more wit than the lot of you put together. Her answer that she came but to consult Doctor Dee is one that I shall remember to the end of my days."

He relapsed into silence, and for a moment or two the only sound was the quickened breathing of his family. Anne looked from one to the other. When were the beatings to begin? Exactly as if she had asked the question aloud, Father answered it.

"Our guest wrested a promise from me that there should be no beatings and no punishments," he said. "I regret it very much but I must stand by it. Now, what can I do to make sure that this shall not happen again? I have ordered and you have disobeyed me. I have warned and you have ignored my warning. There is only one other plea that I can make and I pray God that this one may not fall on deaf ears. You are gentlemen of coat armour. Look at the glass in the window. There are the Washington arms, borne honourably by your forefathers. If you swear by that token that never again will you meddle in such matters, I will be satisfied."

Once more there was silence. Anne glanced at the window. The light was fading. Indoors the hall was growing dark. But her "stars and stripes" stood out against the evening sky. She looked back at the boys again.

Robert stood very straight. "I swear," he said.

"I swear," said Laurie.

Francis took a deep breath. "I swear," he said.

Laurence Washington sighed deeply. "Then that is finished," he said with obvious relief, and stood up. He turned and spoke to Mother in an ordinary voice.

"It would be interesting to learn," he said, "how Sir William Parr got wind of the plan. That is the turning point of the whole matter, and I suppose we shall never know. But I cannot help feeling that God's providence had a hand in it. If the Lady Elizabeth had been caught fleeing the country with Parr, *she*, as well as he, would have gone to the block. Of that I have no doubt at all. It comes to this; whoever the fool was that gave the secret away, without realising it he saved her life."

Sulgrave Church to-day,
Showing the porch built by Laurence Washington ("Father") in memory of
his wife ("Mother")

Postscript

I know that a great many young readers like to be told what is true in a historical story and what is made up. There is a good deal of both in this book, but I will try to disentangle it for those of you who are interested.

To begin with all the principal characters are people who really lived. Laurence Washington and his ten children (there were eleven before the family was complete); Sir John Spencer and his wife, Katharine Kytson, with their target of twenty thousand sheep; Great-aunt Bath, who really did write to the Earl of Pembroke complaining about the theft of a brace of greyhounds intended for the Queen; Sir William Parr, nicknamed by Edward VI "my honest uncle", condemned to death and then pardoned by Queen Mary; Christopher Hatton, who grew up to be one of Queen Elizabeth I's favourite courtiers and held the office of Lord Chancellor; Sir Thomas Tresham, a sheriff of the county, and his grandson Tom; the little party at the Bull Inn, Woodstock, who plagued the life of Sir Henry Bedingfield while Elizabeth was prisoner there; all these characters are true and *could*, I believe, have acted as I have made them act.

Doctor Dee requires a note to himself. He was very much a real person and is not so well known as he deserves to be. He was what we would call to-day "one of the back room boys", and a brilliant mathematician, astronomer and geographer. His planning lay behind many of the great voyages of discovery in the reign of Queen Elizabeth the First; Frobisher, Humphrey Gilbert, Raleigh and possibly even Drake owed much of their success to Doctor Dee. He made a study of astrology as a serious science, and it is quite sad to find that in his old age he fell into bad company and lent himself to crystal gazing and magic of doubtful honesty. But Elizabeth frequently consulted him and when she was Queen visited him at his home in Mortlake, Surrey.

I have to confess that there is no evidence to connect Doctor Dee with Sulgrave. That frankly, I have made up. But it is perfectly true that he frequented the neighbourhood of Woodstock during Elizabeth's captivity, and his letters were smuggled in and out by the Parrys, who were his kinsfolk. It is even suggested by one historian that his presence was one of the reasons why Elizabeth was moved away from Woodstock. Quite certainly a few months later Dee was imprisoned for drawing up the horoscopes and foretelling the future not only of Elizabeth, but also of Queen Mary and her consort, Philip of Spain.

Now let me tell you something about the main plot of the book, Elizabeth's escape from Woodstock and her hiding at Sulgrave Manor. . . . There is a kind of detective story behind it which may interest you.

When I first visited Sulgrave I found there a little book called *The Washington Ancestry* which was on sale at the Manor and in the village. This interesting little book quotes a poem of some ten verses, described as "an Old English Ballad", which tells how, during the reign of Queen Mary, the Princess Elizabeth was hidden in Sulgrave Manor "in a dark niche", while Tresham, on behalf of the Queen, searched for her below. I take no responsibility for the truth of the legend. Some old ballads are founded on fact, others are not. But when I read it I set myself the problem of working out when and how it could possibly have happened.

The ballad does not mention Woodstock. But Queen Mary reigned only for five years; during those five years the only time when Elizabeth was near Sulgrave, and could possibly have been "on the run", was during her imprisonment. Very well; let us assume that she did effect an escape from Woodstock. But why should she come to a remote village like Sulgrave, twenty miles away? What would bring her to the neighbourhood? A little exploring in books revealed that her step-uncle, Sir William Parr, whom she trusted, had his manor nearby. His sister, Queen Katharine Parr, had been like a mother to her. There is no one to whose tender mercies she would be more likely to trust herself. The same books recorded that she did at one time go so far as to contemplate fleeing to the continent. Parr's intimate friends had already fled. So far, so good; the thing was not impossible.

But if Elizabeth did escape from Woodstock and hide at Sulgrave, it is certain that she returned to Woodstock, and that she was not caught. She was not executed, nor punished; nor was anybody else executed or punished for it, as they would have been without doubt if she had been caught. She remained quietly at Woodstock until she was eventually transferred to Hampton Court. It follows therefore, if there is any truth in the legend, that she must have got safely back to Woodstock without notice, so that no record of the episode remains—except in the "Old English Ballad".

Anyhow I have put all these ideas together, shaken them up with some entirely imaginary adventures, such as the old witch and the lost mortgage deed, and the result is the book which you have just read. Perhaps, some of the shots in the dark about Elizabeth's escape may be true. I don't know. No one will ever know. I offer them to you not as history, not even as legend, but purely as story.

Now I have confessed to an invention about Doctor Dee and I

will also confess to one other small device to help the story. In point of fact the Washington family of eleven children included two boys at the beginning and two boys at the end of the tail, whereas I have started off with three boys instead of two. But as only Robert and Laurie, the two eldest, left any mark on history this is not an important change.

Laurence Washington lived peacefully at Sulgrave until his death in 1583. He is buried in the church there. So is his wife and so is Robert who lived until 1619. Laurie became a barrister of Grays Inn and was appointed Registrar to the Court of Chancery.

Sir William Parr got back his honours when Elizabeth came to the throne and became once more Marquess of Northampton. Tom Tresham inherited his grandfather's estate and built the fine Elizabethan house at Rushton which still stands. In his old age Tom had a taste of the meaning of real conspiracy when his son, Francis, was involved in Guy Fawkes' Gunpowder Plot. Fortunately he did not live quite long enough to know of the young man's execution.

Chris Hatton, when he was Lord Chancellor, also rebuilt his house at Holdenby. It is still one of the sights of the county. Sir John Spencer's great house at Wormleighton is now a farm, though many of its former glories can still be traced. His descendents, the Earls Spencer, have lived for nearly four hundred and fifty years at Althorp (where the greyhounds chased the sheep).

I would like to be able to show a picture gallery of all these characters, for portraits, in one form or another, have survived of all of them, except, alas! of the Washingtons themselves. The effigies of Sir John Spencer and Cousin Kit on their tomb in the church of Great Brington, Northamptonshire, are obviously fine likenesses. Great-aunt Bath lies in state in the church at Hengrave in Suffolk, with her three husbands. Sir Thomas Tresham's tomb at Rushton shows him clad in his robes as the last Prior of the Order of St. John of Jerusalem, an office to which he was appointed by Queen Mary the year after the date of this story. His grandson Tom (in his turn also Sir Thomas Tresham) is represented in a portrait at Boughton House, Northamptonshire.

Of Sir Christopher Hatton there are several portraits. The

finest hangs in the Inner Temple, London. It shows him, full length, as a handsome man in his thirties, gorgeously dressed and holding a medallion of Elizabeth I. Holbein drew Sir William Parr; the drawing is in the Holbein collection at Windsor Castle; so is that of the jolly round-faced Thomas Parry. But to me the most interesting of all is the striking portrait of Doctor Dee in the Ashmolean Museum, Oxford. His long pointed beard is white, but his face looks youthful, and there is an alertness in the dark eyes which suggests that, young or old, he was always ready for anything.

All the drawings of Sulgrave which appear in the book were made on the spot, though I have extended the house beyond what remains of it now. Some of it was pulled down after the Washingtons left it, and another wing was built on at the back. But I have shown only those parts which date from the time of Laurence Washington.

Perhaps some day you may go and see Sulgrave Manor for yourselves. You will find it very beautiful and full of interest. You may, perhaps, get a copy of *The Washington Ancestry* and read the "Old English Ballad". If you do so, why not try and ferret out for yourselves the story that lies behind it? Your version will probably be quite different from mine. You will have to consult a great many books and read quite a lot of history. But I can promise you that you will find it very good fun.

Sir William Parr's Garter plate, still broken in two, is preserved in the British Museum.

The sixteenth century pressure cooker can be seen in the West Gate Museum, Winchester.

Many of the other objects pictured in the book are actually in Sulgrave Manor; notably the fourposter bed in the Great Chamber; the child's three-legged chair; and the knife case and the baby's shoe, both of which are Washington relics unearthed when the house was restored.

To end up, I wonder if those of you who know London can

identify the cross roads by Tyburn Gallows mentioned on page 122. The modern names for the four roads are Edgware Road (to Edgware), Bayswater Road (to Uxbridge), Park Lane (to Westminster) and Oxford Street (to London). In short it is— Marble Arch.

Family Tree of the Washingtons

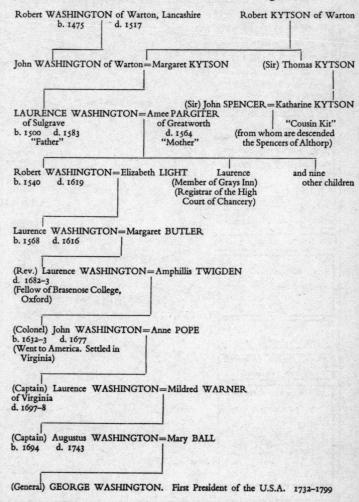

Robert WASHINGTON of Warton, Lancashire
b. 1475   d. 1517

Robert KYTSON of Warton

John WASHINGTON of Warton=Margaret KYTSON

(Sir) Thomas KYTSON

(Sir) John SPENCER=Katharine KYTSON

LAURENCE WASHINGTON=Amee PARGITER
of Sulgrave   of Greatworth
b. 1500   d. 1583   d. 1564
"Father"   "Mother"

"Cousin Kit"
(from whom are descended
the Spencers of Althorp)

Robert WASHINGTON=Elizabeth LIGHT
b. 1540   d. 1619

Laurence
(Member of Grays Inn)
(Registrar of the High
Court of Chancery)

and nine
other children

Laurence WASHINGTON=Margaret BUTLER
b. 1568   d. 1616

(Rev.) Laurence WASHINGTON=Amphillis TWIGDEN
d. 1682-3
(Fellow of Brasenose College,
Oxford)

(Colonel) John WASHINGTON=Anne POPE
b. 1632-3   d. 1677
(Went to America. Settled in
Virginia)

(Captain) Laurence WASHINGTON=Mildred WARNER
of Virginia
d. 1697-8

(Captain) Augustus WASHINGTON=Mary BALL
b. 1694   d. 1743

(General) GEORGE WASHINGTON. First President of the U.S.A. 1732-1799

223

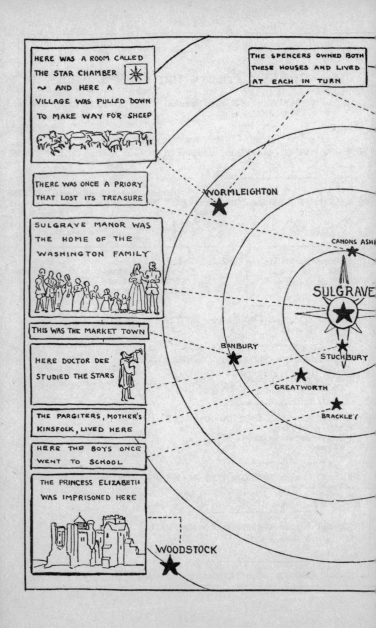

HERE WAS A ROOM CALLED
THE STAR CHAMBER
~ AND HERE A
VILLAGE WAS PULLED DOWN
TO MAKE WAY FOR SHEEP

THE SPENCERS OWNED BOTH
THESE HOUSES AND LIVED
AT EACH IN TURN

THERE WAS ONCE A PRIORY
THAT LOST ITS TREASURE

SULGRAVE MANOR WAS
THE HOME OF THE
WASHINGTON FAMILY

THIS WAS THE MARKET TOWN

HERE DOCTOR DEE
STUDIED THE STARS

THE PARGITERS, MOTHER'S
KINSFOLK, LIVED HERE

HERE THE BOYS ONCE
WENT TO SCHOOL

THE PRINCESS ELIZABETH
WAS IMPRISONED HERE

WORMLEIGHTON

CANONS ASH

SULGRAVE

BANBURY

STUCHBURY

GREATWORTH

BRACKLEY

WOODSTOCK

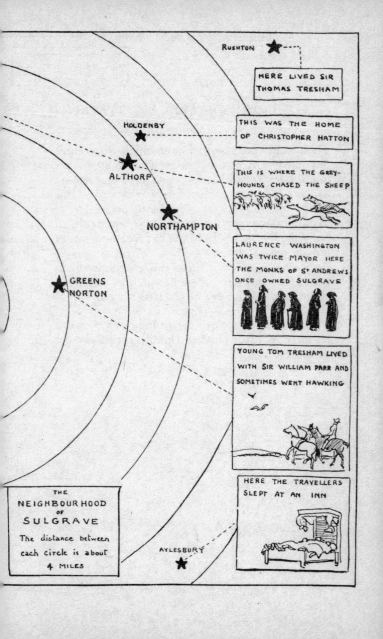

RUSHTON ★

HERE LIVED SIR
THOMAS TRESHAM

HOLDENBY ★

THIS WAS THE HOME
OF CHRISTOPHER HATTON

ALTHORP ★

THIS IS WHERE THE GREY-
HOUNDS CHASED THE SHEEP

NORTHAMPTON ★

LAURENCE WASHINGTON
WAS TWICE MAYOR HERE
THE MONKS OF ST ANDREWS
ONCE OWNED SULGRAVE

GREENS
NORTON ★

YOUNG TOM TRESHAM LIVED
WITH SIR WILLIAM PARR AND
SOMETIMES WENT HAWKING

THE
NEIGHBOURHOOD
OF
SULGRAVE
The distance between
each circle is about
4 MILES

HERE THE TRAVELLERS
SLEPT AT AN INN

AYLESBURY ★

Vivien Alcock

THE TRIAL OF ANNA COTMAN

Thin, sallow and nosy, Lindy Miller is the most unpopular girl in the school. They only let her join the Society of Masks because she was Jeremy Miller's kid sister. When a new girl arrives, the quiet, smiling Anna Cotman, Lindy persuades her to join the Society too. Originally set up to combat bullying, the Society of Masks has become a sinister power group run by bullies. When the gentle Anna challenges their rules, the leaders decide to make an example of her and the terrifying countdown to the day of her trial begins.

Vivien Alcock captures the chilling mood of evil let loose in a school when childish rituals run out of control.

Linda Kempton

THE NAMING OF WILLIAM RUTHERFORD

"Jack! Please help up! Please help us, Jack!"

The little cradle creaked on curved rockers, creak, creak, on the flagstone floor; a tiny cradle of dark brown wood, with carved acorns on each of the corners of the square wooden hood. Figures in long dresses and white bonnets surrounded it. One of them turned her face to Jack.

"Jack, please help us!"

Jack's dream is a frightening and perplexing one. It is so vivid that it seems almost true and he senses that it contains some sort of message for him.

Jack's intuition proves correct and the cradle comes to play an important role in his life, for in a mysterious way it links him with the past, a past so clear and real that Jack begins to live two worlds; his ordinary, everyday world and one in Eyam, an isolated village in Derbyshire, in the year 1665.

As the story unfolds Jack learns his destiny — it seems he *is* the only one who can help.

Penelope Lively

THE DRIFTWAY

Running away from home and their new step-mother, Paul and his sister travel along the Driftway, an ancient road that runs from Banbury to Northampton. For those that can hear them, there are messages to be picked up along the Driftway, messages from people who passed by long ago and had some powerful experience of joy or sorrow that somehow imprinted itself for future travellers.

Paul picks up messages from a boy who has lost his home and family to the marauding Norsemen, a young Cavalier in retreat from the Battle of Edgehill and an eighteenth-century highwayman. The scenes Paul witnesses, and the messages he receives, help him to come to terms with his own problems.

Michael Morpurgo

MY FRIEND WALTER

Bess Throckmorton is more than a little surprised to learn that she is related to Sir Walter Raleigh.

It is not long after this discovery that she meets a mysterious man who takes her to the Tower of London. She is sworn to secrecy and must never reveal his identity. Bess loves her new friend dearly until one day he vanishes, just as her whole life is crumbling. Her father is in disgrace and they have to sell their farm lock, stock and barrel.

It isn't until they hear a news flash announcing the robbery of one of the Crown Jewels that their whole destiny changes.

Penelope Lively

THE GHOST OF THOMAS KEMPE
Winner of the Carnegie Medal

When the Harrisons move to an old cottage in Oxfordshire they are beset by small domestic disasters. Naturally they assume James is up to his tricks again – how can he tell them he is being plagued by the ghost of a meddling seventeenth-century sorcerer, bent on making James his apprentice?

James tries desperately to circumvent the sorcerer's malicious activities, but it is only when he uncovers the reason for Thomas Kempe's sudden reappearance that he finds a way to lay the ghost forever ...

Bel Mooney

THE STOVE HAUNTING

When Daniel's family move to a large rambling house in the West Country, Daniel feels strangely drawn to the old kitchen stove and finds himself sucked inexorably back into the past . . .

The year is 1835 and Daniel's life becomes that of stove boy and kitchen skivvy. Through his friend George, Daniel becomes involved in the plans of the local farm workers to improve their miserable wages by forming a union. But the laws forbid such 'treason' and soon Daniel must try to save his friends from the most terrifying fate of all.

Inspired by the events surrounding the prosecution of the Tolpuddle Martyrs, *The Stove Haunting* provides an absorbing insight into a time of great social change.

Frances Usher

TELL ALICE

At fourteen, Joanna Milford's life is turned upside down when she moves with her mother to a quiet Dorset village to start a new life without her father. Then she finds the diary of Jessie, who, in the 1920s, had lived in the cottage next door. Jessie's elderly brother, Mr Bone, still lives in the cottage – but refuses to talk about Jessie.

Joanna is intrigued by Mr Bone's refusal to talk about his sister and becomes totally wrapped up in the extraordinary story revealed in Jessie's diary, finding that Jessie, too, had an unexpectedly fraught relationship with her father . . .

"engrossing, unpredictable, with insight into the poverty, prospects and rigid social divisions of 1920s England."
Observer